REDEMPTION IN THE KEYS

A Logan Dodge Adventure

Florida Keys Adventure Series
Volume 5

Logan Dodge Adventures

Gold in the Keys
(Florida Keys Adventure Series Book 1)

Hunted in the Keys
(Florida Keys Adventure Series Book 2)

Revenge in the Keys
(Florida Keys Adventure Series Book 3)

Betrayed in the Keys
(Florida Keys Adventure Series Book 4)

Redemption in the Keys
(Florida Keys Adventure Series Book 5)

If you're interested in receiving my newsletter for updates on my upcoming books, you can sign up on my website:

matthewrief.com

PROLOGUE

San Fernando de Atabapo, Venezuela
1999

I stood on a muddy precipice and looked out over the Orinoco River and the flat, dense jungle surrounding it. It was dark, but the cloudless sky above allowed the waxing gibbous moon to cast a humble glimmer over the untouched landscape. After standing by for two days in the heat, humidity, and rain of the Amazonas state, our chain of command had finally given us the green light.

The brief had been long, and I was playing over upcoming events in my mind. At face value, it was relatively simple. Members of a Colombian rebel operation had been bribed by undercover government insurgents to give up the position of one of their facilities. Our intel verified that this was the same group of rebels who were planning an attack on the US embassy in Bogota. Our mission was set: recon and infiltrate.

"Logan," I heard a voice say behind me. I turned and saw Kyle standing with his hands on his hips, his body half glowing from the dim light of the bungalow at his back. "We're moving out."

I nodded and stepped over alongside him. Petty Officer First Class Kyle Quinn was the leading petty officer of our four-man fire team. He stood just over six feet tall, with a lean muscular build and black skin.

"What is it?" I said.

He seemed off, like there was something important on his mind.

He shook his head. "Come on."

We moved side by side into a dimly lit room where the two other members of our team stood beside a table covered with various weaponry and ammunition. Manny Estrada, a short Hispanic second class, was our team medic. Beside him was Lieutenant Nathan Brier, who was command controller, having replaced my good friend Scott Cooper just three months earlier.

We were all dressed in our light combat gear, which consisted of flat jungle khakis and Oakley assault boots. The first part of the mission was primarily recon, so we'd be traveling light. We loaded ourselves up with roughly forty-five pounds of gear each. We grabbed M4 rifles, MP5 submachine guns, Sig 9mms, pig stickers, combat knives, ammunition belts, and our medical and comm gear. I grabbed eight thirty-round magazines for my M4 and stowed them in my belt. We also grabbed some sustenance for the mission: MREs, beef jerky, and canteens filled with water.

Once everyone was set, Nate motioned for us to move out. We moved down a steep hill to the riverbank, where our mode of transport was waiting for us. Down at the end of a short old dock, we boarded a Special Operations Craft—Riverine, or SOC for short. It was a thirty-three-foot-long boat designed for insertion and extraction in shallow-water areas. It had two 440-hp diesel engines that each drove water pump-jets, which meant the thing could haul ass on the water and you didn't have to worry about breaking a prop on the bottom.

The craft, along with two others, had been flown in on the same C-130 Hercules we'd been on just two days earlier. Once in Venezuela, the boats had been rigged to the bottom of MH-47 helicopters with slings and transported to their drop zones. The four of us were to take the craft up the Orinoco River, then head west up the Guainía River roughly twenty-five miles to perform reconnaissance on a Colombian government compound that had recently fallen to the Revolutionary Armed Forces of Colombia, or FARC as they're called. The rest of our sixteen-man platoon would be standing by on the Inirida River, a tributary just ten miles from our target, ready to provide backup in case we ran into trouble.

I moved into my position at the helm. Manny took control of the fifty-cal machine gun, Kyle manned one of the GAU-17 miniguns, and Nate stood beside me, looking through a night vision optic device, or NOD as we called them. I started up the diesel engines and rocketed us upriver. After less than a mile, I turned us to starboard, crossing over the border to Colombia into the mouth of the Guainía. The night was quiet, dark, and still.

Roughly twenty miles upriver, after cruising a series of wide turns, we spotted a small village of raggedy old houses clustered in a field just a few hundred feet from the shoreline. As we came closer, we saw piles of dead bodies sprawled out in the mud.

"Ease up, Logan," Nate said quietly. "Take us to that patch of sand." He motioned towards a small beach in front of the village. "Eyes up. Be ready for anything."

I slowed us to just a few knots, then slid the bow up onto the sand enough that it would stay in place against the steady flow of the river. After killing the engines, I took a quick look at the area surrounding the village. We were in the middle of a dense jungle, making it difficult for us to spot nearby enemies. There was a small hill to the north, but other than that, the horizon was perfectly flat.

We stepped onto the shore and had a look around. It was an awful sight. There had to be around a hundred dead civilians, including women and children. Whoever had come through hadn't left anyone alive. The thing that amazed me was that their bodies were still warm, meaning that they'd only been dead for a couple of hours at most.

Suddenly, I saw movement out of the corner of my eye. It had come from up on the nearby hill, and within a second I had my M4 raised and was looking through the night vision scope. For a moment I caught a glimpse of a guy looking straight towards us. He was there and then he was gone, vanishing into the dense jungle.

"What is it?" Kyle said. He moved beside me and aimed in the same direction as I was.

"Saw someone," I said.

"FARC?" Kyle asked.

I shrugged. There was no way of knowing for sure, but he hadn't looked Hispanic. He'd been far away and discolored by my night optics, but his features had looked more European than anything else. And he'd been wearing a black leather jacket.

Who in the hell would wear a black leather jacket in this heat and humidity?

"I don't think so," was all I said.

We regrouped, then Nate gave the order to head back to the SOC and continue upriver.

"I don't like it," Kyle said. "This doesn't make any sense. I've read detailed reports on every case of FARC activity in this region within the past six months. They don't act like this. They don't slaughter entire villages. Their whole motive is to liberate the people and redistribute wealth. Though civilians have been killed by their attacks, military assets are almost always their intended targets."

"You're humanizing barbarians," Nate said. "Why would you ever give these assholes the benefit of the doubt?"

"I'm not," Kyle fired back. "It's just that this whole thing doesn't make any sense. It's out of character for them. This village didn't matter strategically. These guys aren't stupid; they wouldn't do this just for the hell of it. Also, their infrastructure would have picked up on US movement in the area. If anything, they'd be lying low or drawing back. Especially considering that they're having peace talks with Colombia's president."

Nate's eyes grew wide. "Where did you hear that?"

"Talked to a friend of mine in the Colombian government," Kyle said. "He said that Sureshot was meeting with President Pastrana in the next couple of days. They're having a ceasefire and—"

"Does this look like a ceasefire to you?" Nate said. He motioned back to the boat. "We continue with the mission. We do our job." He eyed Kyle and added, "And we let our chain of command and intelligence officers do theirs."

We boarded the SOC, then I started up the engines and we cruised farther upriver. We came to a big horseshoe turn, and as we finished rounding it, we spotted our target about a half a mile away, nestled into the jungle in a place called Sesema. I hugged the riverbank, then brought us up onto a small stretch of beach surrounded by overgrown jungle. We disembarked, then moved slowly towards our target.

We stopped at a location that had a good visual of our destination and looked around. The compound didn't appear to be very big. It was brick and mortar, two stories above ground, and was surrounded by tall chain-link fences with razor wire. One dirt road led out towards a dock farther upriver, and another road cut northwest through the jungle. Combined, we spotted four bored-looking guards, two up on top of the structure and two at the ground level, walking in circles along the outer fence in opposite directions. All four were carrying AK-47s.

Nate grabbed the radio and relayed the situation to command. We received a quick and decisive order to begin our assault on the outside of the compound.

"That wasn't the plan," Kyle said, looking at Nate like the guys on the other end were crazy.

"Captain," Nate said into the radio, "can you repeat that order? You want us to begin the assault prior to waiting for the rest of the platoon?"

"They're on their way now," Captain Holt said. "Secure the perimeter and begin moving in,

Lieutenant."

Nate looked as stunned as the rest of us. It didn't make any sense for us to move in without the others.

"Aye, sir," he replied, then handed the radio back to Kyle.

Nate looked at each of us for a few seconds, then said, "Alright, you heard Holt. Let's move."

"You can't be fucking serious," Kyle said.

"We're moving," Nate said sternly.

Slowly, we began moving down into the jungle. Everyone except Kyle. He stayed frozen in place. Nate turned, stepped back towards him and stood right in front of him.

"What the hell's going on with you?" Nate said.

Kyle paused a moment, collecting his thoughts.

"A few days ago, I overheard Holt talking on the phone," Kyle said. "I wasn't sure I'd heard what I thought I had, but now I know it's true." He let out a deep breath. "It's an ambush. If we go into that compound, we're gonna be surrounded and killed."

Nate shook his head. "What the hell are you talking about?"

"Look, I don't have all the specifics," Kyle said. "But I do know this: if we go down there, we're gonna die."

"You're saying that Holt is—"

"Yes. That's exactly what I'm saying."

I stood still, my mind racing as I listened to the two guys speak. Kyle had been open with me about his reservations regarding this mission from the beginning. I'd known Holt for years. He was a respected Naval officer with fourteen years of service under his belt. I'd heard of military personnel being involved in corrupt dealings before but couldn't imagine Holt playing a part in it. Especially one that would unnecessarily endanger American lives.

Nate didn't budge an inch. If he was conflicted, he didn't show it.

"We're moving," he said again, stepping just a few inches away from Kyle and staring him down.

Just as Nate turned around, I heard the click of a pistol and watched in utter shock as Kyle raised his Sig and aimed it straight at our command controller. Nate froze when he heard the sound, then slowly turned around.

"What the hell are you doing, Kyle?"

He motioned for us to move back to the boat. "I'm saving our lives," he said flatly.

The four of us stood frozen for a moment. I'd never felt more conflicted in my entire life. I too had felt something was off about the mission, but I'd never expected Kyle to do what he was doing.

"You'll rot in Leavenworth for this," Nate said in a tone that was more worried than angry. "You know that, right?"

"Probably," Kyle said. "But we'll all be alive."

Kyle kept his Sig aimed at Nate for another minute.

When Holt called in for a mission update, Kyle answered, telling the captain that we were heading back downriver and that he could shove his orders where the sun didn't shine.

Holt grew furious, but before he could get a full sentence out, Kyle switched the radio off. Manny and I exchanged glances. Suddenly, we heard the sounds of engines far off in the distance. I lifted my NOD, looked out towards the sound, and saw a group of five large trucks thundering towards the other side of the compound. To the south, I also saw four boats cutting across the surface of the water, heading in our direction. They were far away, but it was clear that they sure as hell weren't fishermen.

"Back to the boat," Nate ordered, his eyes wide.

Kyle lowered his Sig and we booked it as fast as we could through the jungle, heading back towards the riverbank. By the time we reached our SOC, the three boats had closed to within a quarter mile of us. We jumped aboard. I had the engines running, and in seconds we were cruising downriver.

As we accelerated, the guys on the boats behind us opened fire, their automatics rattling across the night air and sending streams of bullets all around us. A few managed to strike the hull of the SOC, but most splashed into the water. They were far away but closing in fast. I brought us up to our top speed and maneuvered to avoid their attack as best as I could.

"Fire!" Nate said over the sound of the bullets.

Manny let loose with the fifty-cal, sending a loud storm of massive rounds exploding back at our assailants. I kept my eyes forward, focusing downriver as I brought us back around the long horseshoe. Only occasionally did I glance over my shoulder to see the status of the gunfight. Manny had taken down one of the boats with the fifty, but the other three were still right on our six.

As the turn sharpened, Kyle manned one of the side-mounted M240Bs and let loose. Bullets continued to fly in both directions. A few managed to hit the armored hull of the SOC, but the well-designed craft continued strong, seemingly unaffected. I turned the helm sharply to the left, then weaved around a thick patch of trees for cover. We were flying down the dark river, not a light or sign of life around us for miles. The humid jungle air slapped violently against us.

For a moment, the gunfire ceased on both sides. Then I brought us out from the trees, and Nate, Manny, and Kyle let loose a torrential downpour straight into the bow and cockpit of the closest enemy boat. I glanced over my shoulder and watched as one of the rounds struck the pilot in the face, causing him to fall forward onto the helm and turn their boat out of control. Trying to perform such a sharp turn at such a fast speed caused the boat to flip and tumble violently, sending the guys on board hurtling through the air.

The two other boats turned sharply to avoid the wreckage, then opened fire on us again. I dropped to the deck, keeping my hands secured to the lower part of the helm as bullets pelted the SOC.

"Ah shit," I heard Manny yell over the sounds of bullets exploding out of chambers and striking all around us.

I glanced back and saw that Manny was hunched over slightly, his right hand pressed to his chest.

"Manny!" I yelled.

Pushing through the pain, he grabbed the fifty-cal with both hands again and let loose a barrage of gunfire with reckless abandon. Kyle and Nate kept to cover and kept firing as well. Looking back, I spotted one of the tangos holding an RPG over his shoulder. I cursed under my breath.

"Hold on!" I yelled just as I turned the helm hard to the right.

The force was brutal. Turning the SOC so sharply at full speed was a risky move, and it almost knocked all of us out into the water. I heard a loud explosion followed by a split second of screeching as the rocket tore through the air and exploded in the part of the river we'd been cruising over moments earlier. The explosion jostled the SOC, nearly toppling it over as I fought to retain control and keep us moving forward.

I heard a loud cry and looked over my shoulder to see that Manny had been struck again.

Without thinking, I let go of the helm and grabbed Nate's shoulder forcefully.

"Take it!" I said.

Seeing the fire burning in my eyes, Nate switched places with me. I moved towards the stern, grabbed Manny from behind, and brought him to the deck. Blood was flowing out from two wounds to his chest. I wanted to help him but knew that if we didn't take these other bad guys down soon, we'd all be dead.

Grabbing hold of my M4, I peeked over the transom and took aim at the first boat in view. Kyle moved in beside me, and we both let loose. I watched through my NOD as one of my rounds flew through the already broken windscreen and tore through the neck of the pilot. As the guys scrambled for control of their boat, we unleashed hell, striking them in their backs and sides and taking the boat out of commission.

That left one boat, and I had just the thing to send it and everyone aboard to the locker. I quickly prepped the M203 grenade launcher attached to my M4. I kept to cover behind the transom as the fourth and final boat closed in. When it was within a few hundred feet, I popped up, took aim, and fired. The grenade burst through the air and struck right in the center of the boat. A deafening explosion followed, sending bodies and shattered pieces of the boat flying in all directions. The fuel tanks went as well, overtaking the boat in flames as it crumbled and crashed to a stop.

Kyle and I took one more quick look around the river behind us and the banks on both sides, but there was nothing except the wreckage of the enemy boats. We knelt down beside Manny, patching him up as best as we could.

"Hang in there," I said as I grabbed his hand in mine.

Nate maintained the SOC at its top speed of just over forty knots. We flew down the river, zigging and zagging our way towards Coco Nuevo, where the Inirida flows into the Guaviare, to meet up with the rest of the platoon.

Manny's eyes began to bulge. I told him again to hang on, letting him know that we'd be able to get him proper treatment soon. But the bleeding was too severe. The flow had slowed, but it had soaked through Manny's clothes and pooled up around us. I'd never seen so much blood.

He took a few labored breaths and looked up at me one more time, his eyes staring deep into mine. Then his head dropped and he went motionless.

ONE

Falcon, Venezuela
Three Days Later

Kyle Quinn's wrists were bound in handcuffs in front of his body as three US Air Force police officers escorted him across the tarmac. Their destination was a Learjet C-21A, a small transport aircraft that would take Kyle back to the States, where he'd face a series of charges against him. It was a hot and humid evening. The dying sun's rays beat down uncontested through a clear western sky, causing a thin layer of sweat to form on Kyle's brow.

His head was a mess. The past three days had been a tiresome and painful blur. With the news of Estrada's death came the story that a Navy Special Forces operative had compromised the mission and was being charged under the UCMJ for failure to obey a lawful order. Even worse, Kyle was also being charged with treason. His personal communications with operatives within the Colombian government were being heavily investigated. There were also reports that he'd been in communication with members of FARC for the past few months.

Kyle continued down the tarmac. Only once did he look over his shoulder at the Special Forces soldiers standing at his back. He made brief eye contact with his friend, Logan Dodge, then faced forward again. He was confident he could count on them to have his back, but the evidence against him was overwhelming. He was facing months of testimonies, trials, allegations, and scrutinized media coverage. Then, in all likelihood, he'd be thrown into prison for the rest of his life.

He shook his head, wondering how in the hell it had all happened. Wondering how such a conspiracy could be orchestrated in the country he loved so much.

The Air Force police stopped in front of the jet's side door. Three guys in suits stood in front of the group. They were big guys with earpieces and sunglasses.

"We'll take him from here," one of the guys said.

The airmen hesitated, waiting to see the guys flash their credentials. Suddenly, Captain Wyatt Holt appeared seemingly out of nowhere.

"They're taking him," Holt said. He was a tall, commanding guy who spoke with rough authority. "I just got off the phone with the joint chiefs. He's to be handed over for the transport."

The airman saluted the captain, then did as they were told. The three suits took control of Kyle, nodded to Holt, then forced him up into the aircraft.

They sat him down in a brown leather chair, then two of the suits headed back down the stairs onto the tarmac. They reappeared a few seconds later, carrying a large metal storage box to the back of the plane.

"This thing weighs a ton," one of the guys said.

They secured it and sat down beside Kyle. After just a few minutes, the side door closed, the pilots fired up the two turbine engines, and the jet took off.

The first hour and a half of the flight was relatively uneventful. Kyle sat in a brown leather seat with his arms shackled. He was surrounded by the guys in suits and no one in the cabin had said a word since takeoff. Through the window, Kyle could see the solid black silhouettes of clouds and the occasional flash of lightning. They'd flown from the calm northern coast of Venezuela into a massive storm that surged over Cuba and into the upper Bahamas.

They were flying at thirty thousand feet over the northern part of the Caribbean when a phone rang in the cabin. It was coming from the pocket of the guy sitting right across from Kyle. He had short black hair and stern brown eyes and he weighed well over two hundred pounds. In his early forties, he was older than the other two suits and was the leader of their group.

He checked his phone, then stood up and moved to the back of the plane before answering. He spoke for just a few seconds before nodding and hanging up. With fast, confident strides, he moved all the way forward and tapped on the cockpit door. It opened briefly and the big guy whispered something to one of the pilots, then the door shut. He moved back to his seat across from Kyle, acting as though nothing had happened.

A minute later, he said something into the ears of the two other guys. Kyle tried but couldn't hear what he said. All three suddenly stood up and ordered Kyle to his feet.

"What's going on?" Kyle asked, trying to sound as defensive as possible.

Deep down, he already knew what was about to happen.

"Shut up and move," the leader said, pulling Kyle to his feet and forcing him to move towards the back of the plane.

The four of them reached the back of the cabin, stopping right beside the bathroom door. Without warning, the leader turned and slugged the suit beside him in the nose. He wailed in pain and placed his hands on his bleeding nose as he nearly toppled over.

"What the fuck was that for?" he said, looking angrily back at the leader of the group.

He shrugged and shot Kyle an evil smile.

"Just following orders," he replied. "Kyle here attacked us midflight. We tried to subdue him but had no choice but to take him down."

He kept his gaze locked on Kyle.

The guy's nose dripped red blotches of blood onto the carpet. He snarled, then eyed Kyle as well.

"Well, then, let's fucking get on with it," he said. "I better get a bonus for that sucker punch."

"We'll all be paid handsomely," the leader said. "You can be sure of that. And you'll be a hero in the media for taking that blow."

Kyle's mind raced wildly. There wasn't going to be a trial; no chance of redemption for him. Those guys were going to kill him and put an end to the entire thing right here and now. He needed to make a move, and he needed to do it soon.

Kyle glanced over at the large metal box for a moment, then the leader met his gaze.

"That's all the intel," he said with a devilish smile. "Too bad you won't be around to sort out the fake shit from the real."

The bloody nose guy grabbed a black Beretta handgun from its holster on his right hip.

"Not out here," the leader said as he pulled open the bathroom door.

The three guys forced Kyle inside the small bathroom and pushed him facefirst up against the wall. The leader pulled a Glock from his waistband and pressed it against the back of Kyle's head.

Time slowed and Kyle could feel his heart pounding in his chest.

"It'll be easier to clean the mess in here," the leader said.

A surge of strength rose forth from deep within him. Just as the guy began to squeeze the trigger, Kyle snapped his head to the left. The 9mm round fired just inches from his ear, exploding out from the chamber and shattering the small mirror in front of him. The sound was painfully loud, and Kyle heard nothing but ringing in his right ear. Before the guy could respond, Kyle forced his bound hands back, grabbed hold of the leader's wrist, and snapped it over his shoulder. The Glock slipped through his fingers and clattered against the floor at Kyle's feet.

Still holding tight to the leader's cracked wrist, Kyle jerked it forward while slamming his head back, shattering the guy's nose with his skull. As Kyle spun around, the leader landed a powerful punch against the side of his face with his left hand. Only slightly dazed from the blow, Kyle bent down, wrapped his hands around the Glock, and put two bullets into the leader's left leg. He yelled in pain and lurched forward. As the two other guys came after Kyle, he used their leader as cover. Extending the Glock around the leader's flailing body, Kyle fired a series of rounds into the chests of the two other guys. Blood splattered out from their bodies and they jerked back, slamming into each other and into a nearby leather seat before toppling over and crashing onto the floor.

Kyle jumped to his feet, kicked the leader across the head, then aimed the Glock straight at his face. A stream of blood flowed out from his mangled nose. He was bent over, his hands wrapped around his bullet-riddled leg.

"Talk, asshole," Kyle said.

The guy struggled to breathe, then spat a gob of gooey blood onto the floor beside him.

"Screw you!" he fired back.

Agitated, Kyle kicked the guy's leg wounds a few times, then aimed the Glock at his right knee.

"Tell me who hired you or I'm gonna blow your kneecap off," Kyle said.

He stared back at Kyle, then grunted and said, "Carson Rich—"

The cockpit door slammed open, and one of the pilots came storming out, holding a Beretta pistol with two hands and aiming it straight at Kyle. He only had a split second to react, and he used it to hurl his body behind the nearby leather chair. The pilot opened fire, letting loose a repetitive barrage of bullets that exploded into the seat and paneling around him.

In the loud chaos, Kyle crawled under the seat, took aim, and fired a bullet into the pilot's right ankle. He yelled in pain and his lower body gave out, causing him to topple over and land hard on the floor.

Kyle fired two more shots, striking the pilot in the chest and forehead. His head blew open and splattered against the leather seat behind him, then his body went motionless.

Kyle rose to his feet, keeping his gaze forward just in case the other pilot decided to make a move.

"Give me the key," he said to the leader.

The battered and bloodied guy handed it over, and Kyle kicked him in the head, knocking him unconscious. Kyle dropped to one knee and quickly removed the handcuffs. Rising up, he moved towards the cockpit with his Glock raised. Before he'd made it halfway through the cabin, the plane suddenly banked sharply to the left. Kyle flew across a nearby seat and slammed against the right-side paneling. He struggled to his feet and felt the plane descending rapidly. Fighting for every inch, he soon grabbed the door and pulled himself into the cockpit.

The pilot was seated. He looked focused and intense as he turned and looked over his shoulder at Kyle.

"Go ahead," the pilot said. "Kill the only pilot left on this plane. Seal your death warrant."

Kyle paused as he kept his Glock aimed at the guy. He'd taken a few flying lessons before but knew that there was no way in hell he could land a plane like this. He glanced over the pilot at the instrument panel, watching as the altitude continued to drop. He needed a plan and he needed one fast. He thought about options, about where they could land to give him the best chance to escape.

"Where are we?" Kyle asked.

The pilot paused for a moment. "The middle of nowhere," he finally said. "A hundred miles or so north of Cuba."

Kyle was in a difficult position, he knew that. The most important thing was to get as far away as possible from the US.

"Turn us around," Kyle said. "Back to South America. And stop taking us down."

Their elevation had dropped to below ten thousand feet. Sheets of rain splattered against the windshield, and lightning cracked all around them.

"How much fuel do we have?"

The pilot tilted his head and pointed towards a gauge. As Kyle leaned closer to read it, the pilot slammed his right elbow into his cheek. His head jerked, and pain radiated as the pilot jumped out of his seat, grabbed the Glock still gripped in Kyle's hands, and slammed it into the wall behind him. It rattled to the floor as Kyle twisted the pilot around and slammed his head into the door frame.

The pilot retaliated, and they scuffled on the floor for a few seconds while the plane flew out of control. The pilot struck Kyle across the face, then choked him, wrapping his fingers around his neck and squeezing with both hands. Just as Kyle felt his consciousness begin to fade, he reached as far as he could behind him and grabbed the Glock, firing round after round into the pilot's chest. Blood spewed out as his body shook and fell to the floor. He went lifeless, his eyes rolling up into his skull as blood pooled around him.

Kyle jumped to his feet and sat in the pilot's seat. The plane had an elevation of just a few hundred feet when he grabbed the controls. He extended the flaps and slowed the engines, trying to lower the plane's speed as much as possible. He pulled back on the controls, but it was no use. They were going down at too steep of an angle and all Kyle could do was level it out as best as he could.

The storm's intensity seemed to grow even worse as rain splattered against the windshield in thick sheets. The occasional flash of lightning allowed him to see the thrashing waves below. He strapped the full-harness seatbelt over his body, and within seconds, the plane crashed into the surface of the angry ocean. The windshield shattered, and water slammed into Kyle as his world went black in a loud and blurry instant.

TWO

Key West National Wildlife Refuge
March 2009

The light of the late-afternoon sun glistened poetically over the clear water around me as I prepared to jump in. I couldn't help but smile as I stepped to the edge of the swim platform. Gripping my pole spear in one hand and my freediving fins in the other, I extended my right leg far out into the water. With a warm splash, the ocean overtook me. I relished the magical transition from the world above to the colorful paradise of sprawling marine life below.

I treaded on the surface just long enough to slide into my fins, then took in a deep breath and dove down. The four pounds of lead weights strapped around my waist allowed me to exert minimal energy while kicking for the bottom forty feet below. Every few kicks, I squeezed my nose and tried to breathe out slowly, equalizing my ears to the pressure. As I torpedoed towards the seafloor, the blur of colors took shape, revealing patches of elkhorn coral and brain coral and parades of various species of fish passing by or swimming to stay still in the current.

When I reached the bottom, the air in my lungs contracted to less than half its original volume as the pressure of just over two atmospheres pushed down on me. With my body relaxed, I stretched out horizontally along the seafloor and scanned the alien-like environment around me. Assimilating into the underwater world as best as I could, I moved slowly and kept my eyes peeled, relishing the hunt.

Through the tiny holes in a large dark red gorgonian, I spotted a hogfish gliding over a patch of turtle grass. Keeping my eyes glued to my prey, I gave a few smooth, strong kicks. I finned slowly alongside it, careful not to spook it as its orange body swam for a cluster of rocks covered in sediment and assorted plant growth. Extending the spear out in front of me, I pulled the band back as far as I could, getting it nice and tight, ready to fire.

I kept my body flat, gliding with the current as I moved in close to the unsuspecting hogfish. As it reached the rocks, it turned sideways, giving me a good target. I took aim and released the spear. The band snapped forward and launched the spear through the water. A fraction of a second later, the single-pronged tip stabbed through the scaly flesh in the small space between its black eyes and its gills, killing it instantly.

The brightly colored fish went motionless, floating aimlessly into the rocks with the spear sticking a few feet through its body. I grabbed hold of the spear and smiled as I turned and finned back towards the surface. On the way up, I spotted Jack swimming roughly fifty feet away from me, his wiry tanned body propelling him through the water like a fish as he searched the bottom for his own quarry.

I surfaced at the stern of my forty-eight-foot Baia Flash named *Dodging Bullets*. Grabbing hold of the ladder, I hoisted my catch up onto the swim platform and slid my mask down to hang around my neck. Atticus, my one-year-old yellow lab, ran over beside me, his tail wagging against the transom.

"Not bad, eh, boy?" I said, scratching behind his right ear.

I'd only had Atticus for a little over a month and had quickly learned of his love for seafood. He looked even more excited than I did for the future meals the fish would bring.

Jack surfaced beside me suddenly. He removed his mask, then slid his long blond hair off his face with his left hand and dropped his fish beside mine. He'd caught a black bass, one of the largest I'd ever seen.

"He was a quick bugger," he said in his usual laid-back tone. "I nearly missed him."

Jack Rubio was one of my oldest friends. We'd first met back in '89 while my dad was stationed at Naval Station Key West. He was born and bred in the Keys and a third-generation conch. He loved where he lived and embraced the island lifestyle as much as anyone alive.

I slid off my fins and climbed up onto the swim platform. Pulling the spear out of the hogfish's head, I held it triumphantly in the air.

"Looks like hogfish is on the menu for a few

days," I said. "Did you see those antennae sticking out from that outcropping?"

I was surprised to see them in such shallow water, given that we were nearing the end of lobster season, and catching bugs was a favorite for locals and tourists alike.

"That's not all I saw. There were a few rows of red-and-white spikes."

"Lionfish?"

He nodded.

Lionfish are beautiful, vibrantly colorful fish that are popular in saltwater aquariums. Though easy on the eyes, the natives of the Indian Ocean and the South Pacific have long venomous spines radiating from almost every part of their body. Their venom is harmful to many sea creatures and can cause extreme pain and paralysis lasting for days for humans. Through a combination of storms and negligent pet owners, these predators have been released over the years and have spread viciously throughout the Western Atlantic and the Caribbean, becoming an invasive species.

"These unwelcome guests showed up here recently and they're spreading like wildfire," Jack said.

I gave Jack a hand as he climbed up onto the deck, then I wrapped both of our fish with an old issue of the *Keynoter* and stowed them away in my Yeti.

"I thought they'd been here for years," I said. "I remember spearing a few off South Carolina back in '05."

"Nah, bro. Not in the Keys. As far as I know, the first ones were spotted just a few months ago. Sadly it was only a matter of time."

I paused for a moment, then turned to face Jack. "I speared a few off Key Largo back when I was driving down to move here. That was back in March of last year. Damn, I would have told someone had I known."

"Really? Well, I wouldn't beat myself up about it. And you've been here for a year is all?"

I nodded. "A year next week."

He shook his head.

"What a year it's been. You know, when you first told me you were moving to the Keys, I imagined you sitting back and relaxing for a while. I think that train of thought lasted about six seconds until you went right into telling me about the Aztec treasure." He laughed, and I couldn't help but join him as I grabbed a can of coconut water from the cooler and took a few swigs. "It's been an exciting year, and you've got the scars to prove it."

He motioned towards the wounds I'd received since moving to the Keys, mainly on my chest. Only a few knife wounds and the bullet wound were clearly visible.

I stepped back down to the swim platform.

"Yeah, well, the only excitement I'm looking for right now is to round up some lions."

Jack smiled. "Don't forget the bugs. If those delicacies think they're making it out of this season alive, they've got another thing coming."

We spent another half hour beneath the waves, rounding up as many bugs as we could find and spearing every lionfish in sight. By the time we climbed back out of the water, we'd bagged five lobsters and three lionfish.

We removed our fins, masks, and weight belts, then rinsed them off with fresh water on the swim platform before stowing them under the half-moon seat around the outdoor dinette. I grabbed a pair of towels from the sunbed. Handing one to Jack, I patted down my body and my dripping brown hair, then slid into a white cutoff tee shirt.

Since the water was still calm and we had the site to ourselves, we decided to have an early dinner right there on the water. I brought out my portable propane grill from the salon and mounted it to the starboard gunwale just aft of the helm. Within minutes we had it fired up, the sound of Jimmy Buffet playing through the outdoor speakers as the smell of sizzling lobster mixed with the fresh salty breeze filled our nostrils. Atticus went crazy at the smell, getting so excited I thought he might have a heart attack.

When we finished grilling, we sat around the dinette and enjoyed the fruits of our labor while taking in the sights. We were anchored over the reef about twenty miles southwest of Key West. We were only a half a mile east of Neptune's Table, a unique underwater ledge where we'd discovered the Aztec treasure almost a year earlier. The southern horizon was empty, just stretches of blue Atlantic as far as the eye could see. To the north, we could see small slivers of the Marquesas Keys, Boca Grande Key, and Woman Key. We could also see a number of boats in the distance along the reef, mainly fishing boats and dive charters.

After filling my stomach with a final bite of lobster dipped in garlic butter, I washed it down with the rest of my Paradise Sunset beer, a local brew from Keys Disease brewery. I gave Atticus the meat from an entire bug, and he rose in joyous surprise as we handed him the leftovers as well. He scarfed down the food in less than a minute, then relaxed on the deck in the shade beside the dinette.

As I leaned back into the white cushioned seat, my iPhone suddenly vibrated to life. Snatching it from the table, I glanced at the screen and saw that I'd received a text message from Angelina.

"How are you getting a signal out here, bro?" Jack said, looking at my phone in amazement.

"I talked to Quincy over at Queen Anne's and he hooked me up with a top-of-the-line signal booster."

I smiled as I opened the message and saw that Ange had sent me a picture. It was of her and two other women holding on to a metal chain as they climbed Half Dome in Yosemite National Park. After spending eight years in the Navy, I had gone to work as a mercenary working various jobs around the world. It was during a job that I'd met Ange, and we'd dated on-again, off-again for years before she'd moved in with me in Key West. We'd been living together for seven months and were rarely apart during that time. The truth was, her visiting California with some old friends was the first time we'd been apart for more than a couple of days since she'd moved to the Keys.

"When does she get back again?"

"A week or so," I said. "Hard to tell for sure. Like me she rarely buys round-trip tickets."

He took a few more swigs of beer, then leaned back and grinned at me.

"You sure have incredible luck, bro," he said. "Ange is quite the woman: beautiful, smart, and quite possibly the most badass girl on the planet."

"Yeah," I said, nodding. "There's no one like her."

Jack paused for a moment, then leaned forward, removed his sunglasses and set them on the table.

"Look, we've known each other for years and we've always been honest with each other. And since your dad's not around anymore, I feel like it's my duty to ask you when you're planning on manning up here."

I looked at my old friend, wondering what he was talking about.

"Manning up?" I said.

"Yeah. With Ange. When are you gonna marry her, Logan?"

I smiled, looked out over the blue ocean and took in a deep breath of fresh air. A moment later, I slid out of the seat, rose to my feet and strode down through the salon door without a word.

"You're not getting off that easy, bro," Jack said, chuckling.

I stepped down into the salon, and headed forward into the main cabin. I moved along the port side, between the edge of the queen-sized bed and the head, reached down, and pulled out the top drawer of my nightstand. Reaching up into a narrow empty space, I grabbed a small hand-carved wooden box, then dropped it into my shorts pocket and closed the drawer.

When I returned to the deck, I saw that Atticus had jumped onto the white cushioned seat beside Jack, who'd just popped open another cold one. He raised his hands in the air when he saw me appear.

"No need for the silent treatment," he said jokingly. "And I mean it in the nicest way possible when I say that you're never gonna do better. And if you think that you—"

He went quiet in an instant as he dropped his gaze down and saw the tiny wooden box I'd set on the table in front of him. With a satisfied grin, he grabbed it and hinged it open. The magnificent four-carat diamond glistened in the afternoon sun, and Jack's mouth dropped to the deck when he saw it.

"This is crazy," he said. "Look at the details here," he added, pointing to the intricate patterns along the edge of the platinum band. "How much did this set you back?"

"It was my mom's," I said. "Dad left it to me in his will. He wrote that he hoped I would find a finger for it one day."

My dad, Owen Dodge, had been a Master Diver in the Navy and one of the most experienced aquanauts I'd ever met. He told me that he'd found the ring in a shipwreck off the coast of Tangier back in the seventies.

Jack set the ring back in the box, then rose to his feet and wrapped an arm around me. After congratulating me, he took another swig from his beer and said, "I guess this means I need to buy a suit, huh?"

"Yeah, right," I replied. "I'm not extravagant, and if I know Ange, she won't want anything fancy either. That is, if she says yes."

"If?" Jack raised his eyebrows. "That woman's crazy about you, bro."

I smiled, then glanced down at my dive watch and saw that it was just past 1900. "Hey, we should get going. Pete said the mic gets hot at sunset."

Jack nodded and killed the rest of his beer.

"Never miss a chance to see the Wayward Suns," he said as he rose to his feet and climbed up onto the bow. "I got the lanyard once you bring up the steel."

I operated the windlass remotely at the helm, bringing up the anchor rode into the locker until the shackle rattled against the rim of the bow. Working slowly, I brought the anchor up, securing it in place. After Jack attached the safety lanyard, he climbed back down into the cockpit and I started up the twin six-hundred-horsepower engines. Within a few minutes I had us up on plane, heading towards Key West with the sun setting at our backs. The Baia has a top speed of just over fifty knots, but I usually like to keep her at her cruising speed of forty.

As we cruised past Crawfish Key off the port bow, my phone vibrated on the dash, indicating that I'd received another message. It surprised me because it was from an unknown number, and when I replied, asking who it was, I got no response.

"Hello, old friend," was all it said.

THREE

We pulled into the Conch Harbor Marina at 2000 and I eased the Baia's hull against the dock fenders at slip twenty-four. Jack stepped onto the dock and I killed the engines as he tied us off to the cleats. He said he'd meet me back there in thirty, then flip-flopped down the dock to where his boat, a forty-five-foot Sea Ray, was moored.

After connecting the shore power cables and freshwater hose, I moved down into the main cabin and took a shower. Even though the ocean temperature in March off Key West averages around seventy-five degrees, there's something about a hot shower after a long day out on the water that feels indescribable.

After stepping out and toweling off, I slid on a pair of cargo shorts and a Rubio Charters tee shirt, then laced on a pair of Converse low-tops. After patting Atticus goodbye and setting out some food and water, I turned on the security system, locked up the salon door, and met Jack on the dock. In the parking lot, we hopped into my black Toyota Tacoma 4x4 and drove over to Salty Pete's Bar, Grill, and Museum. With the sun down and out, leaving the tropical paradise in darkness, downtown Key West transformed into its usual night scene, with tourists walking the streets and island music playing from every corner.

We pulled into one of the last vacant parking spots in the crushed-shell lot beside Salty Pete's. Pete Jameson, the owner of the unique establishment, was an old friend of Jack's and knew the southern Florida islands as well as anyone alive. His place was on Mangrove Street, close enough to attract the Duval tourists but far enough away to maintain a more relaxed vibe.

Moving towards the main entrance of what looked more like a well-renovated house than a restaurant, we pulled open the wooden door and were greeted instantly by the ringing of a bell and the smell of grilled seafood. The place was packed, with almost every table and booth filled and waitresses busily shuffling food, taking orders, and clearing dirty dishes. Pete's was nothing like the rundown restaurant I'd walked into when I'd first moved back to the Keys. It had all new furnishings, windows, and hardwood floors. But the freshly painted walls were still covered with assorted knickknacks, including an old wooden helm, a massive fishing net decorated with crabs and shells, and pictures taken around the Florida Keys over the years, retaining the restaurant's classic charm.

Mia, a former waitress and the newly promoted

floor manager, spotted us from across the busy dining room. She was pretty, with long dark hair she kept in a ponytail, a lean physique, and a small patch of freckles around her nose. She wore a Key lime green Salty Pete's tee shirt, black shorts, and a pair of tennis shoes. Smiling, she waved us over, then pointed towards the large wooden staircase at the back of the dining room.

"They're all upstairs at the center stage table," she said. As we passed by, she added, "Jack, you're starting to scare me. You never used to show up on time for anything."

Jack laughed. "It's Logan's fault. He wears a watch." He pointed at the Suunto dive watch strapped around my left wrist.

The second floor of Salty Pete's was lined with rows of glass cases containing various artifacts Pete had assembled during his years in the Keys. We headed for a large sliding glass door that led out to the balcony, where a small crowd had gathered around the tables and outdoor bar. The door was wide open, allowing us to hear the Wayward Suns as they performed their mic checks on the humble stage.

Pete made eye contact as we stepped out and signaled us over to a round table right beside the stage. He was in his sixties with tanned, leathery skin and a mostly bald head with thin patches of gray hair. He was half a foot shorter than my six foot two, drank enough to maintain an impressive beer belly, and had a metal hook in lieu of a right hand. As Jack and I weaved through the people, Pete slid his chair back and rose to his feet with the springy movements of a much younger man.

"Well, if it isn't the two sons I never had," he said in his rough yet friendly tone. He wrapped an arm around each of us and ushered us to the table. “Where’s the beautiful Angelina?” When I told him that she was away for a week, he said, “That’s too bad. She sure makes this town look good.”

Jack and I sat beside Pete in the only empty chairs on the balcony. A few other locals sat around the table, including Frank Murchison, a brilliant professor who’d been a big help in our discovery of U-3546, the lost German U-boat, and had been by my side while fighting off a notorious Mexican drug cartel for a buried pirate treasure. Harper Ridley, a writer for the *Keynoter* for the past twenty years, also sat at the table.

Pete had an article that Harper had written in the most recent issue unfolded in front of him. Apparently, it was about a new resort being opened up in Key Largo that Pete wasn’t too excited about. They were just at the end of a passionate exchange when Jack and I arrived. I pretended to listen for a few minutes, but really just enjoyed the music and thought about the delicious meal to come.

The table was full of appetizers, and I grabbed a plateful of conch fritters and fried pickles, then filled my glass from a pitcher of their famous Key limeade. Their chef, Oz, a big Scandinavian guy, whipped up some of the best food I’d ever had. One of the waitresses brought over a few Paradise Sunset beers and a mojito just as the music started. The Wayward Suns played a unique combination of reggae and country music, and within minutes they had our island paradise rocking as they sang about exotic beaches, hammocks swaying under palm trees, and beautiful lovers lost.

Sitting on the balcony, listening to the music and enjoying the food among friends, I couldn’t help feeling an overwhelming sense of satisfaction. I found myself missing Ange, though. I brought up the message she'd sent me and zoomed in on her stunning face adorned with brilliant blue eyes and covered by her long blond hair. As I closed the message and was about to slide my phone back into my pocket, I noticed the other message I'd received recently, the one from the mysterious old friend.

As I put my phone away, I looked up and saw a man on the other side of the sliding glass door. He was standing still, staring straight at me. As my eyes focused, I tried to figure out who he was. There was something familiar about his stature, but it was difficult to see his face through the glare from the light of the tiki torches reflecting off the glass. In a moment of clarity, I saw his face. My eyes grew wide instantly and my jaw nearly slammed against the table.

"Shit," I said to myself in a tone that was overshadowed by the sound of the band and the crowd cheering and singing along.

I slid my chair back a few inches instinctively, and faster than a blink, he vanished. It was like he'd never been there at all.

Was I seeing things? Had the years of fighting taken their toll on me? One too many blows to the head, perhaps?

I didn't know how to explain what I'd seen, and there was a part of me that wanted it to be a hallucination.

"You alright, bro?" Jack said, snapping me from my thoughts.

I shook my head softly and blinked a few times before turning my head and making eye contact with him.

"You look like you've just seen a ghost," he added.

For a moment I was quiet. A ghost. Had I seen a ghost?

"Yeah, I'm good," I said. Without thinking, I slid my chair back a few more inches and rose to my feet. "I'll be right back." Then, motioning to my empty Collins glass, I added, "Can you have her bring me another one when she comes by?"

Jack nodded, and I could tell he knew that something was bothering me. Without another word, I moved through the crowd, comprised of a mixture of intoxicated islanders and tourists, heading for the sliding glass door. When I reached it, I took a quick look around before stepping inside.

Other than the balcony, the second floor was devoid of people. It was well lit, so I could see most every corner of Pete's museum and there was no sign of anyone. A strong combination of curiosity and confusion led me downstairs, where the main dining area was still packed with lively patrons.

"Hey, Logan," a low voice said from behind me as I moved for the front door.

I turned around and saw Oz, Pete's large Scandinavian chef. He had long blond hair, wore a dirty apron, and towered over me.

"Hey, did you see anyone come through recently?" I asked.

He shrugged. "It's a busy night. Lots of people coming and going. What do they look like?"

"Never mind," I said, waving a hand in the air and turning back towards the main entrance.

"Are you leaving?"

"Just gonna step out a sec," I said. I pressed my shoulder against the door. "I'll be right back."

A moment later I was out the door, down the steps, and crunching the seashells under the soles of my Converse. I looked around, scanning the area and taking note of every detail. There were a few pedestrians strolling down Mangrove Street, a sunburned guy with a button-up Hawaiian-style shirt here, a woman wearing a sundress and flip-flops there, but no one resembling who I'd seen.

Had he just vanished? Maybe Jack was right. Maybe I had seen a ghost.

I walked towards the end of the parking lot until I reached a row of coco plum bushes and the remnants of a white picket fence. A group of college-aged kids strolled past, taking up most of the street and being about as loud and obnoxious as humanly possible.

Part of the spring break crowd, I thought.

Though Key West wasn't nearly as popular as Miami or Panama City for spring break, it still received a large handful of rowdy college kids every year.

I took one more look around, then turned and headed back for Pete's.

Maybe I hit my head one too many times over the years, I thought as I looked up at what was visible of the balcony, where the Wayward Suns were still playing.

Less than a second after the thought entered my mind, I heard the loud and unmistakable sound of a gunshot.

FOUR

My instincts took over. In the blink of an eye, I bent my knees slightly, whipped my body around, and took cover beside a parked Ford Explorer as I snatched my Sig from my waistband. The shot had come from the other side of Mangrove Street, and I watched as people who'd been walking casually only moments earlier ran frantically away from the scene.

Rising over the hood of the SUV, I spotted movement in an alley between Mike's scooter rental pavilion and the tackle shop beside it. With my Sig held in front of me, I moved towards the street. The glow of the streetlights bled into the alley, revealing the outline of two figures engaged in a fistfight.

As I moved in closer, I could make out minor details of their appearance. One of them wore a black suit, and the other wore shorts, a tee shirt, and a ski mask covering his face. It was clear that both men knew how to carry themselves, but as the soles of my shoes hit the pavement and I closed in to less than a hundred feet away from them, Ski Mask put a quick and painful end to the fight. In a flash of well-timed and meticulous movements, Ski Mask landed an elbow, then wrapped his left arm around Suit's neck and flung his body through the air, slamming him hard onto the pavement.

I was halfway across the street when Suit hit the ground. My Sig was raised, and my eyes scanned the area. I spotted a handgun on the ground beside one of the parked scooters about twenty feet away from where Ski Mask had just body-slammed his opponent. With no way of knowing whether or not there was another gun, I kept my sight locked on Ski Mask.

Suit groaned painfully then went motionless, clearly knocked out from the blow. Before Ski Mask spotted me, I moved into the alley and closed in roughly thirty feet from where he stood with his back facing me.

"Hands in the air!" I barked with my right index finger hovering over the trigger, ready for him to make a move.

Upon hearing my voice, his head snapped sideways and he focused on me, looking like a spooked rabid animal. Seeing the guy closer for the first time, I realized that he had the build of a guy who damned well knew his way around a gym. He had dark coffee-colored skin. He looked to be a few inches shorter than me, and his vein-riddled muscles bulged out of his shirt. He had the lean, muscular legs of a world-class sprinter. Though it was difficult to estimate with the mask on, I judged him to be around my age.

When his eyes met mine, he seemed to relax a

little, which surprised me considering he was also staring into the barrel of a loaded weapon. For a brief moment, I saw what looked like a smile materialize through the narrow cut of fabric around his mouth. Then, in the blink of an eye, he turned and darted toward the back of the alley.

"Freeze!" I yelled as my lower body accelerated unconsciously towards him.

But I knew it was useless. He'd broken into a full-on sprint, and I only had a fraction of a second to weigh the situation and make a decision.

I can't shoot a guy for getting in a brawl, I thought.

I ran down the alley and, upon reaching the guy lying motionless on his back, I quickly checked his pulse. Seeing that he would most likely be fine, I looked up just in time to see Ski Mask disappear around the back of the building.

Rising to my feet, I secured my Sig back in its holster and took off after him. It probably wasn't the smart thing to do, I knew that, but I was never one to just sit by and watch injustice without retaliating. I ran as fast as I could, pumping my arms and keeping my eyes trained ahead of me. I slowed as I hit the corner, my right hand hovering over my Sig as I moved around the back of the wooden building.

Ski Mask was weaving around a dumpster and a trailered Jet Ski as I accelerated towards him. He rolled over the hood of a parked Camry, then made quick work of an eight-foot chain-link fence. I managed to barely cut the distance between us as I slid over the sedan, grabbed hold of the thin metal links, and hurled my body over the top. I landed softly on the sidewalk, bending my knees to absorb the force, and continued the chase. He was fast, very fast, but I knew that there were few people who could outlast me in a foot race, so long as I kept them in view.

I followed him down the sidewalk alongside Fleming Street, heading west. We weaved in and out of worried pedestrians, and Ski Mask almost got rammed by a bicyclist who just managed to brake at the last second, ringing his bell and shouting in anger at both of us as we passed by. My heart was pounding and my adrenaline was pumping as we neared Duval Street. I could hear a mixture of island music and smelled grilled burgers and seafood as we neared the most popular stretch of pavement in the Keys.

When we reached Duval, Ski Mask cut a hard right, wrapping his arm around the trunk of a lignum vitae tree to help redirect his momentum. With reckless abandon, he dashed into traffic, narrowly avoiding a flamingo-colored taxi as its brakes screeched and its horn honked repeatedly. I followed right on his tail and felt a sudden rush of relief as I spotted a white Key West Police Interceptor heading straight for Ski Mask.

The officer braked when he spotted us, causing the trolley to almost rear end him as it screeched to a stop just a few feet behind. My quarry didn't skip a beat. Without a second's thought, he jumped onto the hood of the police car, ran over its hardtop, and hurled his body onto the roof of the red-and-green trolley. The officer switched on his red and blue lights along with the whining siren that dominated the sounds around it.

I watched in awe as Ski Mask, keeping his momentum going, ran along the top of the trolley, then jumped onto the eave on the second story of Margaritaville.

Who the hell is this guy? I thought as I ran past the officer, who I recognized instantly as Deputy Jane Verona. She was just stepping out of the driver's-side door and had her government-issued handgun held with both hands. Fortunately, she recognized me instantly as well from the hours I'd spent at the police station over the past year.

"Call the sheriff," I said, keeping my eyes locked on my quarry. My words were rushed and loud, and my heart pounded in my chest. "There's a guy unconscious back at Pete's."

In a blur of quick movement, Ski Mask disappeared over the edge of the roof just as I stormed through the front door of the iconic island restaurant. Jimmy Buffett was singing the chorus to "Cheeseburger in Paradise," his voice resonating through the speakers and intermingling with the sounds of a full house of mostly intoxicated tourists.

I ran past a confused hostess and nearly knocked over a waiter carrying a tray of wings and mozzarella sticks, who somehow managed to keep it balanced as I maneuvered past him and headed up the stairs. Few people seemed to notice me or care what I was doing as I reached the top step and moved as fast as I could through the sea of people, tables, and chairs.

I ran for a propped-open window on the west wall that looked out towards dark ocean beyond. Without hesitating, I lunged through the window into the fresh evening air and onto a narrow balcony. It was dark and my eyes weren't adjusted to it, but I heard fast-moving footsteps, and as I looked to my left, I saw a dark outline running just a few steps away from me. He was sprinting towards the edge, and it looked like he was going to try and jump the roughly fifteen-foot gap to the roof of the building beside us.

I charged towards him, dug my right foot into the edge of the balcony, and extended my body as far as I could. Just as he was preparing to jump, I tripped him up, slamming my arms into his shins and causing him to collapse hard onto the clay-tiled roof, just inches from the edge. He grunted and groaned as I grabbed hold of his legs and pulled myself up. Positioning myself so that I could take him down with a choke hold, I was caught off guard by a sudden and powerful kick of his heel into my forehead. Pain surged as my head snapped back. I reflexively loosened my grip, and he struggled to his feet. As I shook myself from the daze, he accelerated for the edge and conquered the gap, his body rolling as it made contact with the roof of the adjoining building.

With my forehead burning, I jumped to my feet and watched as he quickly disappeared into the night. I shook my head slightly, and took in a few deep breaths. There was no doubt in my mind that the guy I'd seen through the sliding glass door at Pete's and the one who'd just kicked me in the head were the same person. A man I used to know. A man I'd once fought alongside. A man who was supposed to be dead.

FIVE

By the time I made it back to Pete's, it was nearly midnight, and the Wayward Suns were just finishing up. A small crowd had gathered on the sidewalk, and an ambulance was parked on the corner of Mangrove and Fleming, but the paramedics were just standing beside it, looking like they didn't know what to do. I met Jack in the alley where the fight had occurred and, to my surprise, the guy in the suit was nowhere to be found.

"Jeez, bro, are you alright?" he asked, looking at my forehead.

I knew it probably looked bad, though I hadn't looked in a mirror yet. The blood had dried, but I could feel a mark right where my hairline started.

"Looks worse than it feels," I said. "Did you see the guy in the suit?"

He nodded. "I figured something was wrong by

the look in your eye," he said. "As I headed for the front door, I heard the gunshot, then watched through the window as you chased after that guy. After telling Mia to call the police, I ran over to see if the guy on the ground was alright."

"What happened to him?" I asked, looking up and down the empty alley.

"A car pulled up and a handful of guys stepped out. They picked him up, hauled him into the backseat, then peeled off down Mangrove." He shook his head, reliving the moment. "I tried to figure out who they were, but it happened fast. They pulled up and were gone in less than thirty seconds."

"What did they look like?"

Jack shrugged. "Like the guy on the ground. They were dressed in black suits, all of them well built. They looked like FBI or CIA agents, but I sure as hell don't think they were. They had a hardnosed aura about them, bro."

I scanned the alley, looking for anything that might have been left behind that we could use as a clue. The handgun was gone, and as far as I could tell, they'd even managed to swipe the bullet casing from the ground.

Less than a minute after I made it back, a white Police Interceptor pulled in front of us that had the word "Sheriff" plastered on its side next to the outline of a gold star. Charles Wilkes, head of the Key West police department, stepped out of the driver's-side door. He was wearing his typical dark blue uniform with short sleeves. His tall frame, lean build, and dark black complexion were unmistakable. He was in his late forties, but he moved more like a man in his early thirties.

"I might have to start putting you on the payroll,"

he said as he walked over to us. After we shook hands, he added, "You always seem to be in the right place at the right time, Logan. So what happened here?"

I gave him a brief overview of the situation and the events that had led up to it.

"Any idea who they were?" he asked.

"No," I lied. "Could be anyone. My guess is they were drinking and got into a scuffle."

"And Officer Verona said you chased him? Why?"

I sighed. "I wanted to stop him. I figured it wouldn't be too hard, but I underestimated him."

After giving Charles as good of a description as I could of the guy in the suit and a very generic description of the guy I'd chased, he thanked us and climbed back into his car. Jack and I headed back over to Pete's, and I downed a few glasses of water while the Wayward Suns played their last song for the night. It was about sailing the Caribbean on a cloudless night, with a warm breeze and a sky full of brilliant stars. But I barely heard a word of it as my mind played over the recent series of events.

Even after calling it a night, driving Jack home, and pulling my Tacoma into the Conch Harbor Marina parking lot, the incident was still fresh in my head. I decided to spend the night on the Baia. I liked sleeping on the water; the smells, the sounds, and the peaceful rocking. I often opted to sleep on my boat even though I had a perfectly good house just a short drive away.

It was almost midnight when I grabbed a bottle of tequila and plopped down on the sunbed. Looking out over the water, I saw that only a few other boaters were awake, and I relished the relative quiet.

The reasonable part of my brain tried to convince the rest of me that it wasn't him. That there was no possible way it could be him. He was dead. Gone. He'd been gone for ten years, and he was never coming back.

Then who was it?

In my heart, I knew the answer to that question. In my heart, I knew that it was my old friend and comrade, a man I'd once trusted with my life, a man who'd squandered that trust and turned his back on his duty.

I heard a sound coming from down the dock and it shook me from my thoughts. It was the rhythmic clapping of footsteps, and it was growing louder. I turned my head to look down towards the parking lot and saw a figure approaching. The marina lights went out at ten on the weekends, so I couldn't get a great look at him, but it didn't matter. I knew who it was.

I propped myself up and planted my feet on the deck. I shot a quick glance to my right, making sure my Sig was within arm's reach on the cushioned seat beside me. Turning my attention back to my approaching guest, I watched as he moved with smooth, athletic strides, never once swiveling his head. He kept his gaze forward, looking straight back at me.

The marina had died down; the only sounds were the occasional flapping of lines against masts, the soft splashing of fish breaking the surface to catch an unsuspecting insect, and the gentle rocking of hulls against fenders.

I watched as he walked right up to my slip, and my eyes grew wide when he stepped into the dim light from the cockpit. He was wearing the same thing he had been when I'd chased him a few hours earlier—black tennis shoes, basketball shorts, and a skintight muscle tee shirt. I didn't feel threatened or in danger in any way. No, the only instinct I felt was anger upon seeing his face, which, though I recognized it right away, had clearly aged since the last time we had seen each other over ten years earlier. He had a chiseled jaw, light brown eyes, and short black hair. His face was hardened from a lifetime of fighting, making it clear to anyone who looked closely that this was a man you didn't want to mess with.

"Hello, Logan," he said in his smooth New York City accent.

He spoke in a nonchalant tone, though I could sense the anger deep within his voice.

"What are you doing here, Kyle?"

He gave a heated smirk and bobbed his head slowly. "So it's gonna be like that," he said. A second later, he added, "Alright."

He stepped off the dock onto the swim platform, and I jumped to my feet.

"Get off my boat."

He paused, and raised his hands in the air.

"Is that any way to treat an old friend?" he said. "I mean, shit, it's been like what, ten years?" His eyes scanned around my boat. "Nice to see you're doing so well for yourself." His tone had shifted to sarcastic. "But I guess you were always good at looking out for yourself, weren't you?"

"That's something coming from you," I said. "Look, you wanna talk about what happened, fine. You wanna talk about how you survived and where the hell you've been all these years, fine. But don't come here pointing fingers and blaming me for the mistakes that you made."

"Mistakes?" he said, taking a step towards me and raising his voice. "You still don't have a clue, do you?"

I paused a moment, then bit my lip in frustration. "You know, I stood up for you. I did. I put my ass on the line, my career and reputation at risk, in order to defend you. But I know what I saw, Kyle. I remember what happened like it was yesterday. You violated a direct order and put our entire platoon at risk."

"I saved our platoon!" he fired back. "We would all be dead now if I hadn't done anything. Each and every one of us."

I shook my head. "You and your conspiracy theory."

He stepped closer, moving to within arm's length, and pointed a finger in my face.

"You ignorant piece of—"

Years of pent-up anger surged forth from within me in an instant. My right hand instinctively squeezed into a fist, and in one quick motion, I lunged towards Kyle and hurled my knuckles into the side of his jaw. His head snapped sideways, and he grunted as bone met bone in a forceful and painful collision.

He stepped back, catching himself against the transom, and quickly regained his balance. His face had transformed into a combination of rage and focus. In the blink of an eye, he retaliated. Pressing his heels hard into the deck, he sprang at me like an NFL linebacker coming in for a blitz. I brought my arms up and tried to slide out of the way, but he was too fast. He slammed his shoulder into my chest, knocking the air from my lungs, and body-slammed me onto the sunbed.

He stayed on top of me, and with reckless abandon, he threw punch after punch at my chest. I managed to block a few of them, but the ones that landed sent burning pain radiating through my body.

"Do you have any idea what they did to me?" he said, his words coming out sporadically in between blows. "To my family?"

After redirecting a punch with my forearm, I wrapped my left arm around his neck and lurched his body to the side. I tried to get him in a choke hold, but he was strong, even stronger than I remembered him. We tussled back and forth on the sunbed, exchanging blows for what felt like an eternity.

Suddenly, we heard the ear-rattling sound of a whistle as someone ran down the dock towards the Baia. We shoved away from each other and I lay on my back, my head propped against the edge of the starboard windscreen. We glared at each other and both breathed audibly. The sounds from the whistle grew louder, and when I glanced over at the dock, I saw Gus running frantically towards where the stern was tied up. Gus Henderson owned the marina, a gift passed down from his parents, and he spent most nights on a little bed in the marina office. He was short, pale, and overweight, but he laid down the law in the marina like John Wayne.

I couldn't help but smile as I watched him run towards us wearing only a pair of boxers and a white tee shirt, blowing into his whistle like an angry traffic officer.

"Break it up!" he yelled. "The sheriff will be here any minute."

He finally ceased the painful whistling when he reached the dock beside us. Looking over the stern, his eyes grew wide when he looked at us.

"Logan!" he said. "What the hell's going on over here? Are you alright?"

He eyed Kyle skeptically.

I nodded. “We’re fine.” I rose up and propped myself on my elbows. “Really, Gus? A whistle?”

He shrugged. “Hey, it’s all I had on me.”

There was a brief silence as Gus scanned back and forth between me and Kyle, who was leaning against the dinette.

“Oh, Gus, this is James,” I said, not wanting to reveal his real name. “He’s a… he’s an old friend of mine who’s visiting. We were just having a disagreement.”

Kyle nodded slightly. His face had softened, and we were both relaxing, out of fight mode. Gus just looked at both of us, clearly confused.

“Well, for the sake of my other tenants, can you guys bury the hatchet? You’re waking people up.”

He motioned toward a few nearby boaters who’d switched on their deck lights and stepped out of their cabins to see what all of the fuss was about.

“Sure thing, Gus,” I said. “And sorry for the commotion. Can you call the sheriff and let him know he doesn’t have to come down? Tell him it was my fault and that our next breakfast is on me.”

Gus nodded, but he still looked skeptical of my old friend. He eyed him with a combination of confusion and distrust.

“It’s alright, really,” I assured him. I glanced over at Kyle, then added, “We won’t fight anymore, at least not here.”

He shrugged. “Logan, if this is how you greet old friends, don’t bother stopping by to see me if you ever move away and visit.” I laughed and he added, “I’m gonna go call the sheriff. You guys have a good night, and try to use your words.”

He turned and walked barefoot down the dock,

whistle in hand as he told a few nearby boaters that everything was fine. I sighed and looked over at Kyle, who was looking out at the ocean. I'd calmed down from my initial emotions of seeing him again for the first time. I remembered reading that Thomas Jefferson believed that when you were mad, you should count to ten before speaking, and when you were really mad, you should count to a hundred. Maybe one day I'd learn.

When we made eye contact, I said, "You want some coffee?"

He nodded. "Sure."

SIX

Kyle stepped down into the salon behind me and sat on the white cushioned couch on the port side. I went to work across from him, filling the back of the coffeemaker with water, then setting the filter in place and adding scoops of Colombian medium roast on top of it. As the machine went to work, I sat down on the other side of the couch and angled my body to face him.

"This is one hell of a boat," he said, his eyes scanning every inch of the interior.

"Thanks," I said. "It's a Baia Flash. I bought it when I moved down here a year ago."

Kyle smirked. "You've come a long way from Seaman Dodge and twelve hundred bucks a month."

I nodded, and the salon went quiet for a moment. Part of me still hadn't realized what was really happening. The magnitude of the situation was too much to take in all at once. Though once my friend, the man sitting beside me was practically a complete stranger. There was also the unsettling fact that he was a criminal, a man whose face had been plastered all over the news for years, a man who would be on the FBI's most wanted list if they knew he was still alive.

What the hell was I thinking having him there?

But despite the past, I didn't feel like I was in danger around him, even when we'd been wringing each other's necks.

The boiling water finished flowing down through the coffee, and I poured us both a mugful. Setting Kyle's on the table in front of him, I held mine by the handle and sat back down.

"Thanks," he said.

I took a sip and leaned forward. I had so many questions, I didn't know where to start.

"So are you gonna tell me what happened?" I asked. "Where you've been all these years?"

He shook his head. "What do you mean? I've been hiding, and it made it easier that everyone thought I was dead."

"And now you've decided to come here. Why? If the wrong person recognizes you, you'll be thrown in prison for life."

"I know what I'm doing," he said. "And you're right about that. I wonder, why haven't you called me in yet? Still got my back, Logan?" He said the last words with a sarcastic tone.

"For now, though I think I'll be beating myself up for it later like I did before."

"Like before?"

"Yeah. I stood up for you during all of the debriefs and depositions. They say those things are confidential, but we all know that's shit. I knew my career would never be the same after that. It's one of the biggest reasons I never reenlisted again."

"You didn't have my back in Colombia," he fired back.

"You disobeyed a direct order," I said, raising my voice. "And Manny died because of it."

"We'd all be dead if I hadn't," he said, rising to his feet.

I gritted my teeth as the image of Estrada's face appeared in my mind.

"You should leave," I said in a stern voice. "You shouldn't be here."

"No, I shouldn't, but I have to."

"What are you talking about?"

"I didn't do it, Logan!" He stepped towards me and stared fiercely into my eyes. "They tried to pin the whole thing on me. It was a ruse, the whole mission. It was an under-the-table, greedy deal, and you, me, and our entire platoon would have died had I not disobeyed that order."

I shook my head. "Back to this, huh?" I took another sip of coffee, trying to calm myself a little. "What about that guy in the alley? Why were you beating the crap out of him?"

"Those guys came after us," he said. "They found us, Logan. If they'd just tried to kill me, I wouldn't have cared. I'd have dealt with them and moved on. But those assholes came after my wife and daughters as well."

I was taken aback that someone would try and harm his family. I'd known his wife and had met his daughters a few times when they were babies.

"Are they alright?"

"They're safe. But that's the main reason I'm

here. You can only hide from your troubles for so long. Sooner or later the past catches up with you. And I know if I don't deal with these pests, I'll be running and fighting for the rest of my life."

"Who are they? How did they find you?"

He paused a moment. "I don't know for sure how they found me, but I know they work for Carson. No doubt they're Darkwater."

My eyes narrowed at the mention of her name. Carson Richmond was one of the wealthiest women in America. She owned a handful of casinos and resorts and spent much of her time with the nation's elite in business and politics. She was controversial, and numerous allegations had been made against her over the years, though none of them had ever made it to court. She was also the founder of Darkwater, a high-end private security firm that catered to the world's most elite citizens.

"She's behind everything, Logan. She's the reason we were in Colombia. She tried to kill all of us for her own gain."

I went silent for a moment, thinking over his words.

"So what do you plan to do, Kyle?"

He took in a deep breath and let it out. "I'm gonna bring her down. I'm gonna bring it all down, and I'm gonna bring the truth to light. She and her band of dirty traitors will pay for what they've done."

I finished my coffee and tried to let the words resonate for a few seconds before responding.

"How exactly do you plan to do that?" I asked, genuinely interested.

"I'm gonna find the plane," he declared.

I leaned back into the cushion, caught off guard by the seemingly random response.

"Find the plane?"

"It had intel aboard that I could use to prove that it was all a fabricated lie. If I can find it, bring it up and bring it to light, I can take these people down."

My mind was moving in all directions, but there was one key aspect of recent events that I couldn't wrap my head around. If Kyle was who the media and the government had made him out to be, then why were there people trying to kill him? Why not simply report him to authorities and bring him into custody?

I couldn't find an answer to that question, and it cast a cloud of doubt over my mind. I brought myself back to the moment, to the day the plane went down.

"They scoured the ocean for years looking for that hunk of metal," I said. "No sign of it was ever found. Nobody knows where it is."

"Nobody but me," he said. "But as much as it kills me to say it, I need your help. That's why I'm here."

"Why do you need my help?"

"Because you have a boat, and from what I've read about you in the past year, you have access to decent dive and salvage equipment. Because you can handle yourself in case we encounter more Darkwater. Because you didn't shoot me. And because you haven't reported me to the police."

"And if I don't help?" I said without a moment's pause.

He glanced up at the overhead, rubbed his bare chin, and said, "Then I guess I'll just have to steal a boat, won't I?" He let out a deep breath and added, "Look, if you want to keep your hands clean, I get it. How about you just let me take this and you can report it once I'm a hundred miles away? I'm sure you've got her insured. Regardless, I'm going for the plane, and I'm gonna bring up its contents whether you help me or not."

I glanced at him with wide eyes, and he nodded confidently. For a moment, I stared at him, knowing that if I made the decision to help him, there would be no going back. If he was the criminal liar the rest of the world thought he was, I'd be slated as an accomplice and spend years behind bars. Hell, even if he was telling the truth, that fate would still be probable. But if he was telling the truth, if the whole mission was a conspiracy and we brought it to light, I'd be doing a service to my nation, to my old friend, and to his family.

Suddenly, I heard a voice call my name from out on the dock. I rose to my feet, and walked out into the fresh evening air. Gus had returned and he was standing on the dock alongside Atticus. The curious lab enjoyed hanging out around the marina sometimes, especially in the office. I knew it was mainly because Gus liked to slip him snacks like peanut butter and raisins all the time.

"I think he misses you," Gus said.

Before the words had left his lips, Atticus was already bounding onto the Baia and jumping to me. I leaned over, petting and greeting him as he licked the side of my face.

"You sure everything's alright?" he asked, looking over my shoulder towards the salon door.

"Yeah. Thanks again for handling the sheriff and for watching Atticus."

He waved a hand, told me not to mention it, then said goodnight as he headed back down the dock. Once Atticus relaxed a little, I took in a deep breath and looked out over the dark ocean, trying to make sense of everything that had happened. After a minute, Kyle walked out and stood beside me. I was surprised at how quickly Atticus took to him. Instead of being weary of strangers like he usually was, he simply stared at Kyle then greeted him happily. Kyle petted him for a few seconds then reached a hand out in front of me.

"Here," he said, holding a small folded piece of paper out to me. "An old friend of mine once gave me this."

When I grabbed the paper and unfolded it, I realized that it was a picture of Kyle and me on his wedding day. I was his best man, and in the picture, we both smiled as we posed in our nice black suits and sunglasses with the hills of Southern California behind us. On the back, "brothers in arms" was written in blue ink along with the date, July 1997.

He moved toward the stern of the Baia and prepared to step from the swim platform onto the dock.

"Hey," I said, causing him to stop and turn around. "Why don't you come back inside? We have a lot more to talk about. You can stay in the guest cabin if you want."

I wasn't sure I could trust him or if he was still the man I'd once known, but I didn't know if his place was close by or if he even had a place to stay. I could at least give him a bed to sleep on and listen to what else he had to say.

We talked for another hour before the caffeine wore off and we decided to call it a night. He told me about where he'd been all these years and how he'd managed to stay off the grid by changing his and his family's names. It amazed me how he'd been able to stay in hiding so long, but he'd always been smart and resourceful.

Before I shut the door of the main cabin, I turned back to Kyle and asked what the chances were that the guys who'd tried to kill him earlier would sneak onto my boat.

"Fifty-fifty," he said nonchalantly.

Since it was already almost 0200 and it was just the two of us, we decided not to station alternating watches. Needless to say, I had my top-of-the-line security system fully operational, including the transom sensors and the outer hull metal detectors, which I only used on rare occasions. If anyone came aboard or dove under my boat in the middle of the night, I'd know about it.

With my Sig on the nightstand beside me, I switched off the lights and crashed beneath the covers. After spending years sleeping in jungles and government-issued cots under stressful situations, I had no trouble falling asleep and passed out almost instantly.

SEVEN

Motobli, Liberia

The night air trembled as a distant rumble signaled the arrival of a train. Two young men sitting on metal folding chairs playing poker beside the tracks quickly rounded up their cards and jumped to their feet. They each had a classic AK-47 slung over their shoulder, and they watched as the train hissed and screeched to a stop just a few feet away from them.

It was a calm, humid night, and the lack of wind, combined with the proximity of swamp and dense jungle, meant that the mosquitoes were making their unwanted existence known. Thick clouds covered most of the sky, keeping even the distant glow of the moon from adding any light to the dark surroundings.

The large sliding door of one of the old freight cars screeched open, and a metal ramp was put in place. The car was painted dark green and had big white faded letters that said Wake Corporation across the middle. Casually and without fear, a tall slender white man wearing a long leather jacket appeared from the shadows of the open car and walked down the metal ramp. He had a Don Lino cigar in his right hand and took a few drags as he walked straight towards the two soldiers.

They met the tall guy at the edge of the ramp. They stood still for a moment, facing each other without saying a word.

Finally, one of the soldiers looked behind the tall guy at the train and said, “Have you brought the full shipment?”

The tall guy paused for a moment, took another drag of his cigar, then exhaled.

“Money first,” he replied in a thick Russian accent.

The two soldiers looked at each other, then one of them grabbed a folded-up piece of paper from his pocket and handed it to the Russian. He remained stoic and unaffected as he grabbed the paper, unfolded it, and quickly read it over.

“It is from our general,” one of the soldiers said. “He demands that you take a lower payment for the weapons. Your prices are far too high.”

The Russian crumpled up the paper, then dropped it on the ground and pressed it into the mud under his boot.

“You will pay the agreed price,” he said. “Plus a bonus for pissing me off. Or you will not get your weapons.”

One of the soldiers grabbed his AK-47 and aimed it straight at the Russian.

“We’re taking the weapons,” he said. “Whether

you are alive or dead is up to you."

The other soldier raised his rifle as well, keeping it aimed straight at the Russian's chest. At their backs, a small group of armed soldiers stepped out of the shadows and watched the scene unfold. The Russian was unfazed. He took another drag of his cigar, this one deeper, and blew the smoke into the two soldiers' faces.

Despite his appearance, it wasn't his stature that frightened his enemies most. It was the calm and sinister manner with which he spoke, the look he gave when his blood boiled, and the ease with which he pulled the trigger. He killed without thought or remorse, and at times even without provocation. The most terrifying part was that he appeared to enjoy ending lives, as if he were the devil himself.

Looking them both in the eye, the Russian spat into the mud, then said, "You have made a very grave mistake tonight. And… it will cost you your lives as well as the lives of everyone in this village."

The two soldiers' eyes grew wide, then they glared back at the Russian. They were about to squeeze the triggers of their AK-47s when heavy-caliber rounds suddenly struck each of them and sent them to the mud in an instant. The sounds were loud and ominous, like cracks of thunder waking the sleeping village.

The doors of the other freight cars screeched open, and a flood of well-armed and heavily trained soldiers came bursting out. They fired a storm of automatic rounds into the village, quickly taking down the other soldiers who'd come to help negotiate a better deal. The Russian didn't even blink in the chaos. He looked out over the village, watching as men were mowed down, and continued to puff on his cigar.

When the village went quiet aside from the screams of women and children, a man dressed in full black tactical gear approached the Russian.

"We've taken them out," he said. "Their soldiers are all either dead or have surrendered. Shall we make contact with their general?"

The Russian nodded. They called up the general, told him that they had his men hostage, and let one of the hostages speak with him. He was angry but consented to pay the agreed-upon amount.

Once the transfer of funds had been verified, the Russian turned to his second-in-command. "Now we send a message." He looked deep into the guy's eyes. "Kill everyone."

The man nodded, gathered his troops, and moved into the village. Even when the soldiers dropped their weapons in surrender and pleaded for mercy, the Russian and his men didn't relent. They killed everyone in the village, then set every structure ablaze.

Once everyone was dead, they unloaded the crates of weapons from the train cars and stacked them beside the tracks. The Russian stepped to the side and watched his men at work. His phone rang in his jacket pocket, and he answered it.

"What is your status?" a woman's voice said.

"Minor complications," he replied. "Nothing to be concerned with. The shipment has been delivered without problem. There was disagreement with agreed-upon terms, but we have resolved the issue. The funds have been successfully transferred to the account."

"Good," the woman replied. "I need you on a plane to Cuba."

"Any details?"

"Kyle Quinn is in the Caribbean. I need you to take him out."

The Russian smiled.

"I thought Webb and his team were taking care of it," the Russian said.

"I've lost faith in their ability," she replied. "I haven't called them off, but I wouldn't count on them coming through."

The Russian smirked. He'd always disliked Webb and was happy to see that his team was disappointing their boss.

Webb is a good fighter to be sure, he thought. *But he lacks a certain killer instinct, a ruthlessness that can only be attained from a lifetime of living as I have lived.*

"I need a clean sweep," she said. "Nothing left of him, understand?"

"That will not be a problem. I will contact you when it is finished. I am on my way to airport now."

"No need," she said. "I sent a chopper and it should be landing at your location any second."

As if her words had summoned the helicopter, the Russian heard the sounds of distant rotor blades as they tore through the air.

"You will receive a briefing on the jet," she said. "His current location is Key West, but I suspect he won't be there for much longer. You will fly into Playa Baracoa Airport in Cuba. I have a boat waiting for you there that's fully loaded with arms and explosives."

The Russian smiled. "Consider him dead."

EIGHT

I woke up at 0800 to the sound of my cellphone vibrating to life. After I reached over and turned off my alarm as well as the security system, my head dropped back onto my pillow and I lay in bed for a few more minutes. Morning light radiated through the hatch over my head as I stared at the blue sky above. The hatch was cracked open a few inches, allowing a fresh breeze to sneak in and brush against my face. I could hear the sounds of the marina coming to life, the distant caws of seagulls, the puttering of diesel engines, the muffled voices of boaters as they went about their mornings.

Blinking the sleep from my eyes, I thought over the events of the previous day and couldn't help but shake my head at just how unexpected life can be. One moment you're living your life, feeling like you've got a pretty good handle on things and then wham! The universe throws you a curveball that would make Sandy Koufax proud.

Rolling myself out of bed, I pressed my bare feet onto the deck and slid into a pair of cargo shorts and a gray cutoff tee shirt. I stepped into the head, twisted the faucet, then filled my cupped hands with cold water and splashed it against my face. After toweling off, I moved aft and pulled open the door leading into the lounge. To my surprise, Kyle was already awake. He sat beside the dining table wearing the same thing he'd been wearing the night before and was reading an old framed article from the *Keynoter*.

"Were there any bodies still intact?" he asked as he glanced up momentarily from the newspaper. Seeing my confusion, he turned the article around so I could see it. "This Harper Ridley is pretty good. I'm surprised she hasn't been offered a better gig in a big city."

The article was about U-3546, the German U-boat my dad had found just hours before he was murdered. I'd rediscovered it a few years after, and the photograph was of Jack, Professor Murchison, and me as we dove around its crusted hull 130 feet underwater.

"I'm sure she has." I stepped towards the coffeemaker and filled a mug. "The Keys attract many people willing to trade deep pockets for sandy pockets," I added, stealing a line I'd heard from Charles when we'd first met. "And, yes," I continued, "there were parts of bodies still intact. The enclosed stagnant water in different sections prevented some from decomposing completely. We strived to be as respectful as possible and never released any photographs of bodies."

Kyle only nodded and continued to read as I sat

down on the other side of the couch. I took a few sips of the warm coffee, then set the mug in front of me.

"How long you been up?"

"A few hours," he replied.

I was surprised I hadn't heard him since I usually woke up at the slightest disturbance.

He set the framed article on the table and paused for a moment.

"Well?" he said, raising his eyebrows at me.

"Well, what?"

"Don't play dumb with me, Dodge. I don't have time for it. Are you going to let me use your boat or not?"

The salon went quiet. I'd been thinking it over all night and, despite how foolish and reckless it was, had come to a decision.

"If you think for a second that I'm going to let you take my boat, you're out of your mind," I said, then leaned forward, grabbed my mug, and took another sip.

Kyle shook his head and rose to his feet.

Just as he was about to tear me a new one and stomp off, I added, "Without me too, that is."

He paused, then tilted his head and looked me in the eyes. I saw the makings of a potential smile, but he quickly wiped it away.

Nodding, he said, "Alright."

"But I have conditions," I said. "Mainly, I'm in charge. We'll work as a team to find this plane, but I'll have the final say."

"Fine," he said, though he didn't exactly sound excited. "What else?"

"I want to know everything that you do about the situation. Everything you've heard about our mission in Colombia, and everything you know about Carson

Richmond and Darkwater's involvement."

"That it?"

I nodded and finished off the rest of my coffee. Rising to my feet, I stepped starboard and opened the fridge.

"You hungry?"

I warmed up a few poppy seed and blueberry muffins from Key's Knees Bakery, then blended up a strawberry, mango, and banana smoothie with a few scoops of whey protein powder. While we ate, I grabbed a rolled-up chart and spread it out on the table in front of us. I also snatched my laptop from a nearby locker and booted it up.

"Alright," I said, swallowing a bite of warm muffin. "Where are we heading?"

Kyle leaned forward and placed a finger on the chart. He was pointing at a stretch of blue ocean between Southern Florida, Cuba, and the Bahamas.

"Cay Sal?" I said.

He nodded, and I wasn't surprised. After their flight had crashed ten years ago, the US and Bahamian governments had spent months searching for the wreck. Though a few pieces were recovered, including a good-sized chunk of its tail, most of the plane was never found. The plane had been on a course for Miami, if I remembered correctly, and it had lost contact with air traffic controllers just north of Cuba.

"It's a good thing my armory's stocked," I said.

Cay Sal Bank, the westernmost of the Bahamian Banks, is a long way from nowhere. It's a modern-day No man's land, a place frequented by pirates, poachers, and refugees, where only the brave and well-prepared dare venture.

"Don't tell me you're scared," Kyle said with a

grin. “Haven’t you been fighting the FARC? I’d take on a band of modern-day pirates over Colombian rebels any day of the week.”

He was referring to the six years I’d spent as a mercenary after getting out of the Navy. Though I’d been hired for various jobs around the world, most of my time had been spent in Colombia and other South American countries.

“You’re forgetting about Darkwater,” I said. “They’ll follow us and it’s only a matter time before we’ll have to fight them off.”

We finished the rest of the food, then formulated a plan of action. We both agreed that we should leave as soon as possible and made preparations for the long voyage ahead of us. Though Cuba oftentimes tries to claim Cay Sal as their own, the bank is considered part of the Bahamas. In order for us to cruise into Cay Sal legally, we’d have to clear customs, and the closest place to do that was the Bimini Islands, 170 miles northeast of Key West. From there, we’d refuel and cruise over a hundred miles south to Cay Sal.

Before casting off, I checked over all of my gear, including specialty salvage gear like my magnetometer, underwater metal detectors, scuba equipment, and my two sets of Draeger rebreathers. The Baia has built-in side-scan sonar, which, though designed to allow me to navigate through shallow cuts and reefs, would also be useful during our search for the wreck. Fortunately, my onboard safe contained many of my firearms, including an extra Sig, an MP5N, and my Lapua sniper rifle. I also had a good supply of ammunition and stacks of various currencies, including a stack of Bahamian dollars and Cuban pesos, just in case we made it that far south.

Once I had all my gear in order, I filled up the freshwater tank, then removed the mooring lines and started up the engines. Cruising slowly, I brought the Baia over to the fuel station and filled up the 370-gallon tank. Though it was still expensive in the Keys, I knew that fuel would cost an arm and a leg in Bimini, so I wanted to minimize the amount purchased there. Since the maximum range of the Baia at cruising speed was just short of three hundred miles, I decided to fill my spare tank as well. It would be nice to have an extra supply on hand just in case.

As I filled the spare fifty-gallon tank, Gus walked over and handed me a package.

"That's strange," I said. "I didn't order anything. Who's it from?"

"It doesn't have a return address," Gus said, pointing at the label as he handed it over to me. "Going on a trip?" He eyed Kyle skeptically.

He was standing beside the cockpit, leaning over the dinette as he scanned over charts.

"Yeah. Hey, have you seen Jack this morning?"

Gus nodded. "We had breakfast at the Pelican. He should be over on his boat."

When I finished filling up, he told me he'd add it to my monthly bill. I thanked him, started up the engines, then pulled away from the fuel station and up alongside the stern of the *Calypso*. I spotted Jack as he was preparing his boat for an afternoon charter, setting up fishing rods, filling coolers with ice and beverages, and rinsing the deck. His fifteen-year-old nephew, Isaac, was up on the flybridge and called to us as we approached.

Jack, who was wearing nothing but a pair of boardshorts, turned and set a fishing pole along a row of others.

"Good morning, Jack," I said.

His smile quickly shifted when he spotted Kyle sitting beside me.

"Oh, Jack, this is James Evans," I lied. "He's an old friend from the Navy."

Kyle stood, walked over to the starboard gunwale and shook Jack's hand.

Jack looked at me, confused. "Good to meet you. Where are you guys off to?"

I moved just a few feet from Jack and said, "We're gonna do some diving near Cay Sal."

Jack's eyes grew wide and his confusion only increased. Having spent his entire life in the Keys, Jack knew as well as any man alive the dangers associated with boating around Cay Sal. Though by no means a guarantee, the chances of encountering criminals were greater there than just about anywhere else in the Caribbean.

"Look, I don't want to lie to you," I said, keeping my voice low enough to be muffled by the sound of my idling engines. "But I also don't want you to know the truth. For your protection and for…" My eyes shifted towards Isaac, who was messing with the electronics up on the flybridge. "There's something that we've got to do. Just do me a favor and don't tell anyone where we are. Just say we're in the Gulf for a few days or something."

"Should I be worried, bro?" he said.

"About me?" I laughed. "No. But if it makes you feel better, I'll have my sat phone with me and I'll try to give you a call once a day."

"What about Ange?"

"She doesn't need to know," I said. "She would come down here right away if she knew what was going on, and I don't want that."

"I had breakfast with Gus this morning and he said that you two were brawling last night," he said, glancing at Kyle. "And now you're going on a trip together to Cay Sal?"

My mouth opened to give a reply, but I knew that it would be impossible for me to explain everything. It was difficult for me to comprehend myself, let alone try and get someone else to.

"We have a history," I said. "But we need to do this. I need to do this." I patted him on the shoulder. "I'll keep in touch. If all goes well and we don't run into trouble, I should only be gone for a couple of days."

I stepped back onto the swim platform of the Baia.

"You know, questioning whether or not you'll run into trouble sounds pretty funny coming from you," Jack said with a chuckle. "Just try not to get captured by a drug cartel."

Kyle looked at me questioningly.

I smiled and said, "I'll do my best."

NINE

At just after 1000, we cruised out of the marina. It was a slightly overcast day, and even though it was March, the temperature was already over seventy degrees. When I brought us out of the no-wake zone, I hit the throttles, causing the propellers to tear through the water and rocket us up to our cruising speed of forty knots.

Off the port bow, we passed by Mallory Square, the bustling waterfront plaza known for its street performers, sunset celebrations, and carts selling everything from conch fritters to natural sponges. To starboard, the tiny Sunset Key blurred past as we cruised south. We flew around Fort Zachary Taylor, then headed northeast along the Keys, making a beeline for the Bimini Islands across the Straits of Florida.

The prevailing wind blew in from the east at just

four knots, allowing for a smooth passage as we tore over the Atlantic.

Kyle grabbed the mysterious package and cut into it beside me.

"Mind if I use your shower?" he asked, grabbing and pulling out a stack of folded clothes from the package.

I shook my head. "You always did bag me on how predictable I was."

"Yeah, well, I hoped for the use of your boat. You tagging along is a surprise."

He dropped down into the salon and took a shower in the guest head. In the solitude, I looked out over the water and thought briefly about my life. I'd moved to the Keys to get away from the action and relax, and yet again I found myself venturing into an unknown that promised nothing but danger. Maybe it's true that you can't escape who you are, that the universe clutches you and pulls you back just as you think you've drifted on to something else. Or perhaps blaming destiny is a cop-out, and my experiences have been a result of decisions I've made. I've always preferred the latter, believing wholeheartedly that I am captain of my soul.

Half an hour later, Kyle appeared wearing a fresh cutoff tee shirt and a pair of grey swim trunks. We spent most of the five-hour voyage getting reacquainted as best as we could. I gave him a brief history of everything I'd done since we'd last seen each other in Venezuela, and he told me more about where he'd been and how he'd managed to survive the plane crash.

"They tried to kill me midflight," he said, a resoluteness burning from his eyes as he stared off into the seemingly endless blue. "They were gonna blow my brains out at thirty thousand feet."

He went on to explain how he'd managed to fight off his captors and take them out using their own weapons. The only problem was that the pilots were shot in the process. One had died instantly, and the other had had a hard time keeping the plane in the air. Within minutes, the plane had gone down, crashing into the Caribbean during one of the worst storms of the year.

"Surviving a plane crash is crazy in and of itself," I said. "But how did you manage to survive after that and stay undetected?"

"I'll be the first to admit there was a lot of luck involved, though it was far from easy," he said. "Cay Sal is one of the worst places in the Caribbean to be stranded. Just ask any of the thousands of refugees stranded here every year."

"I'm guessing you ran into some?"

He nodded. "A handful of Haitians whose raft had crashed into the Dog Rocks. Fortunately, we managed to haggle our way onto a smuggling boat. The only problem was that it was heading for Miami."

I raised my eyebrows. "And you still went along?"

"I wasn't exactly surrounded by options. I'd been without food and fresh water for two days, and those smugglers were the only ones who'd come close enough for us to talk to them."

"So you rode with them all the way to Miami? And then what?"

"After dropping off the Haitians and Cubans, they cruised back to Puerto Rico. It was there that I was able to call in a few favors from a friend. I got a fake passport and driver's license, then got in contact with Grace."

I paused a moment. "How did she take all of it?"

"She cried a lot," he said. "But she's an amazing woman. Many women wouldn't stand by their husbands through such an ordeal."

I glanced down at the GPS and redirected our course with a slight touch of the helm.

"She believes me," he said, shifting his gaze towards mine. "And soon enough you will too."

A few hours after we'd left Key West, we heard the sound of a low-flying airplane soaring through the air, heading the same direction that we were. It was one of those elongated seaplanes with added rows of seats and couldn't have been more than a few thousand feet up.

"What do you make of that?" Kyle said, eyeing the plane suspiciously.

I shrugged. "Don't know. Could be just a tour or special flight of some kind."

We watched as it continued northeast and disappeared into the horizon. Soon after, I switched on the autopilot, kicked back, and enjoyed the ride through the straits.

We reached Bimini, the three-island chain consisting of North Bimini, South Bimini, and East Bimini, at just before 1500. We cruised straight for the Bimini Big Game Club Marina located on the eastern shore of the north island in Alice Town. As I motored into the marina, I flew the yellow quarantine flag, then docked and disembarked with a folder containing the boat's registration, our filled-out immigration cards and passports, and a maritime declaration form. There had been times in my life when I'd entered foreign waters illegally for the sake of secrecy, but it was generally a good idea to have the law on your side.

Since I'd already printed and filled out the forms and had all of our documentation in order, it only took fifteen minutes. Once we were cleared, I paid the fee and topped off the Baia's fuel, replacing what I'd burned on the crossing from Key West. I ordered a couple of mahi Reuben sandwiches to go from the marina bar and grill along with their famous seafood sampler. Carrying the brown paper bags of food, I made my way to the end of the dock, where the Baia was temporarily tied off beside a rundown Catalina sailboat.

When I reached the Baia, I stepped aboard and headed down into the salon. Atticus greeted me before I'd reached the bottom step, happy to see me as usual. Looking around, I saw no sign of Kyle, who'd been sitting topside when I left. I checked every interior space and heard only silence in response to my calling his name.

Where the hell did you go? I thought, shaking my head.

I looked through the port window and noticed a seaplane moored just down the channel from us. It looked identical to the one we'd seen flying overhead earlier that afternoon.

I set the bags of food on the table, then told Atticus to stay and headed back up to the deck, shutting the salon door behind me. As I reached for my cellphone in my front pocket, I spotted three guys standing on the dock near the stern. They were wearing black suits, even though it was in the upper seventies, and were staring at me behind sunglasses so dark that they completely concealed their eyes. They stood frozen and ominous, as if they were waiting for me to make a move.

My right hand intuitively gravitated casually over my right hip, where I usually kept my holstered Sig. My gaze widened when I didn't feel the familiar hard polymer grip. Carrying firearms on your person is illegal in the Bahamas, and I reminded myself of the unfortunate fact that I'd locked up my weapons prior to meeting with the customs officials.

Since I wasn't armed, I had two choices: either make a break for the main cabin and get to my weapons as quickly as I could, or try and take them out the old-fashioned way. I made up my mind in a decisive second and stepped towards them naturally, cutting the distance between us.

"We're coming aboard," the guy in the middle said authoritatively. He was the biggest of the three and spoke in a distinctly Australian accent. His pale head was devoid of hair and reflected the tropical sun into my eyes. He brushed aside the left flap of his white jacket, revealing a handgun holstered to his chest. Without another word, the three of them stepped aboard the Baia with Baldy leading the way. These guys didn't give a damn about proper boating etiquette. They were there for one reason and one reason only.

Baldy motioned behind me and said, "Inside. We would like to speak with you about your friend."

There was no doubt in my mind that the only thing they wanted to do below deck was put a bullet in my head. I didn't have time to think about whether or not they'd already confronted Kyle. I had only a few seconds to make my move.

Feigning compliance, I nodded and turned around slowly. These guys were well trained, I was confident of that. I knew I'd have to be at the top of my game if I had any chance of bringing all three of them down by myself, especially considering that all of them were undoubtedly armed and I wasn't.

I took two slow steps forward, passing right between the cockpit and the dinette.

"And no sudden movements," Baldy added.

I could feel his presence just a few inches behind me. Just as the words left his mouth, I spun around and slammed my right leg into his knees. His body lurched sideways, his feet flying out from under him, and his head crashed against the edge of the dinette.

Before his body hit the deck, I lunged towards the guy behind him. He was smaller than the other two but looked like he was solid muscle. He managed to land a left hook to my side, causing a mouthful of air to burst from my lungs. I blocked his second attack, diverting his fist into the back of the helm chair while rearing back to throw a punch of my own. I landed a solid right uppercut. My knuckles slammed into his chin, snapping his head backward with a crack of bones, and sending his body crashing onto the transom.

Focusing on suit number three, I realized that he'd moved back a few steps, increasing the distance between us. He held his Walther P99 in one hand and quickly raised the barrel towards me. I knew that he had me beat, but I didn't care. With reckless abandon, I dropped down towards Baldy, who lay sprawled out unconscious at my feet. I reached for the handgun still holstered under the left flap of his jacket, expecting to feel an extreme surge of pain and hear the sound of a gunshot at any moment.

Just as my hand gripped Baldy's Glock, the sound came, followed by two more in rapid succession. But instead of a trio of ear-rattling bangs, I heard the unmistakable sound of suppressed 9mm gunfire. The burning pain of lead exploding through my flesh never came, and as I gripped the Glock and turned to face my enemy, I saw a trail of bullet wounds winding up his midsection. His body collapsed, his arms dangling over the starboard gunwale as three streams of blood swiftly drenched his undershirt, turning it from white to dark red.

I jumped to my feet, held the Glock out in front of me and scanned the dock and nearby boats for more enemies as well as the source of the gunfire. I instantly spotted Kyle kneeling on the old Catalina moored next to the Baia. As we made eye contact, he jumped onto the dock, took a quick look around, then strode onto the swim platform.

The short guy whose jaw I'd broken shook to life and tried to struggle to his feet.

"Don't even think about it," I said, zeroing the Glock onto his face.

His eyes filled with anger as Kyle disarmed him from behind, pushed him to the deck, and pressed a knee into his spine. I grabbed two ultra-strength zip ties from a small locker outboard of the helm and handed them to Kyle.

"Nice to see you've still got the edge," he said while tightening the plastic bindings around Shorty's wrists and ankles. He glanced at the bullet-riddled guy beside us and added, "Still need me to save you, though."

"I had him no problem," I said as I dropped down and bound Baldy as well. Moving aft, we grabbed hold of the bleeding thug and flapped his lifeless body down onto the deck beside the others.

"Don't let anyone see that," I said, motioning toward my Sig clasped in his left hand.

He knew as well as I did that Bahamian law

requires personal firearms to be kept under lock and key at all times.

"What now, Captain?" he said, raising his eyebrows.

I slid the Glock into my waistband and took another look around the marina, this time keeping an eye out for observant passersby rather than hostiles. By some incredibly fortunate combination of luck, the lack of people near the dock, and the fact that we were at the end, nobody seemed to have noticed our little live reenactment of a *Die Hard* scene.

"Cast off the lines, will you?" I said as I moved into the cockpit.

We'd lingered long enough, and no matter what we chose to do with our unwanted guests, it was best that we got a move on as soon as possible. Once Kyle had us loose, he jumped aboard and I started up the engines. Kyle searched our prisoners more thoroughly, emptying their pockets and depositing their contents onto the dinette as I slowly eased us away from the dock and into the channel.

Once we reached the open water, I gunned the throttles, quickly bringing us to our top speed of just over fifty knots and leaving a long trail of white behind us.

TEN

We cruised south past Gun Cay and the Cat Cays, putting as much distance between us and Bimini as possible. When we were twenty miles south of Alice Town and had the ocean almost entirely to ourselves, I slowed the Baia to her cruising speed to conserve fuel. Kyle was sitting on the half-moon cushioned seat beside me, going through what little the three guys had in their pockets. Glancing over, I saw a few extra magazines, wads of various currencies, a key ring with two brass keys, and a flip-style cellphone.

"No wallets," Kyle said. "In fact, no identification of any kind. I guess that's to be expected, though."

"Can you hack into the phone?" I asked.

"Yeah," he replied confidently. "But it would be a hell of a lot easier to just force these guys to tell us the code."

A few minutes later I slowed us to an idle, then killed the engines. We tossed the dead guy overboard after putting a few dive weights in his pockets so he'd sink. Then I rinsed down the bloody deck with the freshwater hose while Kyle kept a steady eye on the other two. Tiger and bull sharks were prevalent in those waters, so I had no doubt that within twenty-four hours, there wouldn't be much left of his corpse. Once I had my deck restored, I sprayed Baldy's face with the cool water, waking him up. He looked around, wide-eyed.

"What the hell?" he said angrily, not fond of the manner in which I'd woken him up. He tugged at his hands and legs and realized that he was bound. Glancing at Shorty, who hadn't made a sound since we'd duct-taped his mouth, he asked, "How did you guys let them best us? And where's Blake?"

"He's dead," Kyle said, leaning against the sunbed and aiming Baldy's Walther back at him. "And you guys are dead too if you don't start talking."

I expected Baldy to be silent, to keep information from us and protect it with his life like most trained professionals are taught to do. Instead, he spoke freely, as if we were having a chat over coffee.

"What could I possibly tell you that you don't already know?" he said, shrugging.

"Who sent you?" I asked.

He shook his head. "If you two don't already know the answer to that question, then you're incompetent."

"Says the guy whose ass just got handed to him," Kyle shot back.

I took in a deep breath, then let it out. Staring into Baldy's eyes, I said, "Darkwater?"

"Of course," he replied.

"I thought they were security," I said.

"Primarily, yes. But Darkwater doesn't just handle private security," he said. "There's a branch that deals with tracking and taking down high-value targets. Quinn is a criminal, a traitor. And you're helping him, so what does that make you?"

Kyle bent forward and pressed the muzzle of Baldy's handgun into his forehead.

"You have no idea what the hell you're talking about," he said, raising his voice and gritting his teeth. "You aren't aware that the whole thing was a setup? That they were planning to murder sixteen Naval Special Forces personnel in order to spark a conflict that would benefit them financially?"

Baldy cleared his throat, then paused a moment, wanting to choose his words carefully. "I don't know anything about that. You really think that they tell us big-picture stuff? I get a call, I complete a task, I get paid. That's how it works."

Kyle relaxed a little and brought the Walther back, leaving a red circle on the failed assassin's forehead.

"What else do you know about us?" I asked.

Baldy's eyes scanned over to me. "Nothing about you," he said. "Though I wish I'd known something. Maybe I could've been ready for that sidekick."

I couldn't help but give a slight grin. The truth was that beyond the hand-to-hand combat I'd learned in the Navy, I hadn't received extensive formal training in jiujitsu. I had my sparring sessions with Ange to thank for that.

"And all I know about you is what everyone has read," he continued, looking back at Kyle. "That you disobeyed direct orders in the line of duty, and two

Americans were killed because of it. That you tried to take over the plane while being moved to the States, but your plane went down, killing everyone aboard. Well… almost everyone, at least."

I watched Kyle closely as the words came out of our captive's mouth and could see the anger that they caused.

"What's the code for your phone?" I asked, changing the subject.

"If I tell you, will you let us live?" he replied.

"You'll tell us or we'll blow your brains out right here!" Kyle barked.

He hesitated a moment, then said, "Four-three-six-two, but it's a prepaid, mate. Haven't had it for more than a day. Not sure how much help it will be."

"We'll be the judge of that," I said as Kyle grabbed the phone and keyed in the code.

He glanced up at me and nodded, indicating that he hadn't lied to us.

"Alright," I said, rising to my feet. "This guy has nothing else for us. Let's get rid of them."

Baldy's expression shifted from nervous to enraged in the blink of an eye.

"You said you wouldn't kill us," he said.

Kyle turned back to face him, looking like he wanted to beat the crap out of the guy.

"Stop," I said, placing a hand on Kyle's shoulder. Facing Baldy, I added, "We never said that. Now shut the hell up and don't move a muscle."

Using the charts and satellite images, I found a location that would serve nicely and started up the twin 600s. I punched the throttles, sending us flying over the turquoise waters of the northern Bahamas, heading south. Twenty minutes later, a tiny speck of land appeared on the horizon. As we motored closer, the sorry excuse for an island took form, allowing us to see a small patch of rams horn bushes growing out of the sand just a few steps away from the crashing waves. The island couldn't be larger than a basketball court, and that was with the ocean at mid-tide.

I killed the engines a few hundred feet from the shore.

"Alright, this is your stop," I said, eyeing Baldy as I strode aft.

He looked over his shoulder at the island.

"You can't be serious, mate," he said.

"Of course I am," I said, aiming my Sig at his chest and pulling him up to his feet. "An hour ago you were trying to kill us. You're lucky we're not putting bullets in your chest and feeding you to the sharks like your buddy."

Kyle lifted Shorty to his feet, then ripped the tape from his face.

Breathing heavily, he spoke for the first time. "We'll die anyway if you leave us here!"

We forced them to the swim platform, pushing them right up to the edge.

"Fishermen pass through these waters," I said. "You guys probably won't be there more than a day or two if you keep watchful eyes."

"And if you are lucky enough to be found," Kyle said, "you'd better get the hell out of the Caribbean. If you come after us again, I'll kill you. Understand, mate?"

Without another word, Kyle and I performed a pair of front kicks, slamming our heels into their backs and sending their bodies tumbling forward and splashing into the shallow crystal-clear water. Their heads submerged for a second before they both planted their feet in the sand and straightened their upper bodies out of the water.

"There's some limestone on the other side of the island," I said. "It'll make quick work of those zip ties."

I started to turn around and head for the cockpit, but Baldy's voice caused me to pause.

"There's something else you should know," Baldy said as he tried to blink the saltwater from his eyes.

"We're listening," I said.

"I want water," he said. "If you give me water, I'll tell you."

"You'll tell us and then we'll give you water," Kyle fired back.

The big guy sighed, realizing that was the best offer he was gonna get.

"Alright," he said, raising his hands in the air. "There's someone else coming after you guys. Someone with a little more of a reputation than the three of us."

"Who is he?" I said.

"I don't know his name," he said. "But they call him the Russian Devil. He's the most… well known of all of the operators working with Darkwater and also the one people know the least about."

The name rang a bell in the back of my mind. In my years working as a mercenary, I'd heard the name brought up a few times, and never in a good light.

I walked over to the cooler, grabbed a bottle of water, and tossed it to Baldy.

"Just watch your backs," he added. "I'm sure he'll run into you guys sooner rather than later."

I nodded and glanced at Kyle. I could tell that he recognized the name as well, but we didn't say a word. Instead, I moved into the cockpit and started up the engines, and the small island quickly became nothing more than a dot on the horizon at our backs.

ELEVEN

We still had eighty miles of ocean to traverse until we'd hit the northern section of Cay Sal Bank, and another sixty miles beyond that to the location where Kyle said the plane wreck was located. I put the Baia on autopilot at her cruising speed with a south-southwest heading. Our first order of business was sustenance, as we'd only had occasional snacking to keep us going since breakfast that morning.

I climbed down into the salon and grabbed the two brown paper bags that had spots of grease stains bleeding through. After reheating and plating the food, I brought it topside and we ate while lounging around the dinette. I'd kept Atticus locked in the main cabin since the confrontation, so he was excited to come topside and see what was going on. He sniffed the deck for a few minutes, then turned his attention to the food Kyle and I were chowing down on.

The mahi Reubens were incredible. Fresh mahi-mahi marinated in secret island spices and grilled to perfection between fresh Bimini bread with swiss cheese, coleslaw, and thousand island dressing. The seafood sampler contained a variety of island favorites including lobster bites, fish fingers, and cracked pepper shrimp, which we dipped in a homemade spicy cocktail sauce.

We enjoyed our meal under a brilliant blue sky, with the tropical sun warming us from over the starboard bow and fresh ocean air in our lungs. After a few minutes of eating, I heard a loud splash ahead of us. Straightening my body, I tilted my head and directed my gaze just forward of the port bow, where a small pod of dolphins was swimming. I stood up and slowly eased back on the throttles, bringing us down to just fifteen knots. They looked like bottlenose, and knowing that they had a top speed of twenty, I was hoping to get them to put on a show. The sentient beings didn't disappoint. They noticed right away when the Baia slowed and swam just forward of the bow, splashing into the water ahead of us one after the other.

Kyle and I both laughed and stood, watching the magnificent show as we finished off the rest of our food. I'd heard of dolphins jumping in front of large yachts and freighters but had rarely heard of them doing so in front of a boat as small as *Dodging Bullets*.

"A good omen," I said.

After a few minutes, the pod shifted off towards the east, jumping and waving their flukes at us. As they disappeared from view, I brought us back up to forty knots, wanting to reach Cay Sal before nightfall.

I grabbed us both a couple of coconut waters

from my Yeti to wash it all down, then grabbed my laptop while Kyle went to work on Baldy's cellphone. I did a quick generic Google search of our new adversary, the Russian Devil. After reading a few news articles, I was only able to solidify what I already knew: that he was a deadly assassin and that he was great at staying in the dark. There wasn't even so much as a blurry picture of him.

"Find anything?" I asked, glancing at Kyle, who was looking frustrated as he pressed buttons on the flip phone.

He shook his head. "You?"

"Nothing we don't already know," I said.

As I finished off the rest of my food, I cleaned my fingers with a napkin, then slid my sat phone out of my front pocket. We needed intel, and I knew exactly the man to call. I brought up his contact info and pressed call, and Scott's voice came over the small speaker after the third ring.

"Hey, Logan," he said. "Is this an emergency?"

"Not really," I said. "Just looking for some info."

I heard a group of people talking in the background and I could tell that they wanted his attention.

"Alright. Look, I've got an important meeting, so I need to make this quick. What do you need?"

"I need whatever intel you can scrounge up on the assassin known as the Russian Devil."

Scott paused a moment, then said, "Okay. I'll get this to Willy and have him give you a call."

"Thanks, Scott."

Kyle's eyes darted to mine when he heard me say the name. His face displayed a combination of confusion and amazement.

"You bet. If I had more time, I'd ask what you're

up to." He spoke to someone beside him, then added, "Just be careful. If you need any backup, I'm just a call away."

We ended the call and I slid my phone back into my pocket.

"Don't tell me that was who I think it was," Kyle said flatly.

He'd been eyeing me with a questioning gaze since I'd mentioned Scott's name. Scott Cooper and I had known each other since I'd first arrived to my SEAL team. He'd been my division officer, and our hard-headed personalities had clashed at first, but we soon made up and became good friends. After the Navy, he'd gone into politics and was currently serving as a senator representing the state of Florida. You would think that after trading up his rifle for a briefcase, he would stay away from action and adventure, but Scott was a unique breed. He'd gone on and even instigated more than one adventure with me since I'd migrated to the Keys.

"He's one of my most trusted friends," I said. "And I didn't say anything about you, did I?"

"He's a politician," Kyle said. "None of them are to be trusted. And in case you forgot, he didn't exactly back me up when the shit hit the fan."

"He did everything he could," I said, then shook my head as I stared off into the horizon. "He vouched for you. He put his career on the line for you even though there was a mountain of evidence against you."

"Falsified evidence," he shot back.

We went silent for a moment. I took in a deep breath and sighed.

"Look, we need all the info we can get on this guy," I said. "And if it comes down to it, Scott has a long list of valuable connections. He's also saved my ass more than once in the past few years." When he started to interject, I cut him off. "And remember, you agreed to my being in charge."

Kyle stood, then moved forward toward the steps down into the salon.

"Alright," he said before disappearing, "but if this comes back to haunt us, don't say I didn't warn you."

"It won't," I assured him confidently before he dropped out of view and shut the hatch behind him.

Roughly an hour after depositing our guests on their own private island, I noticed a shift in the weather.

The wind, which was blowing in from the east-southeast, had picked up strength and was now gusting in excess of twenty miles per hour, creating a carpet of whitecaps ahead of us. Far in the distance to the south, a mass of dark clouds had moved in and extinguished the blue sky.

My phone vibrated to life in my pocket and I pulled it out. It was CIA Deputy Director Wilson, a man who'd helped Scott and me on more than one occasion over the past year. As usual, Wilson didn't waste time on pleasantries. He cut right to the chase.

"I don't know what kind of situation you're in," he said in his rich Georgia accent. He paused momentarily as if giving me a chance to explain what was going on. When I didn't, he continued, "But this Russian Devil has been on our radar for some time now."

"What can you tell me about him?"

"Well, as I'm sure you've learned on your own, he's very good at staying under the radar."

The whitecaps were getting a little too big for my

liking, so I put my phone on speaker, switched off the autopilot, and grabbed hold of the helm.

"Hey, is everything alright?" Wilson asked.

"Yeah, I'm fine. You were saying?"

"So, what we do know is that his real name is Drago Kozlov. He's been doing major jobs around the world for over twenty years, mainly working for criminals. We believe he's in his mid-forties, is well over six feet tall, and has a frame like a fence post. Unfortunately, we don't have any pictures of the sumbitch." He paused for a moment. "Logan? Did you get all that?"

"I did," I said. "Thanks. Is there anything else?"

Even over the strong gusts of wind, I could hear him sigh on the other end.

"This guy is trouble, Logan," he said, his tone shifting. "Wherever he goes, people die, and usually more than necessary to complete his job. All evidence points to him being a genuine psychopath who also happens to be one of the most highly trained killers on earth."

Great, I thought, shaking my head.

I'd known that he was bad news from the moment Baldy spewed out his name, but when the deputy director of the CIA sounds worried, you know it's serious.

I was about to thank him and end the call when he said, "One more thing—he's had multiple run-ins with our agents over the years, and the consensus is that he likes his knives. Prefers to kill with a blade if possible."

I took a mental note, and thought about what he'd just said.

Multiple run-ins? Maybe he wasn't as dangerous as I was imagining him.

“Is there any way I could talk to one of those agents?” I said. “Just to see if I can learn anything about his tactics?”

Wilson paused a moment. “No. You can’t, because they’re all dead. He killed all of them.”

I swallowed hard, then thanked him.

“Like I told Scott earlier, we really want this guy, Logan,” he said. “If you feel like letting us in on whatever’s happening, I’d be happy to offer the support of the Agency.”

I told him I’d be in touch with him soon, and we ended the call. I appreciated their offers, but how could I tell them what was going on without bringing up Kyle? They were friends and I trusted them, but telling them that I was working with a believed-dead fugitive was out of the question. They worked for the government, and even if they did understand, I couldn’t put them in that kind of position.

“This guy Drago sounds like he’s really fun at parties,” Kyle said as I put my phone into a small locker beside the helm.

I smiled and we both looked out over the horizon in front of us.

“There it is,” I said, pointing at a strand of jagged rocks jutting out of the angry ocean.

The clouds overhead appeared much larger and had shifted to a menacing, dark black color. We were heading right into the thick of it.

“You were saying something about an omen,” Kyle said, his eyes wide as he gazed upon the coming storm.

TWELVE

We cruised through the strong winds and heavy rains without much trouble and reached the long strand of rocks known as the Elbow Cays just as the storm passed and the sun was sinking into the ocean. The sky had cleared as the monster ran away, heading northwest towards the mainland of Florida, and giving way to a brilliant streaking sunset.

I gazed over the horizon at the clear waters of Cay Sal Bank, watching as the surface twinkled with the dying evening light. The westernmost of the Bahama banks, Cay Sal is located between Cuba, Andros Island, and Southern Florida. With a surface area of just over two thousand square miles, it is one of the largest atolls in the world. The Bank is littered with almost a hundred rocky islands ranging in size from three hundred acres to barely scratching the surface at low tide. Most of the islands are desolate, with only light patches of vegetation and the occasional flocks of birds.

As we watched the sunset, North Elbow Cay came into view, marked by its long and narrow shape and a sixty-foot stone lighthouse jutting up near its center. Built by the Spanish in 1839, the light had gone out in the 1940s but had been reactivated during the seventies for a short time when the Bahama police set up the island as a lookout for drug smugglers. Today, the lighthouse, and what remains of the few scattered houses around it, are nothing more than remnants accessed only by brave tourists and refugees, the latter oftentimes carving their names into the old stone.

I kept us cruising at just twenty knots as we moved towards Elbow Cay. I glanced back and forth between the radar and depth readings, the side-scan sonar, and the surface of the water, careful to avoid the numerous cuts and reefs. As we approached the northern tip of the cay, I spotted something on radar. It was big, and it was heading north into the strait. A few seconds later, two more echoes appeared behind it.

"Check this out," I said, glancing up from the screen and motioning Kyle over.

He moved beside me and stared down into the screen.

"Looks like a cluster of boats," he said. "What do you think?"

I shrugged, "Could be a number of things."

I brought up the VRM or variable range marker, which allowed us to see that the echoes were just under nine nautical miles away from us. Keeping our course, I brought us along the eastern side of Elbow Cay. The steep, rocky island formed a handful of natural coves, which would provide as good a place as any to drop anchor and hunker down for the night.

"There's more of them," Kyle said, shaking his head. "Smugglers would never travel in such large numbers in daylight. My money's on a bunch of fishing boats."

It made sense. Cay Sal, being somewhat isolated from general human populations, offered exceptional fishing. And while it was common to see commercial fishermen, it was also common to see poachers catching whatever they desired without regard for marine life or regulations. Regardless of who they were, it was unlikely that they'd give us trouble so long as we kept our distance. Still, there was something about the small flotilla that made me feel uneasy, and by the time we spotted a suitable cove, I'd counted nine vessels in all.

The winds were still in the upper teens, making it a welcomed relief from the chop as we cruised slowly into the protection of the cove. The mooring site would suit our purpose well, having a relatively narrow opening of just a hundred feet or so, but widening out enough for us to anchor without worrying about the Baia drifting around with the wind and colliding against the jagged rocks surrounding us. The sky grew dark as the last glow of sunlight vanished behind the cay. I killed the engine, then dropped the anchor and paid out enough line to keep us secure. Since we were only in about ten feet of water, I dropped seventy feet of chain to do the trick. My side scan sonar indicated a few shallow rocks, but none were close enough for the Baia's hull to strike, even if she somehow shifted 180 degrees in the night.

We kept a sharp eye on the boats as they maintained their course, watching on the radar screen as they cruised within a few miles of our position, then continued northwest along the edge of the bank. It wasn't long before the flotilla cruised out of range, disappearing from the screen entirely.

I grilled up some lobster, a large grouper filet, and a pile of chopped-up garlic potatoes for dinner. We ate out around the dinette while going over maps and depth charts of the area. The sky calmed considerably as the night progressed, and a first quarter moon cast a silver light over the water and rocky island beside us. It was quiet, with only the sounds of lapping waves and the occasional caw of gulls on the shore.

We decided to call it a night around 2300. I turned off the dim topside lights, then locked up the salon door and switched on the security system. I told Kyle I'd see him in the morning, then moved forward into the main cabin with Atticus at my heels. After brushing my teeth, I pulled off my tee shirt and plopped onto the queen-sized bed. Atticus took up his usual position at the foot of the bed as I plugged in my phone and set the alarm for 0500. We'd debated going looking for the plane in the dead of night but decided against it when we read that most illegal activity around Cay Sal Bank took place at night.

I turned off the overhead light, then collapsed onto my pillow. Within minutes, the deep welcomed sleep after a long day on the water overtook me.

Atticus crawled beside me and licked my face, waking me up half an hour before my alarm went off. I reached up and petted him behind the ears.

"What is it, boy?" I said.

He wagged his tail and tilted his head back and forth between me and the hatch a few times. I'd never owned a dog before Atticus and I'd only had him for a few weeks, but it was clear what he wanted.

Patting his head, I said, “Okay.”

Rolling out of bed, I slid my phone into my pocket and secured my Sig on the right side of my waistband. I lumbered into the head, splashed cold water on my face, then moved into the salon and started up the coffeemaker. There was no sound coming from the guest cabin, but I saw a faint glow under the door, letting me know that he was already awake.

Does that guy ever sleep? I thought as I opened the salon door and climbed topside with Atticus right at my heels.

He ran straight for the swim platform and quickly did his business over the side. When he was finished, he crawled up onto the sunbed and I followed suit, relieving myself over the port side as I stared out over the ocean.

Thankfully, the weather had cleared up even more. The small cove we'd called home for the night felt more like a lake it was so calm, and I felt only a hint of eastern wind brush against my damp face. It would make the search and any subsequent dives much easier. When I finished, I grabbed my night vision monocular from a locker and moved along the side railing towards the bow. Standing against the forward railing that only reached my shins, I scanned over the landscape that was green-hued through the lens of my monocular. I couldn't see much because the rocky shore rose up vertically at a ninety-degree angle in places and extended some fifteen feet into the air. Lowering the monocular, I took in a deep breath of ocean air, then stepped back down into the cockpit.

I switched on the radar, and as it booted up, I

opened my laptop and brought up the weather forecast for the day. Partly cloudy with a high of seventy-four degrees, wind speeds up to eight miles per hour, and a ten percent chance of precipitation.

"Looks like a good day to blow some bubbles, eh, boy?" I said.

Atticus was sprawled out with his head over the back of the sunbed, staring at me quizzically. When the radar screen materialized with an image of the surrounding area, I rose to my feet and looked it over. Everything looked as it had the night before until I looked closer at the southwest part of the island. There was a large inlet and what looked like a boat anchored just a few hundred feet from shore. I brought up a screenshot I'd taken the night before to compare, and sure enough, the echo wasn't there. Whoever it was, they'd arrived in the middle of the night.

I glanced over at Atticus. "You feel like going for a walk?"

Just as the word *walk* left my lips, he jumped to his feet and eyed me with eager anticipation. I walked back down into the salon just as Kyle was stepping out of the guest cabin. He was wearing the same black shorts but had changed into a skintight gray workout shirt. He looked like he'd been up for hours and was holding a stack of papers in his hands.

"You sleep at all?" I asked.

"A little. How's the water?"

"Like glass compared to yesterday." I nodded towards the charts in his hands. "We'll head over to the search area and put the magnetometer in the water once the sun pops up."

He nodded, and I moved into the main cabin and threw on a blue tee shirt. Reaching into the back of my closet beside my large safe, I grabbed a pair of two-way radios and my Northside water-resistant tennis shoes. I put them on, tightened the laces, then reappeared in the salon as Kyle filled a mug with coffee.

"What's going on?" he said, eyeing the radios and seeing my focused expression.

"There's something on radar. A boat on the other side of the island. Must have pulled in last night or early this morning."

His eyes grew wide and focused on mine.

"Drago?"

I shrugged.

"No way of knowing who it is, but Atticus and I are gonna go check it out." I handed him one of the radios and added, "Cellphone signal is a joke around here."

He looked at the radio for a moment, then said, "You sure you don't want me to come with?"

"Yeah. We're just gonna have a look. Keep that Walther close by."

He lifted his shirt slightly, revealing the pistol secured to his waist. I gave a brief nod, and stepped up onto the deck. Atticus was beside the transom and had a difficult time containing his excitement. I was impressed that he was doing so well being cooped up and understood why he wanted to go ashore so badly. Before he'd died, my neighbor in Key West had often taken him out on the water, though rarely for longer than an afternoon.

"The echo's only about half a mile to the southwest," I said. "We should be able to see it up by the lighthouse," I added, pointing to the highest part of the island in view. "Shouldn't be gone very long."

I stowed my night vision monocular, the radio,

and my Sig in a waterproof backpack, then moved aft and plopped down onto the starboard edge of the swim platform. While holding my bag over my head, I lowered myself into the gin-clear seventy-eight-degree water. The water rose up to my shoulders as I planted the soles of my shoes on the sandy bottom. I waded towards the shore, then grabbed hold of a jutting rock and pulled myself up out of the water.

Turning back, I called to Atticus, who jumped happily into the water with a splash and swam over to me. I threw my backpack over my shoulders and climbed the nearly vertical slab of sharp-edged limestone. Atticus, having found an easier route, climbed up onto the shore fifty feet away from me and reached the top before I did. He shook the water from his fur, then wagged his tail and watched as I caught up to him. He had a proud look on his face, and he seemed to really enjoy beating me.

"You're one smart pooch, you know that?" I said, patting him on the top of his head and taking a look around.

Most of the island was desolate and completely devoid of anything other than jagged rock. But as we moved closer to the lighthouse, patches of green-brown vegetation littered the landscape, including cacti and various tropical bushes that were more brown than green. Atticus trotted off a short ways ahead of me, smelling everything in sight. After a quarter mile or so of walking, we came to the ruins near the base of the lighthouse, long-ago-abandoned structures built to house the lighthouse keeper and whoever else was there. I grabbed my Sig from the waterproof backpack and slid it into my waistband. I'd heard many stories about Cay Sal, and none of them had happy endings.

There were scattered articles of clothing, remnants of old rafts, and abandoned food containers all around me. It was an important reminder of the frequency with which refugees used the island, and I knew that there was a pretty good chance that I wasn't alone. I could only imagine the horrors these people had experienced that drove them to risk their lives so dangerously in order to escape their homelands. They had my sympathy, but that wouldn't stop many of them from killing me and stealing my boat if given the chance. When pushed to utter desperation, people can do vile things in order to survive. I'd seen it many times in my life, and it was why I rarely went anywhere unarmed, even if that meant breaking Bahamian law.

Atticus barked and shook me from my thoughts. Glancing his direction, I saw that he was standing at the base of the lighthouse just a short ways away from me. I quickly cut the distance between us and saw that he was staring at what looked like the remains of a cooked bird beside a makeshift fire pit. There were hundreds of birds flying near the beach and nesting nearby. I knelt down and placed my hand over the ashes. They weren't hot, but it was clear that whoever had cooked the meal had done so within the past couple of days.

"All the more reason to make this quick, eh, boy?" I said, moving around the lighthouse and preparing myself for an encounter.

My Spanish was pretty good, and if they didn't attack me, I was hopeful I could try and help them in some way. That is, if they were still on the island. When I reached the other side of the lighthouse, I looked out over the western shoreline to the south. The sun was just starting to glow over the eastern horizon, but not enough to be of much help. I could see a dark outline of the shore and the faint glow from the moon over the water but couldn't spot anything on the water at the spot where the echo had been on my radar.

I grabbed my monocular from the backpack, scanned along the coast, but still saw nothing but rocks and waves.

That's strange, I thought as I brought my scope down. *It's like whatever was there simply vanished into thin air.*

I heard the shuffling of paws and realized that Atticus had run ahead a few hundred feet and was sniffing a pile of rocks. When I moved towards him, his head snapped to the side and he gazed out over the water. Following his gaze, I saw movement at the southern tip of the island and peered through my scope to get a better look. It looked like a large fishing trawler, and judging by the size of its wake, it was cruising away from us at nearly twenty knots. Unfortunately, it was too far away for me to read the blurry words on its stern or see any details of the two guys whose outlines I spotted out on the deck.

"Looks like a false alarm," I said, then gave a quick whistle, turned around, and headed back towards our cove with Atticus right behind me.

THIRTEEN

Drago Kozlov stood at the stern of the sixty-foot trawler. He kept his gaze focused on the island as his thighs leaned against the transom. In his right hand, he held a half-empty bottle of Mamont eighty-proof vodka. In his left, he held a Cohiba that had been dragged down to a stumpy remnant that nearly burned his fingers. His long black hair blew across his face, but his dark eyes stared unblinking.

The aft door opened slowly, and Solak stepped out. He wasn't surprised to see Drago wearing his usual dark attire and his leather overcoat, even in the morning heat of the Bahamas. In the two years he'd known the Russian killer, he'd never once seen him without it.

"Using the fishing convoy was an excellent decision," Solak said, standing a few short paces behind Drago.

The previous night, they'd cruised alongside a group of Cuban fishing boats and had spotted their target's boat at the northern part of the atoll. Locking their target's position on a digital map, they'd waited a few hours before looping back and dropping anchor on the other side of the island.

"A simple tactic," Drago said flatly, "but an effective one."

"And now we move?" Solak said. "They will know where we are."

"If what I've been told about his training and experience is correct, I have little doubt that he has been aware of our presence for some time now. But this does not concern me." Solak stared at his companion, then continued, "At worst, given our location, they may suspect that we are poachers, nothing more. Even the most cynical of experienced professionals would not suspect this hunk of metal to be anything more than ordinary fishing boat."

But it was no ordinary fishing boat. Carson Richmond had strong connections in the Cuban underworld, having worked alongside drug smugglers and human traffickers to sell and distribute illegal arms across the Caribbean for years. Beneath its decrepit exterior, the sixty-foot trawler was a smuggler's dream. Top-of-the-line electronics, a powerful radar, and in the engine room, two eight-hundred-horsepower Mercruiser engines that combined to push the big boat through the water at speeds of up to forty knots. She also had spare fuel tanks, allowing a maximum range of over five hundred miles.

Solak shook his head as he watched them cruise away from the island.

"We should have just killed them both while they

slept!" he said.

Drago paused a moment, then lifted his left hand to his face and inhaled what little life remained of his Cohiba. The heat singed the skin around his fingers, but he didn't seem to notice. Pain, like death, was no longer a concern of his. He welcomed both and at times wished for death to overtake him. It was this aspect of his character that made him so different from his fellow assassins, and so deadly.

"Use your head, Solak," Drago said. "Why do you suppose that they are here of all places?" When Solak couldn't come up with an answer, Drago continued, "They are looking for the plane."

Solak paused a moment. "But I thought that plane went down a hundred miles from here, on the northeast part of the bank."

"That is what was believed to be true based on the plane's flight plan. But it lost contact. It could have flown off course due to storm. Regardless, the plane was never found, and now we know that Quinn was the only survivor."

Solak was beginning to see the logic in Drago's decision making.

"Miss Richmond spent a fortune looking for that plane," Solak said.

"Yes," Drago said, then gave a few raspy coughs. "Imagine how satisfied she will be when I call her and tell her that not only have I killed Quinn, but I've found her plane as well. We will be able to charge a generous sum in exchange for revealing its location."

Drago took a final drag of his cigar, then exhaled. He held the burning nub in front of him and glanced at his red fingertips before flicking it into the white wake below. Turning his gaze back to the island, he scanned over its rocky, desolate terrain and thought he could see the dark outline of a man standing near the base of the old lighthouse.

FOURTEEN

Watching every step with careful precision, I made my way back across the coarse landscape towards the cove where the Baia was anchored. As its white deck and dark blue hull came into view, the sun was just starting to appear over the water to the east. I stopped for a moment when I reached the edge where the rocks angled dangerously towards the water below. The view looked like a picture straight out of a fancy travel magazine, the Baia floating in vibrant turquoise water surrounded by steep rock faces with a backdrop of dark blue.

I took a few deep breaths, enjoying the scene before me, then climbed down. Having learned from my intelligent canine companion, I took his route and reached the lapping ocean with ease, barely having to use my hands at all. I waded into the water and Atticus splashed in, swimming ahead of me and climbing up onto the swim platform.

"What'd you see?" Kyle asked.

He was standing beside the sunbed, staring down at me through a pair of sunglasses. Atticus shook the water off a few times, then I set my bag over the gunwale and climbed up beside him.

"Looked like a fishing boat," I said. Kyle handed me a towel and I dried off. "But it was too far away by the time I saw it to get any specifics."

"They went on the move just a few minutes after you left." He stepped towards the cockpit and glanced down at the radar display. "They're still heading south. They won't be in range much longer."

Once my upper body was mostly dry, I grabbed my tee shirt from the drybag and threw it on. I stepped around the transom and looked at the screen beside Kyle.

"It was around sixty feet long," I said. "And it looked old. I saw a few guys out on the deck, but they were too far away to notice specifics."

"Poachers?"

"Maybe. Either way, it doesn't look like they'll be any trouble." With my backpack slung over one shoulder, I moved towards the salon door. The smell of cooked sausage and eggs wafted into my nostrils as I stepped below deck.

"Smells like your cooking's gotten better," I said, grinning back at Kyle as I looked over the food. "I guess it couldn't have gotten any worse."

"You're welcome," he fired back. He raised his palms in the air, then laughed and added, "And it sure beats the hell out of MREs."

He handed me the radio, and I stowed both back in the main cabin closet. We made quick work of the food and I downed a mug of coffee before getting all of our gear ready for the day. By 0700, I brought the anchor rode up with the windlass and slowly secured the anchor in place, then Kyle attached the safety line. I brought the twin engines to life with a low roar and cruised out of our small cove. The red needle on the fuel gauge indicated that the Baia was just over half-full. The fifty-gallon tank I'd filled in Key West would give us some leeway, but we'd still have to keep an eye on it if we were going to eventually reach the nearest marina in Marathon.

Once we cleared the rocks, I turned the helm to port, putting us on a northerly course. I slowly brought the Baia up on plane, cruising us over the calm water with ease. The sun shone brilliantly across a cloudless eastern sky, so I grabbed a pair of Oakleys from the dash and slid them over my eyes.

It was a perfect day to be out on the water, and within fifteen minutes, we reached our destination at a spot where the atoll dropped off into the dark blue waters of the strait. Looking out over the horizon, I could see the Dog Rocks to the southeast and the Muertos Cays to the southwest, both island strands nothing more than desolate slabs of rock barely peeking out of the water.

I eased down to just a few knots and glanced at my depth gauge on the dash in front of me.

"We're at two hundred and fifteen feet here," I said. "At the edge of the atoll, it quickly drops off to well over six hundred. We'd better hope this plane isn't there, because that would mean we'd be cutting this trip short. I don't have the equipment to dive that deep."

The truth is, diving deeper than a few hundred feet can be very dangerous, even for experienced divers. Most people who die scuba diving do so in deeper water. I had my two Draeger rebreathers aboard, which would allow us to dive deeper for longer periods of time than using air or enriched air, but even rebreathers have their limits.

"It was dark when the plane crashed," he said. "After making my way out of the plane, I floated on the surface for a few minutes after it sank. I remember looking down and seeing the faint flashing glow of one of its taillights. From the research I've done, even a light as powerful as one of those in the best viz conditions wouldn't be visible more than three hundred feet down."

I smiled and nodded. I had to hand it to him, he'd certainly done his homework. I guess ten years in hiding had afforded him that luxury.

I idled the Baia then moved aft. My Proton Mark 3 magnetometer sat on the sunbed, and we powered it up, then ran a quick diagnostic to make sure it was working properly. It looked like a fancy yellow torpedo, its aquadynamic shape allowing it to cut through the water with ease. It worked similar to a run-of-the-mill metal detector that you see guys walking around with on the beach sometimes, just with a much better range.

Once all the checks came back satisfactory, I connected the cabling to the stern cleats and dropped it into the water. In the past, using a magnetometer to search the seafloor at hundreds of feet down required extensive mechanical equipment. But my top-of-the-line mag was so light and its cabling was so thin that I was able to tow it behind the Baia. Still, since the Baia wasn't designed for salvaging, I connected the cabling to both cleats just in case.

Kyle let out the cable slowly as I eased up on the throttles. I performed a quick calculation to decide how deep we would drag it and came up with one hundred feet down. From there, I was confident that the mag could pick up large remnants of the wreck within a five-hundred-foot radius along the seafloor, which would be the width of our lanes while searching. The problem was the plane had gone down in a storm, which meant that it was more likely to be scattered along the ocean floor. However, a relatively large intact part of the fuselage, or a wing, or an engine would leave a large magnetic field distortion for us to pick up.

When the cable went taut, we booted up the laptop, which would make a sound whenever the device picked up metal and identify its location on a digital map. I adjusted the audible indicator's baseline to ensure that smaller objects wouldn't set it off. I also had the Baia's built-in sonar up and running and connected it to the laptop as well. Using the sonar and magnetometer combined, we'd end up with a digital replication of the seafloor in addition to markings indicating metal objects.

Usually, as had been the case with the search for the *Crescent* and the *Intrepid*, I'd start off by creating a large grid using sonar and then sweep through with the mag. But this time was different. Though it had been dark when it had crashed, Kyle was confident as to the plane's general whereabouts. We also didn't have weeks and an unlimited fuel supply to find what we were looking for, as had been the case before.

"All set," Kyle said, giving me a thumbs-up as he looked down at the laptop screen.

Atticus sprawled out beside Kyle on the cushioned seat around the dinette as I pushed us up to ten knots. The yellow mag torpedoed through the water behind us, and the sonar gave readouts of the ocean floor below.

While Kyle kept a sharp eye on the laptop screen, I kept my eyes peeled over the horizon and routinely scanned a 360-degree arc using Ange's binoculars. An hour into our search, I spotted a pair of echoes on the radar screen but soon realized that it was only a couple of center-console sportfishing boats. For the most part, we had the ocean to ourselves, but I knew that could change in a hurry.

By noon, the mag had identified a few metal objects, but none were in the same ballpark size-wise as a major piece of a wrecked plane. Neither Kyle nor I felt the least bit discouraged, though. I hadn't expected to find the wreck in the first few hours. Even if you have a solid idea where to find something, the ocean is underestimated time and time again, even by the most seasoned salvagers. We'd managed to do three passes along the same lines since early morning. That meant that Kyle would have had to remember where the plane had gone down to within fifteen hundred feet or so, not exactly easy considering he had been floating in swells in the dark and that it was over ten years ago.

We ate a working lunch of lobster rolls, using leftover lobster and some white bread, along with a side of potato chips. The wind started picking up a little around 1300, but the sky was still clear aside from a few scattered clouds. By the time the sun began to sink into the water, we were slightly dejected. The mag had yet to pick up anything large enough to be a significant part of the plane.

Kyle sighed and leaned back into the cushion.

"Maybe there's something wrong with the mag?" he said, looking aft over the transom.

I shrugged. "Not likely. That's what the

diagnostics are for." He shook his head, growing irritated. I added, "These things take time. It's a big ocean."

"Yeah, but it's down there. I know it's there."

I rose from the helm seat and reached overhead, stretching my body.

"Keep an eye on her," I said, stepping towards the salon hatch. "I'm gonna put on more coffee."

"How's the fuel, anyway?" he asked, shifting off the half-moon bench and moving towards the helm.

"We're fine. We'll be tight if we haven't found it by morning, though."

I used the head, then filled my coffeemaker with its limit of Colombian medium roast. Opening the small fridge, I grabbed a plate of grouper filets and heated them up in the microwave. Then I melted a little bowl of butter and sat in the galley, snacking on the fish and watching as the water boiled and drizzled down over the grounds. I let my mind wander, thinking about what we'd have to do if we didn't find the wreck.

Should I still help him? I thought. *And what if we return and come up dry again? What then*?

I believed Kyle when he said that the wreck was there somewhere. Though he'd made some borderline decisions during our time serving together, he wasn't one to make up something like that.

I finished off more of the fish than I wanted to, eating unconsciously. Waking myself from my thoughts, I realized that the coffeemaker was done and moved towards it.

"Logan!" Kyle shouted from topside.

Freezing in my tracks, I quickly headed up the steps and onto the deck above.

"What's going on?" My eyes went first to the

laptop. Once I saw that there was nothing abnormal displayed, my eyes darted towards Kyle's.

He motioned towards the radar, and I saw an echo on the screen about seven miles southwest of our position. I grabbed the binos from the dashboard, then moved aft and focused on the horizon. Within a few seconds, I spotted the source of the echo.

"You're not going to believe this," I said as I peered through the binos.

"What? Is it that trawler?"

I nodded. "The one that was heading south this morning towards Cuba." I stepped back towards the cockpit, then handed Kyle the binos and glanced down at the radar screen. "Now it's making waves on a northeast trajectory. Whoever these guys are and whatever they're up to, they seem to like skirting the edges of our radar."

"They don't even have nets in the water," Kyle said, looking out towards the trawler. After a few seconds, he added, "What's the game plan here? You wanna cruise over there and introduce ourselves?"

He said the last words with a grin, then lowered the binos and looked over at me. I paused for a moment, wondering what to do next and considering everything from going over there and confronting them John Wayne style or just letting the Bahamian Coast Guard handle it. Suddenly, a high-pitched ping broke the silence. It came from the laptop and caused both Kyle and me to huddle over its screen in a fraction of a second.

"Shit, that's big," Kyle said.

He was right. The object being detected appeared to be roughly fifty feet long and looked like a wing. Just as I was about to idle the engines, another ping rattled across the ocean air, this one even louder.

Keeping our eyes glued to the screen, we watched as an object over a hundred feet long came into view.

Kyle smiled from ear to ear and placed his hand on my shoulder.

"That has to be the fuselage," he said. "There's no way that isn't the fuselage."

FIFTEEN

I idled the Baia, then checked our depth and saw that it was right at two hundred and ten feet. I had six hundred feet of anchor rode, meaning the best that I could do letting all of it out would be a three-to-one ratio. The boating handbook recommends at least seven to one, but I was confident that, so long as the weather stayed calm, the Baia would stay in place.

While Kyle kept his eyes on the laptop, I grabbed the binos and took another look at the pesky trawler. The light of the dying sun cast a glare over the water that made it more and more difficult to see them. All I could see was its dark silhouette.

"Looks like he's turned a little," I said. I looked down at the radar and added, "They're heading east now. Away from us."

Kyle looked out over the water and nodded.

"It looks like they don't want anything to do with

us," he said. "Let's drop anchor and get in the water."

After a long day of searching, I was glad that we'd finally found something and was just as anxious to get into the water as Kyle was. But my instincts told me that seeing the trawler again wasn't just a coincidence. I thought about Baldy and how he'd said that the Russian Devil, who we'd learned was Drago Kozlov, was after us. His reputation of being unpredictable and mysterious was well established.

I watched as the trawler's echo faded off the radar screen, then turned to Kyle, who'd grabbed both sets of rebreather gear and carried them up onto the deck.

"We'll only need one," I said sternly. He looked over at me with a confused expression on his face, and I added, "We need to have someone on the surface just in case that trawler or some other boat comes near." I stepped towards him and grabbed one of the rebreathers. "I'm going down, Kyle. You stay up here and keep a sharp eye on things."

"The hell with that," he said. "If anyone's going down there, it's me. You don't even know what you're looking for, and you don't know where it is. I do."

I wanted to remind him that he'd agreed to my being in charge, but he was right. He could explain what the electronics looked like and where they were, but it wouldn't be as effective as him going. He'd been on the plane and had seen its layout and the storage devices.

I took in a deep breath and let it out. Usually, in a situation like this, I'd just send my underwater drone down to investigate, but there was no denying that what we were looking at was the main part of the plane. One of us had to go if we were going to try and recover the electronics.

"Alright," I said. "You go down. You remember how to use this, right?"

I handed him the rebreather. It was a rhetorical question, of course. We'd been trained to use all sorts of diving methods in the Navy: scuba, various rebreathers, and surface-supplied air. We'd been trained so heavily that we were able to don the gear blindfolded in heavy crashing surf. The only easy day was yesterday and it pays to be a winner, those were the mottos that had driven us to be the best in the world at what we did.

I climbed up onto the bow and released the anchor's safety lanyard. Moving back down into the cockpit, I used the sonar to find a suitable anchorage site near the wreck, then fired up the windlass and splashed the anchor away. I killed the engines and let out all six hundred feet of rode. Once we were anchored down, I moved aft, where Kyle was reeling in the towfish cable. He'd already coiled up most of it, and just as I reached the transom, the yellow mag broke the surface. I stepped down onto the swim platform, wrapped my hands around its frame, and hoisted it up onto the deck. After doing a quick integrity check and seeing that it hadn't been damaged, I shut it off and temporarily stowed it up against the starboard gunwale along with the coiled cable.

As Kyle calibrated the rebreather, I opened a locker beside the dinette and pulled out a black mesh bag containing fins, masks, and weight belts. Stepping down into the salon, I moved into the guest cabin and grabbed a large 3mm full body wetsuit. I carried it with me topside and went through the final calibrations of the rebreather with Kyle. It took a few minutes to make sure that each tank was filled and properly pressurized, that the scrubber was working properly, that none of the connections were blocked or leaking, and that the gases were being mixed properly.

Once Kyle was done, we traded places and I performed a few dummy checks, just in case. He grabbed the wetsuit, then stepped down onto the swim platform and submerged it, making it easier to put on. Removing his shirt, he slid into the dripping wetsuit, then grabbed a pair of fins from the mesh bag along with a black full-face dive mask. He spat into the glass frames of the mask and rinsed it out in the ocean, a simple yet incredibly effective means of preventing the mask from fogging. Once I was finished, I helped Kyle into the gear and tightened the straps, making the rebreather snug.

He moved to the swim platform and plopped down onto the transom. I took one more look around with the binos but saw no sign of the trawler. The sun was almost gone, just a sliver above the horizon, and the sky was growing darker and darker with each passing second. Kneeling on the deck, I reached deeper into the locker beside the dinette and pulled out my dive flashlight, which was fully charged, handing it to Kyle. He strapped it around his left wrist, then slid his bare feet into the fins and secured the mask over his face.

Usually, an ordinary dive mask works fine, but I wanted us to be able to communicate, so I'd opted for him to use the full-face. I did a quick check using my handheld radio in the cockpit to make sure he could hear me.

"Loud and clear," he replied through the speaker and gave me a thumbs-up.

Looking down at the radar, I saw that, for now, we had the nearby ocean all to ourselves.

"Alright," I said, performing a final check of his gear. "It's two hundred and ten to the bottom. Let me know when you have positive identification of the plane. Even at that depth, you've got plenty of bottom time with this setup. Just be careful, and don't get caught on anything if you enter the plane."

"When I enter the plane," he said through the com. He rose to his feet, then stepped toward the edge of the swim platform and added, "Piece of cake, Dodge."

Glancing over his shoulder, he nodded, then took a big step and splashed into the water. He bobbed on the surface for just long enough to tap his right fist on the top of his head a few times, signaling that everything was fine, then dropped down beneath the surface. I watched him descend for a minute, then grabbed the mag and rinsed it down on the swim platform using the freshwater hose.

Once finished, I grabbed the binos, climbed up onto the bow, and had another look around. After seeing nothing, I stepped back down into the cockpit and opened the salon door to let Atticus out. He rushed out onto the deck and sniffed around, curious what all the excitement was about. I sat down in the cockpit and kept a steady eye on the radar. Atticus eyed his tennis ball which sat in a cupholder on the dash, then grazed his head against my leg.

"Not right now, boy," I said.

After a few more minutes passed, the small radio came to life with static, followed by Kyle's voice.

"I have a visual of the plane," he said. After a few breaths, he added, "It's the main part of the fuselage. The tail broke off and is nowhere in sight.

The other hit we had looks like part of a wing."

With the radio up to my mouth, I held the talk button down.

"Can you get inside?"

After a short pause, he replied, "I might be able to get in through the side door. Swimming over the main section now."

I petted behind Atticus's ears while keeping the radio raised in front of me, waiting for more information. The distant sun sank completely into the water, disappearing in a spectacular light show that covered every color of the spectrum from dark red to light orange. The sky around me grew darker in an instant, and I grabbed my night vision monocular, exchanging it for the binos, which I placed back in the small locker beside the helm.

"Nose looks like hell," Kyle's voice said over the speaker. "Cockpit windows are shattered and the frames are bent, but this looks like my best bet. I wanted to get in through the side door, but it's pressed up against part of a rocky ledge."

"Roger that," I said.

He swam in through the cockpit, narrating his movements and what he was seeing every few seconds. As we'd expected, he told me that the plane was an absolute mess. Tangling wires, sheared metal, and debris everywhere. He finned his way to the back of the plane and lifted a few panels that had broken off and rested against a seat. After a few minutes of silence, I was about to say something when his voice came over the speaker.

"Logan, I found it," he said, sounding less excited than I expected him to be.

"Great," I said. "Let's get it up and get the hell out of here."

After a short pause, he said, "Thing's heavy as hell." His words were rushed, and I could hear his heavy breathing. "I can't get it out of here by myself."

I sighed and glanced over at the other set of rebreather gear.

"Alright, stay there," I said. "I'll be right down."

As I stepped towards my other rebreather, he said, "Thing's got to weigh over a hundred pounds."

Over a hundred pounds? I thought.

My mind went to work, thinking of ways to haul up something so heavy from so deep below water. Suddenly, an idea popped into my mind, but as I checked my rebreather, I quickly realized that there was something wrong with the calibration. It was giving me an error code, and I didn't have time to deal with it.

Perfect timing, I thought.

Moving into the guest room, I exchanged it for my BCD. It took a few trips to bring everything up, but I soon had my BCD, two tanks of trimix, and one regular air tank resting on the sunbed. Trimix is a special blend of Oxygen, Helium, and Nitrogen that's specifically designed for deep diving. Reaching into the overhead of the guest cabin, I also grabbed a deflated and folded-up yellow emergency raft that had come with the boat when I'd bought it.

"Alright, boy," I said, motioning towards Atticus.

I ushered him down into the salon, then closed the door and locked it. After changing into my wetsuit, I strapped my dive knife around my left calf, then took out a mask and fins from the mesh bag still resting on the dinette. Grabbing my BCD, I did a few quick checks, then strapped on the two trimix tanks and hooked up the regulator. I sat on the edge of the sunbed, brought each strap over my shoulder, then tightened the Velcro and pulled the straps snug. I grabbed my other full-face mask, powered it on, and tested it. When I heard Kyle's reply, I defogged the lenses and donned it. I grabbed my other flashlight, strapping it around my wrist, and sat on the transom. After donning my fins, I grabbed a small dry bag, put my Sig inside, and clipped it to my BCD. Then I grabbed the deflated emergency raft, a coil of nylon rope, and my extra tank of air.

Standing up on the swim platform, I looked one more time out over the empty horizon, then took a big step out into the water. I kept my BCD stowed with the weights in its flaps, so with no air in the bladder, I entered negatively buoyant and sank right away. Glancing at my dive watch, I was able to see my depth as I descended. When I reached fifty feet down, I switched on my flashlight.

After a few minutes of descending and equalizing the pressure, I caught my first glimpse of the seafloor and the plane wreckage. The entire rear of the plane was completely torn off along with both of its wings. The cockpit was smooshed in, and the sides of the fuselage were broken in places and scratched to hell. I met Kyle in the cockpit.

"Told ya it's a mess," he said. "You should leave your fins here," he added. "We'll be walking this thing out."

He pointed to where his fins were stowed under a stone in the silt. I removed them one at a time, then placed them beside Kyle's. I also set the spare air tank, the coiled nylon rope, and the deflated emergency raft alongside them.

Kyle glanced at the equipment I'd brought down for a few seconds and smiled.

"Smart thinking," he said, then motioned me to

follow him inside.

Using my hands and controlling my buoyancy via my breaths, I followed Kyle up and through the shattered cockpit. After we navigated our way to the middle of the fuselage, he pointed towards a large metal storage container with piles of debris beside it. He moved to the backside of it, then we both grabbed onto a handle, one at each end. He wasn't kidding about the electronics being heavy. It was a pain getting them to the front of the plane and out through the torn-up cockpit, even with the two of us. By the time we got it out, I'd been down for twenty minutes.

Grabbing hold of my pressure gauge, I figured I had only about ten more minutes left at that depth. Even with two tanks filled with trimix, diving down to two hundred feet means the gases compress to nearly one-seventh the volume that they were at the surface, giving the diver very little time to hang out at that depth. It also didn't help that I was lifting a heavy object, making me use up even more precious air than I normally would have.

Carefully, we carried the metal box down onto the seafloor and went to work. Grabbing the nylon rope, we looped it through the box's handles, underneath, then through the other side. We did this three times, making sure that the box would be held in place, then looped and tied the nylon ends around the corners of the life raft, distributing the weight as much as possible.

Once the raft was secured to the box, we spread it out on top, making the whole thing look like a big jellyfish. We donned our fins, then Kyle held the makeshift contraption in place and I reached for the full tank of air in the sand beside me. Once the tank was under the raft, I used my left hand to support the cylinder, then grabbed the pillar valve with my right.

Here goes nothing, I thought, then turned it slowly counterclockwise.

The valve cracked open and air spewed out, bubbling up towards the surface and becoming trapped under the raft. Within seconds, the bottom of the raft filled with a pocket of air and rose up like a hot-air balloon, causing the nylon connections to go taut. I continued to fill, keeping a watchful eye on the edges of the raft and making sure that it wasn't going to tear. The positive buoyancy of the air soon prevailed and lifted the metal box from the seafloor.

Kyle glanced over at me and said, "You're a genius. Enjoy that, because you'll probably never hear it again."

I was about to laugh, then stopped myself. Checking my pressure gauge again, I saw that I barely had enough to make it to the surface and perform my safety stop.

"I need to head up," I said, and when he looked over at me, I motioned towards my pressure gauge. "You got this alright?"

The box had already lifted a few feet off the seafloor without any assistance. With Kyle steadying it and finning it along, I reasoned he should have no trouble bringing it up alone. Especially since the more it ascended, the more the air trapped under the raft would expand and the faster it would travel.

"Let some air leak out over the edges if it goes too fast," I said. "I'll see you at fifteen feet."

He gave the OK signal, then I looked up and finned briskly, with big smooth kicks, towards the surface. Keeping an eye on my depth via my dive watch, I stopped at fifteen feet down, then started a five-minute timer. Performing a safety stop is important at the end of every dive, especially when you go down below a hundred feet. Failing to stop drastically increases your chances of decompression sickness, or the bends as it's referred to.

Keeping myself neutrally buoyant, I took in my surroundings. I could just barely see the light of Kyle's flashlight below, and above I could see the Baia's hull jutting into the water about a hundred feet away on the surface.

As I floated, wondering if it would be easier to swim the metal box over or move the Baia closer, I heard the distinct sound of a boat engine and a propeller cutting through the water. My heart raced, and I searched the surface for the source. Sound travels much faster in water than in air, making it easy to hear sounds from much farther away. However, this also makes it almost impossible to identify which direction the sound is coming from, since to figure that out, our brain uses the time it takes for sound waves to travel from one ear to the other.

"Logan, do you have a visual?" Kyle said.

My eyes scanned back and forth towards the surface and the twilight sky above. The sound was growing louder and louder, and after a few seconds, it materialized into a boat that was skirting across the water in the corner of my eye, heading towards the Baia.

SIXTEEN

I kept my eyes trained upward and locked onto the boat. It was small, no more than twenty feet long, and it looked like a rigid-hull inflatable, or RHIB, as they're called.

"Kyle," I said into the speaker. "It's a RHIB."

I watched as it cruised around the Baia, then moved back towards the stern, slowing to just a few knots.

"Who is it?" Kyle asked, like there was a way in hell I was supposed to know.

"It's slowing aft of the Baia," I said. "I'm gonna pop up and check it out."

"Wait for me!" Kyle said. "I'm almost up to you."

Not that I didn't want Kyle's help, but the second that raft hit the surface, it would be a massive target and give away our position. I glanced down at the timer and saw that I still had a minute and a half left.

I guess I'm gonna have to risk it.

I had no way of knowing who they were or what they wanted, but one thing was certain: I wasn't about to let them board my boat without my permission.

The RHIB idled just aft of the Baia as I loosened the straps on my BCD, pulled apart the Velcro waist strap, and slid it off my back. If any of them had half a brain, they'd already know where I was from my bubbles rising up to the surface. After venting enough air for the BCD to remain neutrally buoyant, I took a final inhalation, then pulled the regulator from my mouth, grabbed my small drybag, and swam towards the bottom of the Baia. Just as my body cleared the hull, a bright spotlight pierced down into the water from above.

Once I reached the port side of the Baia, I ascended slowly, exhaling some of the air from my lungs to prevent overexpansion. Rising slowly out of the water, I exhaled the rest of my air, then took in a slow, quiet breath. I reached for my mask and slid it up over the crown of my head. My body was hidden from the guys in the boat by the Baia's port gunwale. As I moved slowly aft, I silently removed my Sig from the drybag and held it up out of the water with my right hand. I grabbed hold of the swim platform with my left and peeked around the corner, catching my first glance of our guests.

My first realization was that they sure as hell weren't Bahamian Coast Guard, and whoever they were, they weren't there to make friends. There were two men, one sitting all the way aft with a hand on the tiller of what looked like an idling 75-hp Yamaha; and the other was standing all the way forward and shining a spotlight into the water near where I'd been ascending just a few moments prior. Both guys were armed. The guy up forward aimed what looked like an M4 into the water with his right hand and shoulder while he adjusted the spotlight with his left. The guy aft had an MP-5 SD6 strapped across his back and a handgun in his right hand. I couldn't make out any details of their appearance in the darkness, but judging by their mannerisms, they had some training.

Suddenly, the guy operating the tiller spoke. I was roughly fifty feet away, but it sounded like he was speaking Russian. The guy forward replied, and I was able to distinctly discern the word *nyet*, which means no in Russian.

Shit. I guess Baldy had been telling the truth after all.

I brought my Sig up and rested the barrel on the edge of the swim platform. I knew I only had a few seconds before Kyle and the raft would reach the surface.

Time to send the Russian Devil home.

I lined up my front and rear sights on the guy standing up forward. With my finger on the trigger, I clicked off the safety and took in a slow, deep breath. Suddenly, he yelled out something in Russian and adjusted the position of his M4. I knew that he must have spotted our makeshift salvage contraption. With a smooth, quick motion, I pulled back on the trigger. The hammer slammed home, sending the 9mm round exploding from the chamber. The sound rattled across the calm evening air as the bullet struck the guy up forward in the chest.

In rapid succession, I sent another round his way, the second striking him just below the neck. His body lurched forward, spinning the spotlight and casting a pillar of bright light straight up into the night air. As the guy fell forward, his M4 exploded to life, sending a stream of bullets splashing into the water below. After a fraction of a second of firing, his body tumbled all the way forward, collapsing over the bow of the RHIB, and he let go of his rifle.

I redirected my attention to the guy seated at the stern. In a flash of movement, he snapped his body around and yelled out a curse in Russian as he aimed his handgun in my direction. Just as he spotted me, I fired off two more rounds. The first struck the right side of his chest, causing his body to jerk violently. The second put him straight to bed in an instant as it exploded into the side of his skull, spewing blood and bone onto the inflated rubber gunwale beside him.

Following the report of the rounds, the scene around me turned eerily quiet as the two guys lay motionless. I kept my Sig raised for a few seconds, just in case. When it was clear that both men were down and out, I held my Sig up out of the water and kicked towards the black RHIB. Just as I made it to the starboard tube, I reached for the bow and quickly switched off the spotlight, which had still been shooting a beam high into the night sky. After what had just happened, the last thing I wanted was to draw more attention than the gunshots already had.

Once the light went out, I noticed air bubbles rising up to the surface near where I'd left my BCD. Swimming forward, I held my mask against my face and peered down into the water. The concave raft was just a few feet beneath the surface but was losing air.

That guy must have shot it with his M4 when he went down.

There was no time to think of a plan. At the rate the air was bubbling out, it would all be gone and the box would sink to the bottom in a hurry. Looking down, I saw Kyle kicking beneath the metal box, working hard to keep it afloat. I took in a deep breath, dove down, and finned towards him as fast as I could. Grabbing hold of the metal box alongside Kyle, I motioned towards the RHIB and we both kicked as hard as we could, willing the box towards it. There was no way we could make it to the Baia before all of the air escaped, which meant that our only chance to get it out of the water was to use the black inflatable.

After a series of strong kicks, we reached the edge of the RHIB. Rising out of the water, I wrapped my right arm around one of the pontoons and held one of the metal box's handles securely with my left. Kyle pulled off his rebreather gear beside me, leaving me to keep most of the weight up by myself. I felt every muscle across my body flex and tremble as I gritted my teeth and forced myself to hang on.

Once Kyle was out of the gear, he grabbed onto the other handle, taking some of the weight off and easing the pain in my fingertips. Keeping my left hand clasped to the handle, I pulled myself up onto the pontoon using my right leg, then rolled over onto the thick plastic hull. Fortunately, we'd chosen the side opposite to where the two dead guys had collapsed, so we wouldn't have to worry about the small boat tipping over.

After removing my fins, I adjusted my grip on the side of the boat, making sure I was secure, then leaned over the side.

"Alright," I said, making eye contact with Kyle. "One…two…three!"

I pulled as hard as I could while Kyle kicked and pushed up. With a strong, quick movement, we jerked the heavy-duty box out of the water, slid it over the pontoon, and thumped it onto the deck. After helping

Kyle get the rebreather gear out of the water, I fell back against the starboard pontoon and breathed heavily.

"Holy shit," Kyle said as he pulled himself out of the water and plopped down beside me. He slid out of his fins and looked around the boat, breathing as heavily as I was from sheer exhaustion. The deep dive, lugging the metal box out of the plane, and hoisting it up into the boat had taken its toll on both of us.

"Way to make a mess," he said, glancing at the two bleeding dead guys.

"Next time I save your ass, I'll make cleanliness a higher priority," I fired back along with the best attempt I could make at a grin. Tilting my head to look at the monstrous metal box beside me, I added, "What the hell's in this thing anyway? It feels like a box of bricks."

"Things that are going to bring the truth to light," Kyle replied in between quick, deep breaths.

Summoning my strength, I sat up and looked around. I felt beyond tired and dehydrated, but we weren't done yet.

"Let's get this hunk of metal onto the Baia," I said. Then, looking down at the two dead guys whose blood was pooling at our feet, I added, "We've got to figure out what we're going to do with these two."

"Sending them both to the bottom is my vote," he said. "You think one of these jerks is the Russian Devil?"

I shrugged as I moved for the Yamaha outboard that was still idling.

"I heard them speaking Russian," I replied. "We should search them real quick before we get out of here."

"You sound like you're in a hurry."

"This boat has a short range," I said. "Which means that the mothership must be somewhere nearby."

As the words came out of my mouth, I could tell Kyle was wondering why he hadn't thought of that himself. Fatigue and deep diving don't mix. The combination can have bad effects on your wits.

He looked around us while I put the motor in forward gear, then twisted the throttle on the end of the tiller. Just as we began to move, Kyle snapped his head towards the bow, then held a hand up in the air.

A second later, he pointed out over the bow and said, "I hear something."

My eyes darted in the direction he was pointing and tried to focus through the darkness. The patches of cloud covering the moon made seeing anything difficult, but I could just make out the large black outline of what looked like the fishing trawler we'd been suspicious about. I cursed myself for not noticing it sooner, but the sound of the idling Yamaha must have drowned out the noise of its engines as it approached.

My eyes grew wide as the trawler cruised towards us at an unbelievable speed. I tried to accelerate out of its path, but with all four bodies along with the metal box, the small RHIB was most likely right at the limit of its load capacity, causing us to ride low in the water. With my right hand still gripping my Sig tightly, I accelerated our small boat as fast as it could.

In an instant, the trawler slowed just a few hundred feet away from us, and I spotted a man standing stoically on the bow. Through the darkness, I saw a plume of smoke coming from his mouth, then realized that he was holding something both unmistakable and terrifying over his left shoulder.

"RPG!" I yelled.

Kyle snatched the M4 from the deck and raised it just as I raised my Sig. But before either of us had time to take a shot, a rocket exploded violently from the launcher. My heart pounded as I instinctively hurled my body over the port gunwale. In the corner of my eye, I could see Kyle diving as well as the rocket-propelled grenade hissed through the air. In the blink of an eye, the grenade made contact with the center of the RHIB and exploded, sending a painful shockwave into my body and scorching my back as I splashed into the water.

I grunted as the pain overtook me and felt disoriented in the dark thrashing water. The force of the explosion had knocked the air from my lungs, but I forced myself to swim deeper, not wanting to expose myself. There was a high-pitched ringing in my ears, my back burned, and my side felt like I'd been hit by a series of Mike Tyson haymakers. I opened my eyes to the sting of saltwater and saw a burning glow radiating from the surface above. I heard the sounds of the trawler's propellers as they pushed the enemy boat along and could barely make out its hull through my blurred vision.

Suddenly, I felt an arm grab hold of mine and jerked my head sideways. I still couldn't see very well but realized that it was Kyle and that he was pointing towards something in the water ahead of us. Focusing my eyes forward, I spotted my BCD still floating lifelessly at fifteen feet down. It looked to be about thirty feet away, fortunately having drifted in the same direction as I'd motored the RHIB.

With my lungs aching for air and my body

feeling like hell, I swam alongside Kyle towards the BCD. Forcing myself to keep moving and pushing through the pain, we eventually reached it and took turns taking a deep breath of much-needed air. My vision slowly cleared, but the ringing in my ears persisted. I looked up towards the surface just in time to see strands of automatic gunfire splashing into the water, the rounds breaking apart just a few feet over our heads. By the sporadic nature of the bullets, it wasn't clear whether they saw us or not. But one thing was clear, they knew that neither of us had been killed by the grenade blast.

Knowing that it was our only hope of getting out of this mess, I'd managed to maintain my death grip on my Sig even while diving into the water and during our short swim. We both looked around us, trying to come up with some kind of plan.

Whatever we do, we need to act fast, I thought as I glanced at the pressure gauge, which indicated that the tanks were dangerously close to being empty.

We kept a sharp eye on the trawler and, as I'd expected, it slowed to an idle between the burning RHIB and the Baia. Tilting my head towards Kyle, I motioned for the stern of the trawler. We each took one more deep breath and took off into the darkness, using the light from the slowly extinguishing flames to guide us.

When we reached the stern, I pulled my dive knife from its sheath strapped to my left calf and handed it to Kyle. At the count of three fingers, we rose up out of the water, making as little noise as possible as we grabbed hold of whatever we could get our hands on for support. As soon as Kyle started to pull himself up towards the top of the transom, a man yelled out something in Russian from up on the flybridge, and a second guy swiveled his MP5 towards Kyle. Before he could level his weapon, Kyle lunged forward, grabbed hold of his shirt, then jerked him over the stern and slammed him into the tip of my dive knife. The blade cut through his heart, killing him almost instantly.

As Kyle hurled the guy into a front flip and splashed him into the water, I took aim and put two rounds into the chest of the guy who'd yelled out a second earlier. He pulled the trigger of his M4 and shot a burst of rounds into the air as his body jolted sideways, flew over the starboard side of the trawler, and splashed into the water below.

More voices came from both inside and from the bow of the trawler, and Kyle and I knew that we had to move quickly. Wrapping my hands over the transom, I pulled myself up as fast as I could, brought my legs over, and planted my bare feet onto the deck. In a flash of movement, Kyle snatched the MP5 from the guy he'd impaled, then climbed up and hit the deck beside me.

We both saw movement coming from inside, and Kyle moved towards the aft door with his MP5 raised. Just as we were about to breach, a series of automatic gunfire erupted from inside, shattering the windows and causing us both to drop to the deck. I rolled to my left towards the port gunwale, seeking cover behind the metal bulkhead. Just as I reached the port bulwark, a pair of long arms grasping a blacked-out AK-15 came into view just a few feet ahead of me. It was being held by a tall, lanky guy wearing a large black leather jacket and having midnight hair that reached well past his shoulders. I hadn't gotten a good look at him before, but he had the same general appearance as the guy who'd blown up the RHIB with the RPG.

Just as we spotted each other, he aimed his AK towards me and pulled the trigger. I just managed to extend my hand at the last second and grab his wrist, forcing the barrel to look anywhere but at me. Bullets exploded out, missing parts of my body by less than a foot as they rattled against the transom behind us. My left arm shook as I muscled the beast at bay. I gave a strong push, then, with my right hand still gripping my Sig, raised it up towards his chest. Before I pulled the trigger, he caught me off guard, using my momentum against me as he spun around and shoved me onto the deck against the metal gunwale. In a quick retaliation, I snapped my right leg across the front of his body, knocking the AK out of his hands and sliding it forward on the deck.

I raised my Sig and managed to fire off a single round, the bullet flying inches from my assailant's face as he dropped down on top of me. Before I could fire another shot, he grabbed me by the forearms and, using his falling momentum, spun me around and slammed my Sig onto the deck. Sharp pains shot up from my right hand as my Sig came loose and rattled against the transom behind me.

I was amazed at how fast and efficient my enemy was and knew without question who he had to be. The Russian Devil. Drago Kozlov. One of the most feared assassins on earth.

His reputation preceded him. He was strong and fast, and he clearly had years of extensive training. But beyond his physical abilities, there was something deeply menacing about the guy. His pale face showed no emotion, and as he turned to face me, his dark eyes looked like portals into hell. I felt a faint recognition upon seeing his face up close. I couldn't place it in the heat of the moment, but I swore that I'd seen him before.

Before my Sig had come to a stop, he reached beneath the left side of his black leather jacket and pulled out a silver blade that glistened under the deck lights. He sliced the sharpened steel towards my body as I twisted and pummeled him across the face with my right foot. Seeming to be only irritated by the blow and nothing more, he came back with another strike, this time stabbing the blade towards my chest. I rolled and forced the blade aside, causing it to stab into the deck beside me.

Jumping to my feet, I managed to avoid a few more stabs of his blade before his clenched fist struck me in the side. As I lurched sideways, he sliced the blade through the air, the steel cutting a deep gash in my left shoulder. I grunted, trying to brush off the excruciating pain. As he came in for a finishing blow, I shuffled to my left, grabbed hold of his shirt, then spun him around and slammed his head into the bulkhead. I could tell he was slightly dazed from the blow and used it to my advantage. Without hesitating, I twisted him around, and hit him with a strong front kick. His body flew forward and he nearly tumbled onto his face.

"Logan!" Kyle shouted from the other side of the boat.

I turned around, took a few steps aft, and snatched my Sig from the deck. Glancing over at Kyle, I saw him standing with the MP5 in one hand and my dive knife in the other. Two dead guys lay bleeding and motionless at his feet.

As we both turned our attention to the port side, I heard a loud order barked in Russian across the night air. I ignored the pain from my shoulder as blood dripped down my wetsuit. I turned to look back down the port bulwark, this time with my Sig raised and with Kyle at my six, but Drago had vanished. I glanced at Kyle, then took a step forward. Just as my bare foot hit the deck, a loud roar grumbled from below. The trawler suddenly accelerated at an unbelievable rate, causing the bow to rise high into the air and sending Kyle and me falling backward.

We both lost our balance for a second, nearly tumbling over before stabilizing ourselves against the transom. I didn't know how the old and decrepit-looking trawler managed to move so quickly, but it definitely had some unbelievable upgrades in the engine room. In the chaos of the boat accelerating and Drago vanishing, we hadn't noticed that one of the bleeding guys Kyle had taken out had somehow managed to rise to his feet. He was a big guy, built like a tank, and he looked pissed off.

Just as we looked his way, I saw that he'd snatched a long metal pole and was swinging it towards both of us. We only had time to raise our arms to try and absorb the brunt of the blow, but the pole was heavy and he was swinging it like a big leaguer at a home run derby. The pole slammed into us, causing our legs to brace against the transom and our bodies to hinge. Our upper bodies jolted backward and we spun almost 360 degrees before splashing into the white, bubbly water of the trawler's wake.

Disoriented in the strong current of the churning water, I broke the surface and turned around to look at the trawler, which was already nearing forty knots as it cruised away from us. Through salty, blurry eyes, I spotted a dark figure climb up onto the flybridge with an AK in his hands. It was Drago.

"There he is!" I shouted over the thrashing of the water and the roar of the engine.

Kyle treaded beside me and we both took aim, firing round after round towards the blacked-out devil. He shot a few rounds back at us as well, the bullets striking the sea and splashing around us. As the trawler cruised far away into the night, I saw at least one of our rounds hit home. Drago jerked sideways and collapsed onto one knee. Seconds later, he dropped out of view and the trawler disappeared into the darkness. Soon even the low hum of the engines faded away, and we were left alone in the calm after the storm.

SEVENTEEN

"Well, that was fun," Kyle said between quick, deep inhalations.

I nodded, then wiped some of the dripping water from my brow.

"What the hell?" I said. "I thought you took that guy out."

He shrugged. "Me too. He went with the old hook bar to the chest. Oldest trick in the book."

Kyle kicked his body up higher in the water, then quickly checked the rounds left in his magazine. I didn't have to count. My fifteen-round mag had three rounds left, a fact that caused my body to turn instinctively towards the Baia. She was still floating peacefully, her bow pointed towards us, into the slow-moving current.

"I don't understand why he isn't coming back to try and finish us off," I said as I turned back and glanced towards the dark horizon where the trawler had vanished.

"Maybe he wants to replenish his numbers," he said, glancing over at the two dead guys floating in the water. "Not a lot of good it'll do."

My body relaxed as the adrenaline began to wear off. I became increasingly aware of the pain radiating from my left shoulder, then motioned towards the Baia.

"Come on," I said, then swam on my right side towards the stern.

Kyle slung the MP5 onto his back, then freestyled, reaching the swim platform a few strokes ahead of me. He climbed up the swim platform ladder and looked out over the water.

"This day just keeps getting better and better," he said, motioning towards the few burnt pieces of the RHIB that floated in the water behind us.

Needless to say, the metal box was nowhere in sight.

After climbing aboard, Kyle extended a hand to help me up.

"Damn," he said as I rose up to my feet. "I sure hope that looks worse than it feels."

"Yeah, the saltwater really eases the pain," I said sarcastically.

Dripping water and small amounts of blood onto the deck, I grabbed a small towel and pressed it against my shoulder.

"Be a friend and hand me that first aid kit under the helm," I said.

Kyle moved forward, then bent down and opened the small locker.

"Let me stitch it up," he said, grabbing it and placing it on the dinette beside us.

I heard feet shuffling and barking coming from below deck. Grabbing my keys out of my wetsuit pocket, I slid the brass one into the salon door. Atticus came bolting out, clearly excited by all the commotion. He placed his paws against my chest and looked around. After sniffing the deck for a few seconds, he jumped back to me and looked at the blood coming out from my shoulder and soaking part of the towel.

"I know," I said, petting him behind his right ear. "I'll be alright."

As Kyle opened up the first aid kit, I moved down into the main cabin. Stepping into the closet, I pressed my right thumb on the scanner of my biometric safe and punched in the code. I grabbed two more mags for my Sig along with my MP5 SD6 assault rifle. As I stepped back up onto the deck, I heard the radio crackle to life.

"*Seas the Day* to Baia Flash," an older man's voice said through the radio. "Logan, are you okay?"

Kyle glanced over at me, but my face showed nothing but utter confusion. I had no idea who was contacting us, though his voice sounded vaguely familiar.

I stepped towards the cockpit and grabbed the radio.

"Baia Flash to *Seas the Day*," I said, holding down the talk button. "With whom am I speaking?"

After a short pause, the man's voice returned.

"This is George Shepherd," he said. "Captain of *Seas the Day* and former captain of *Island Dream*."

Hearing his name took me back instantly to my first few days back in Key West last year. *Island Dream* was the name of my boat before I'd purchased it, and George Shepherd was the man I'd purchased it from. He'd painted over the name to allow me to choose a new one, and I'd christened it *Dodging Bullets* a short while after. George had been a surgeon living in the Keys and, after retiring, he'd sold the Baia and bought a sailboat to cruise around the world with his wife.

I smiled and brought the radio back up close to my mouth. Kyle was still looking back at me, confused. I debated telling George to sail away as fast as he could but knew that that was probably not the best idea considering that there was an angry and heavily armed Russian assassin out there somewhere.

"George, you wouldn't happen to know anyone who could take care of a knife wound, would you?"

"With this wind, I should reach your anchoring in half an hour," he said. "We heard the gunshots and the explosion, and we saw the spotlight in the sky. Looked like a war zone." After a second's pause, he added, "Can you manage your shoulder until we get there? If it's serious, I've got a small dink and outboard I can drop in the water."

"Appreciate it, George. The pressure seems to be holding it fine."

"Alright. ETA in thirty. We're a forty-four-foot catamaran. Don't shoot us."

I laughed when the last three words came over the radio.

"Roger that," I said. "Over and out."

I stuck the radio onto its clip beside the helm, then turned back to Kyle. He was still shooting me a confused look.

Shaking his head, he said, "You've only been living in the Keys for a year. Seems like you know everybody."

I grabbed my canteen from the dinette and took a

few swigs.

"He used to own *Dodging Bullets*," I said. "I bought it from him back when I first moved."

"And… we can trust him?"

"He's not gonna arrive standing on his bow with a rocket launcher if that's what you're wondering."

He shrugged, then motioned towards my shoulder. "Seems to be contained well enough." He bent down, then stepped down towards the salon. "You got another rebreather, right?"

Atticus cocked his head at the question. Even he seemed to realize that it was crazy.

"Yeah, but it needs calibration work. Why?" I said, shaking my head.

"Because I'm heading back down. I wanna see if the box is still intact."

"You're kidding, right? Kyle, it was a tool storage box, not an explosion-proof safe. There's no way it survived a head-on collision with a rocket-propelled grenade."

"Well, I'm gonna make sure. We came all this way. I'm not about to let a little hiccup stop me."

A little hiccup? I thought.

He didn't wait for a reply. As he turned and continued down into the salon, I placed a hand on his shoulder.

"Wait. I've got a better idea." I squeezed my way past him. "Just wait up here and keep an eye out. I'll be right back."

When I reached the bottom of the steps, I hooked a sharp left and moved into the guest cabin. After opening the big locker on the starboard side, I reached inside and pulled out a plastic hardcase. Back topside, I set the hardcase on the sunbed, unclasped the hinges, and pulled it open. Kyle's reaction was just as

I'd hoped.

"I didn't know you had one of those," he said, leaning over me for a better look.

Inside the case was my commercial-grade underwater drone, complete with top, bottom, and forward/reverse thrusters. It also had a series of high-powered LEDs and three built-in cameras. Secured in the foam base beside the drone were four hundred feet of coiled-up yellow tether and a remote control with a built-in digital display.

After turning it on and checking to make sure that the battery was full and that everything was working properly, we set it in the water beside the swim platform. Once it was submerged, I powered up the top thrusters, propelling the small ROV downward.

"That thing's awesome," Kyle said.

"It comes in handy," I said, then handed him the controls. "Here. It handles pretty well."

Kyle was always a quick learner, and after less than a minute, he was piloting it like a pro. I plopped down on the cushioned seat beside Atticus. Sliding the first aid kit in front of me, I pulled out a small stack of gauze pads and some disinfectant. After taking care of the wound, I pressed the towel back against it and tightened it using one my leather belts. Once finished, I took a few more swigs of water, then leaned back and scanned the eastern horizon. The clouds had opened up a little, allowing the moonlight to cast a silver glow over the water.

"I have a visual of the seafloor," Kyle said. He was sitting on the sunbed with his feet propped up and his upper body hunched over the ROV's controls. "Looks like I owe you a new rebreather," he said, holding the screen up so I could see what remained of the destroyed piece of expensive diving equipment.

I waved him off and reached for my night vision monocular. "I already scratched it as a loss. I was looking to upgrade them to newer models soon anyway. Any sign of the box?"

I turned on the monocular, then looked east. Far in the distance, I saw the outline of a twin-hulled sailboat, its boom rising high into the air. It looked to be just a few miles out. While waiting, I grabbed my Sig along with an old rag and took it apart, rinsing each piece with freshwater and drying it off to prevent it from rusting.

Kyle suddenly dropped the controls in his lap, then leaned back.

I sighed and said, "Nothing left?"

He tilted his head and looked out over the horizon. "Nah. Just bits and pieces, burned and scattered all over the bottom."

He set the controls on the sunbed, then rose to his feet. Standing against the starboard gunwale, he looked out over the horizon. His breathing was heavy, his eyes narrowed, and his blood was probably just a few degrees shy of boiling.

"Hey," I said. "I'm sorry. But it'll be alright."

"How the hell can you say that?" he said, keeping his eyes peeled out over the water. "These people have been doing this for years. They came after me, and recently my family as well."

We both fell silent for a minute. I swear I could hear his heartbeat pounding in his chest. Not knowing what else I could say and deciding that he needed space, I put my Sig back together and slid off the bench.

"You should change out of that wetsuit and grab a shower," I said.

If he heard me, he didn't show it. After a few more seconds of silence, he turned to look at me, his eyes still narrowed and his brow furrowed. He quickly brought the drone back up to the surface, washed it down, then stowed it back in the hardcase. As he carried it forward, he stopped right beside me.

"I need to use your sat phone," he said.

I motioned towards where it sat on the dashboard in the cockpit. Grabbing it, he disappeared through the salon door.

EIGHTEEN

Seas the Day pulled slowly along the starboard side of the Baia fifteen minutes later. She was a beautiful forty-four-foot Lagoon with sleek white hulls, big windows that wrapped all the way around the galley and cockpit, and a large trampoline up forward. She looked new and immaculately taken care of, which didn't surprise me. The Baia had been in near-perfect condition when I'd purchased her, even though she had been two years old at the time and he'd put over a thousand hours on the engines.

"Ahoy, Captain Dodge," George said. He was standing against the thin port railing.

George was in his early sixties. He was average height, had a dark tan, and his hair was all salt and no pepper. Clearly taking to retired life well, he looked to have lost some weight since I'd last seen him. He was wearing a pair of white linen shorts and a blue polo shirt, and he was barefoot.

"Ahoy, Captain Shepherd," I replied, playing old sailor with him. "When you said your name, my jaw hit the deck so hard I think it made a dent."

He laughed and tossed me a line, which I secured around the starboard stern cleat.

"Well, my reaction was probably about the same when I heard all of the commotion, then saw my old boat through the lenses of my binoculars. Just ask my wife."

He tossed me a second line, which I secured to the bow. We each tossed over a few white fenders so our hulls wouldn't slam against each other. A petite Asian woman who looked like she was in her early fifties stepped out from the open sliding glass door. She was wearing a loose purple sundress.

"He looked like he'd just seen a ghost," the woman said.

"Logan, this is my wife, Rachel," George said. "Rachel, this is Logan Dodge."

"Pleasure to meet you, ma'am," I said.

"Likewise," she replied. "But just Rachel is fine. Where's the other guy? We saw two of you."

"He's not feeling well," I lied. "I think he passed out on the couch."

George grabbed a red-and-black duffel bag from the deck beside him, then stepped down to where *Seas the Day*'s port swim steps were floating just a few feet from the Baia's swim platform.

"Request permission to come aboard," he said.

I stepped down and held out my right hand. "Come on over."

In just a few seconds he had me seated beside the dinette and was riffling around in his duffel bag. At his direction, I loosened the belt and pulled off the towel, allowing him to see the wound. He quickly sanitized his hands, slid both into latex gloves, then softly removed the gauze. Grabbing a flashlight, he pulled part of the sliced wetsuit away and examined it further.

"Wow. That's pretty deep," George said. "You're lucky that you were wearing a wetsuit. The pressure of the neoprene prevented excessive bleeding." He set the flashlight down on the dinette, then grabbed a needle and thread. "Alright, go ahead and pull this down to your waist."

Reaching behind me, I ripped the Velcro at the base of my neck apart then pulled the zipper down. I winced slightly as I pulled the neoprene away and down to my waist, revealing my bare chest, which was covered in a thin layer of blood. George went right into doctor mode, first disinfecting the wound, then stitching me up with the efficient and perfect movements of someone who'd done it thousands of times in his life.

"You're lucky that you weren't cut another inch deeper," he said. He snipped the end of the thread, then placed the needle into a plastic hazardous waste disposal compartment in the bag, followed by the gauze and then both of his gloves. "Alright, that should do ya. I would recommend that you avoid any strenuous activities for at least a week or two, but judging by what I've read about you, I'm sure you wouldn't listen."

I smiled and raised my eyebrows. "What you've read?"

He motioned towards his catamaran. "We've got a laptop on board, and I read the *Keynoter* whenever I'm feeling homesick. You've been a busy guy this past year, and I'm willing to bet that Harper Ridley and the other writers haven't figured out everything you've done."

I laughed and thought briefly about my last year in the Keys. It had been a busy year. In fact, I thought about what day it was and realized that the following day would mark exactly one year since I'd moved to Key West.

"So are you gonna tell us what happened or what?" Rachel said.

She was still standing at the stern of *Seas the Day*, watching everything that we were doing.

George grinned. "My wife is the direct one out of the two of us. Though I'm curious as well, considering our peaceful night on the water suddenly turned into a war zone."

I briefly examined the skillful work he'd done stitching up my shoulder, then slid off the seat and rose to my feet.

"We were diving when that trawler cruised up on us," I said. "We'd seen it since yesterday evening and had grown suspicious. My guess is they were after the Baia. Fortunately, we were both armed and managed to fend them off."

I was glad that the bodies had drifted far enough south that they could no longer be seen. Dead, bloodied bodies in the water aren't exactly a nice sight to look at.

"How many more were still onboard?" George asked after thinking for a moment.

"I think just two," I replied. "Though I shot one of them, so I doubt they'll be back here anytime soon."

I slid my wetsuit the rest of the way off, then stepped down onto the swim platform and rinsed off using the freshwater hose. Once I had the blood washed away, I toweled off, then grabbed my tee shirt from the corner of the sunbed and threw it on.

"Do you know who they are?" Rachel asked.

I shrugged. "Local criminals is my guess. These waters aren't exactly the safest around." After a few second's pause, I added, "Did you guys call the Coast Guard?" I assumed that they probably had as soon as they'd heard the gunshots.

"I was about to," George said. "Then I grabbed my binoculars and recognized my old boat. Then I recognized you as well."

Part of me felt immensely relieved. The last thing I wanted was for a Bahamian Coast Guard patrol to engage a potential threat without knowing what they were getting themselves into.

"What brought you both to these waters anyway?" I asked.

"We're on our way to Saint Pete," he said. "Our daughter-in-law is due in the next few days and we don't want to miss it. We were fifty-fifty whether we were going to just fly out from Nassau, though now it appears that may have been the smarter course of action." He glanced at his wife, then turned back to me and added, "You guys hungry? Rachel made stew and it's incredible."

I could actually feel my mouth water and hear my stomach grumble. We hadn't eaten since lunch, and it'd been a busy couple of hours.

"That sounds great, thank you," I said. "Let me check on my friend and see if he wants some."

George nodded, grabbed his duffel and headed back over to his boat.

"I'll warm it up," Rachel said. "It might make your friend feel better."

Opening the salon door, I stepped down and saw

Kyle seated with one foot propped up on the table. He was staring off into space with my sat phone resting beside him.

"You want some food?" I said, and he just shook his head. I noticed my sat phone beside his foot and added, "Who'd you call anyway?"

"Murph," he said flatly.

My eyes narrowed with interest.

"You serious? He still work for the NSA?"

"Not anymore. He left a few years ago. Does mainly freelance stuff now, and he recently started his own tech company."

Elliot Murphy was a tech wizard whom I'd only met a few times during my time in the SEALs. He'd designed, created, and patented many of the high-tech gadgets we utilized and was also one of the best hackers in the world.

"I haven't spoken to him in years. But you've kept in touch?"

He nodded. "He's the one who helped me find you. He's also the reason I'm not behind bars right now. Helped me make it out of Cuba with a new passport and IDs."

I paused a moment. "You're pretty good at disappearing," I finally said. "I hadn't even noticed you'd left when their cat approached."

"I've been a living ghost for ten years, Logan," he said. "It comes naturally now. So what exactly is the plan with Drago? He's still gonna come for us."

"We track him down and we kill him. Simple as that."

"And then what?"

I shrugged. "I don't know, Kyle. We go back to living our lives."

"Yeah, easy for you to say."

"What do you wanna do? You said that the data on that plane was the only way we could prove your innocence and prove who the real guilty parties are."

He paused a moment, then said, "I didn't say that was the only way, I said it was the best way."

Just then, Atticus came trotting down the stairs behind me. He slid past me and plopped down at my feet.

"So what did you guys talk about?" I said.

Kyle took in a deep breath, then let it out.

"We talked about plan B," he said. "Since the original plan is shattered to pieces at the bottom of the ocean, we talked about another way to bring them down." When I just looked back at Kyle, confused, he reached into his pocket and pulled out what looked like a normal flash drive. "This is called the Plague. It's Murph's newest invention, and it's the fastest and most efficient hacker in the world."

I raised my eyebrows, and he went on to explain how that little flash drive could hack and make copies of some of the most protected computers in the world.

I thought over his words for a few seconds.

"You're going to go after her, aren't you?" I said.

"I told you, Logan, I'm finishing this. One way or another. I'm sick of hiding. I'm sick of running. I'm sick of me and my family living like fugitives. It's time to end this."

NINETEEN

After discussing possible plans of action going forward with Kyle, we decided to head back to the Keys. The Baia was running low on fuel, and with the electronics destroyed, there was no reason for us to stay in Cay Sal and attempt to further search the plane. I didn't like the idea of George and Rachel sailing across the Florida Straits by themselves with Drago on the loose, so I requested to join them on their crossing. They agreed over a quick bowl of some of the best beef stew I'd ever had, then I headed back over to the Baia to grab a few things.

"Bring this over to your friend," Rachel said, handing me a sealed plastic container full of stew. "If he's anywhere near as hungry as you were, he's going to appreciate it."

I thanked her, then climbed back over to the Baia and met Kyle in the salon. After setting the stew on the counter in the galley, I moved forward into the main cabin, grabbed my black Camelback and filled it with two extra mags for my Sig, my night vision monocular, my satellite phone, and a long-sleeved tee shirt. Throwing it over my right shoulder, I stepped back into the salon.

"Keep in touch via the VHF," I said.

"See you back in Key West," he replied.

I nodded, then motioned towards the container of stew. "That's for you, by the way." Turning aft, I added, "Keys are on the dash."

"Thanks, Logan," he said when my foot hit the first step. I tilted my head to look back at him and saw his eyes staring into mine. "Thanks for doing all of this."

It caught me slightly off guard. Kyle had never been the sentimental, appreciative type. But I guess both of us coming inches from death had given him a little perspective on the present situation. My ears still rang a little from the explosion that had almost killed us.

"I will draw on every remaining ounce of strength to protect my teammates and to accomplish our mission," I said, quoting a small portion of the Navy SEALs creed. "You're welcome."

He gave a slight nod, then I turned and headed up topside. Atticus jumped to his feet when he saw me and hopped up onto the sunbed. He seemed to really enjoy all of the stuff going on. Blazing guns, explosions, and a bleeding owner didn't seem to faze him very much.

"You're the perfect dog for me," I said as I scratched under his chin. "You need to stay here."

I stepped down onto the swim platform.

"How's he with small dogs?" George asked. He

was standing right across from me beside his boat's helm.

"Never had any problems," I replied.

"Well, he's welcome to come with us. Wally likes company."

I turned back to look at Atticus, who was staring back at me, his head cocked sideways.

"You want to stay here or come with me?" I pointed at the Baia, then over at *Seas the Day*. I'm not sure how dogs understand, but I think it has just as much to do with body language as it does verbal communication. His ears rose slightly and he jumped down onto the deck beside me, his tail wagging against the transom.

"I think that's a yes," I said.

Bending down, I wrapped my arms around his legs, lifted him up and extended his body towards *Seas the Day*. I was planning to just set him down on the port swim steps, but George came down and grabbed him. It amazed me how limber, strong, and well balanced he was, but I guess living on the water does that to you. I remembered a trip I'd taken Down Under for a training exercise with the Aussies back when I was in the Navy. As we pulled into Sydney harbor, we saw handfuls of sailboats being piloted by leather-skinned men in their seventies who moved like they hadn't aged in decades. You're kept busy at sea, handling lines, rigging sails, charting courses, and performing maintenance on everything from the engines to the washing machine. *Seas the Day* was only a year old, but even new boats have issues from time to time.

Once Atticus was aboard, I jumped over and climbed up into the cockpit. Setting my bag on a nearby bench, I turned and saw that Kyle had popped up onto the deck. He quickly untied the forward and aft lines and cast them over to me. I gave a quick wave, then he vanished back down into the salon. He was as untrusting as they came, but given his situation, it made sense for him to try and maintain a low profile.

"Your friend looks kind of familiar," George said.

"Yeah," I replied, "he looks like Allen Iverson, but with about forty pounds of muscle packed on."

It hadn't been a sudden, quick-witted response. Back in the SEALs, Kyle had looked so much like the dominating NBA point guard that his nickname had been AI.

"That must be it," George said with a smile. "I saw Iverson play at the 2001 All-Star game in D.C. He made the impossible look easy that night."

I felt a surge of envy. That had been one of the best games ever played, and I'd only been able to watch the highlights on a tiny old television with bad reception.

Wally came out from the sliding glass door right at Rachel's heels. The Boston terrier's eyes grew wide upon seeing Atticus, and the two moved in close and inspected each other. After a few seconds, Wally turned back inside and Atticus followed.

"I guess they're friends now," Rachel said.

"You Sox fans?" I said.

I thought it was kind of clever that they'd named their Boston terrier after the Red Sox mascot.

Rachel smiled. "For life. Thank God for the '04 season."

I nodded. To this day, it had been one of the most incredible things I'd ever seen on television. George went on to explain how Rachel was from New

England and they'd met there in college.

George and Rachel went to work in a smooth symphony of orchestrated movements, bringing the mainsail with the halyard, positioning the boom, and tightening the sheet in place. The cat had top-of-the-line features, making the process of setting sail an easy one with mechanical winches to do most of the work. I offered my help, but in less than thirty seconds, they had the main full of wind and the hulls cutting through the water. We had nine knots of wind blowing up from the southeast, so they put us on a broad reach as we set our course for Key West.

Seas the Day moved through the water like a dream, and I decided right then and there that if I ever decided to purchase a sailboat, it would be a Lagoon catamaran. At Rachel's insistence, I helped myself to another bowl of stew from the crockpot, then sat down on one of the cushioned benches at the stern. As I ate, George put our destination into the cockpit monitor and switched on the autopilot.

"Should make Key West by nine a.m.," he said. "You wanna get some sleep?"

I looked out over the dark horizon. Drago and his trawler were still somewhere out there. I felt very protective of George and his wife. After all, the crossing wouldn't have been nearly as dangerous had it not been for Kyle and me.

"I think I'll stay up a while longer," I replied. "I saw your coffeemaker in the galley. You mind if I brew a pot?"

"Stay put and eat," Rachel said from inside. "I'll bring it out to you. How do you like it?"

I told her with cream and sugar, then thanked her and took a few more bites of stew. It really was some of the best I'd ever had, with tender marinated beef, soft carrots, potatoes, and onions all covered in delicious gooey flavor. When I finished, Rachel stepped out holding a thermos and mug. Exchanging them for my bowl and spoon, she headed back into the salon, then forward into the galley.

"Amazing woman you've got there," I said.

George smiled, then sat down a few feet away from me.

"Yes, she is," he said. "Why she settled for me remains one of the greatest mysteries of life."

I filled a mug with coffee, then took a sip and offered the thermos to George, which he quickly declined. Rachel came back out and we sat for a few hours, them talking about where they'd been and me talking a little about my life since moving to the Keys. This was a practice run, they told me. They'd been sailing around the Caribbean and down along the eastern coast of South America for almost a year, preparing for a voyage around the world that they expected to last three years.

"We want to take our time," Rachel said. "To see and to feel as much of the world as we can. Especially the quiet places where few people go."

When midnight rolled around, they both rose, stretched, and headed inside.

"You sure you don't want to sleep?" George said. "The guest cabin is really nice, and the autopilot will alert us if anything comes up. This boat's been piloting itself more than we have this past year."

I thanked them for their offer but told them I'd rather stay out a little longer. I had no doubt that the guest cabin was nice, but I didn't want to risk anything happening. George told me there was plenty of liquor in the galley if I wanted, then they headed inside and shut the sliding glass door. That left just me, Atticus, and Wally. The dogs lay on either side of me as we cruised over the small rollers of the straits.

Fifteen minutes after they went inside, I saw an echo on the radar about six miles behind us. Soon after that, I saw the Baia flying through the water at her cruising speed of forty knots. We'd decided that he would wait a while before leaving Cay Sal, just so our two boats could stay as close as possible in case something happened. Kyle stood at the helm and waved towards me as he flew by. I waved back, then nestled back into the cushions.

I grabbed my sat phone and made a quick call to one of my old friends, Wade Bishop. Wade worked for Mobile Diving and Salvage Unit Two, an expeditionary mobile unit that was homeported in Little Creek, Virginia. They were widely regarded as the experts of underwater salvage. The guys over at MDSU 2 had been vital in many past high-profile salvage operations including TWA 800, the ironclad USS *Monitor*, and the space shuttles *Challenger* and *Columbia*. More recently, they'd played a key role in the preservation and identification of U-3546, and they'd also helped recover and dispose of the biological weapon lodged in the seafloor beside it.

We talked for a few minutes, catching up a bit, then I told him that I knew where the lost Air Force C-21A wreck was located. He paused for a moment, then asked me how in the hell I'd managed to find it. I told him it was a long story, then sent over the coordinates.

"You think you could convince them to bring the *Grasp* to the Bahamas and take a look?" I asked.

The USNS *Grasp* was MDSU 2's 255-foot salvage and rescue ship.

"We're off Wilmington right now," Wade said.

"I think I could convince Sprague to head down that way, especially if I mention your name. That guy holds you in high regard." I was surprised, since I'd only interacted with Commander Sprague a handful of times. "I'll keep you posted, Logan. Thanks for the tip. You want us to give someone else the credit for this find like the last time?"

I thought for a second. "Best to abstain from any credit at this time. Or you guys could just take it, I don't really care. But do me a favor and let me know if you guys find the flight recorder."

Flight recorders are oftentimes mistakenly referred to as "black boxes." In reality, the devices are usually painted bright orange to make them easier to spot following a crash. I doubted that such a classified flight would have even turned it on, especially since Kyle said they tried to kill him, but it was still worth a shot.

I thanked him for his help, ended the call, and returned to my quiet evening on the deck. Every half hour or so, I'd stand up, stretch, and do a full survey of the horizon using my night vision monocular. It was a nice night out on the water, and I enjoyed the solitude and the quiet of cruising under sail. The moon reflected down over the water, and even with the breeze at my side, I was comfortable in my shorts and long-sleeved tee shirt.

I dozed off a few times, but never for longer than a couple of minutes. The coffee did its job for the most part. When I'd get really tired, I'd climb up onto the bow and do squats, planks, and full-range sit-ups with the surf spraying against my body. I wanted to do push-ups as well but figured it wouldn't be the best idea considering the state of my left shoulder.

At 0230, the cockpit radio crackled to life.

Atticus and Wally stirred at the sound and I rose to my feet.

"*Dodging Bullets* to *Seas the Day*," Kyle said between the static.

Stepping over to the helm, I grabbed the VHF and held down the talk button.

"*Seas the Day*, go ahead," I said.

"I've got a beat on Drago. Saw an echo half an hour ago and I have visual. He's cruising northeast at twenty knots."

I snatched a notepad and pencil from the dash.

"What are your coordinates?"

He gave me a combination of latitudes and longitudes, then said that the trawler was nine miles southeast of his position.

"Thanks," I said. "I'll get right back with you."

Setting the radio in its holder, I moved aft and grabbed my satellite phone out of my Camelbak. Clicking through the contacts, I came across Wilson's name and pressed call. After apologizing to the deputy director for waking him up, I told him that I had a positive location on Drago Kozlov.

"Don't worry about it," he said, his tone shifting drastically. "Just give me a second."

A moment later, I gave him the coordinates along with the other info Kyle had given me.

"Can you track the trawler's position and give me updates? Especially if he decides to turn around and head south?" I asked. "I'm on my way to Key West now, and I'll be ready to go after him then."

"Already having my people run the info into the system. We should have confirmation of the target any second." After a short pause, he added, "Alright, we have it. I'm gonna call the Coast Guard and let them know what's going on."

"No!" I said, more loudly than I meant to. "I mean, I wanna take this guy down myself."

Wilson sighed. "They're big boys, Logan. They can take care of themselves."

"I know that, but I've already encountered him. I have an advantage."

There was a moment's silence as he thought it over. The truth was, though I'd worked with Coast Guard many times before and knew that they were experts at their jobs, I was a little concerned. Just the previous summer, I'd been surrounded by a Cuban gang on Loggerhead Key while trying to protect an innocent family. The last day on the island, a Coast Guard helicopter had flown in to pick us up, only to be blown to bits before it could land. The look on their faces as I swam aboard to try and save them still burned in my memory.

"Alright, fine," Wilson said. "But if he gets away, I'm blaming you."

"Fair enough."

"We'll be in touch."

The line went dead, and I placed the sat phone beside me. Grabbing the radio, I hailed Kyle and told him that the trawler's position was being tracked. He acknowledged, then told me that he'd see me at the marina. After placing the radio back down, I grabbed a blanket and sprawled out on the cushion beside Atticus and Wally. If Drago was being tracked, I was going to try and get at least a few hours of much-needed sleep.

TWENTY

My eyes opened as a strong gust of fresh sea air blew across my face. I rubbed around my eyes for a few seconds, then looked out over the water. The sky was still dark, but judging by the time, the sun would be making its grand entrance any minute. My hand gravitated to my sat phone, which indicated that I'd received a message from Wilson.

"Trawler in channel in north Key Largo," it said. "Will keep you posted."

I set the phone back on the cushion, rose to my feet, and looked out in all directions. I'd only managed to get four hours of sleep, but it had been restful and deep nonetheless. I'd always liked sleeping on the water, to the peaceful rocking of a seagoing vessel. I stepped up onto the bow beside the trampoline and looked out to the west. The Lower and Middle Keys were specks on the horizon, and I expected that given the wind speed, we'd reach Key West in a few hours.

I moved back down to the cockpit and slowly opened the sliding glass door. As quietly as I could, I tiptoed into the galley and started up another pot of coffee. I had no doubt that I was in for another long day, what with Drago hanging out on my turf. I couldn't think of any reason as to why he would be there.

Why would he not cruise back to Cuba? I thought as the boiling water dripped down over the coffee grounds.

Whatever he was doing there, I resolved to find out as soon as possible.

Once the coffee was brewed, I refilled the thermos and stepped back outside. Atticus and Wally opened their eyes groggily, but seeing there was nothing exciting going on, they went right back to sleep.

I sipped the coffee while facing aft and watching one of the most spectacular sunrises I'd ever seen in my life. A jaw-dropping display of vibrant colors, streaks of light, and sparkling reflections across the water. I had nothing to distract me except Mother Nature as we sailed closer and closer to Key West, so I let my mind wander to Kyle, Drago, Carson, and how I was going to tell Ange what I'd been up to the past few days.

An hour later, George and Rachel came out and started on breakfast. Rachel made waffles that were so good they didn't need syrup and topped them with slices of banana and mango. After eating, George switched off the autopilot and brought us manually across what little remained of the straits.

At just after 0900, we cruised around Fort

Zachary Taylor at the southwest tip of the island, then past Mallory Square and a Carnival cruise ship tied off at the dock. With the flick of a few switches, George furled the mainsail, started up the cat's twin fifty-five-hp engines, and motored us into Conch Harbor Marina. He eased the starboard hull against one of the day moorage slips, and I grabbed my bag and hopped off. Atticus said goodbye to his new friend, then jumped onto the dock beside me. Turning around, I prepared for George to throw me the ropes so I could tie off *Seas the Day*. Instead, he kept the engines running as they both moved against the starboard gunwale.

"You're not stopping?" I asked.

"We're pretty set on supplies," George replied. "And we're both eager to reach Saint Pete. Maybe we'll see you on the way back."

I nodded. "It was good to see you again, George. And it was nice meeting you, Rachel."

She reached over the gunwale for a quick hug.

"Hopefully it's not a year before we see you again," George said.

I grinned. "I'd fly halfway around the world for more of that cooking."

"I'm spoiled," George said as he moved back towards the helm.

"It was nice meeting you too," Rachel said.

I waved as George turned *Seas the Day* around and motored back out of the harbor. After a short walk towards shore, then across and down an adjoining dock, I spotted the Baia tied off at slip twenty-four. After talking with Kyle for a few minutes, I grabbed a quick shower, changed, then called Wilson for an update. He informed me that the trawler had stopped over for a few hours at an island in the Upper Keys near north Key Largo. Then, at around 0300, the trawler left, heading south. Currently, he said that it was moored just off the coast of Knockemdown Key, on the Florida Bay side. He sent me a satellite image verifying their location and said that the trawler hadn't moved for a few hours.

He's making his way to Key West, I thought.

He was going to try and remedy his failure in Cay Sal. I assumed that he would opt for a subtler approach the second time around. A poisoned drink. A sharp knife to the neck while we slept. A quick round from a silenced handgun. Then again, he would be pissed off after our first engagement, and I thought it might affect his reasoning, even with his experienced track record. Regardless, we weren't about to wait around for him to make a move.

"What island did it stop at?"

There was a slight pause, and I heard Wilson clicking a few keys on his keyboard.

"Looks like it's a privately owned island," he replied. "Richmond Key. Ever heard of it?"

My eyes widened slightly at the mention of the name. I didn't know much about Richmond Key, but I did know that it was located in Card Sound between North Key Largo and the southern mainland of Florida. I also knew that it was privately owned by none other than Carson Richmond. I wasn't surprised. If deep down I hadn't believed Kyle, I would probably have never traveled with him to Cay Sal to look for the plane. But hearing Wilson's words solidified Kyle's story. Carson Richmond was behind everything. She wanted us dead, and she was a woman accustomed to having things her way.

After a few more quick exchanges, we ended the call. He informed me that he'd already notified the

Coast Guard and that they too were tracking the trawler but had orders to keep their distance and not to engage unless it was absolutely necessary.

Kyle was sitting on the outside dinette across from me and had been listening in on our conversation. He grabbed my spare Sig from his waistband and inspected the chamber.

"You ready for round two?" he said, his lips forming a confident grin.

I nodded, my face resolute. Though it would have been easier to sneak up on the trawler at night, I didn't want to give Drago that much time. It was clear that Kyle didn't want that either. I'd been thinking of a plan since Wilson had told me where the trawler was hiding out, and an idea suddenly came to me.

I moved down into the salon. Atticus was standing over his empty water bowl, so I quickly topped it off along with his food, and his head dropped into each dish, his tail wagging happily. I stepped into the main cabin, rummaged in the closet, and pulled out a faded Miami Marlins ballcap that had been left there by an old girlfriend, along with one of those functional wraparound hats you always see park rangers wearing. Then I grabbed a long-sleeved tee for Kyle, and two thin windbreakers.

I stepped back up into the cockpit and set the clothes beside Kyle.

"This being your first time in the Keys," I said, "I think it's high time I showed you a few of the sights. How are you on a kayak?"

I made a quick phone call to a boat rental shop, then we prepped our gear. I walked Atticus over to Gus at the marina office and he agreed to watch over him for the afternoon. When I made it back to the Baia, I climbed aboard and finished getting my gear ready.

"Taking off again, huh?" a voice I recognized as Jack's said from the dock.

Turning around, I saw him standing just a few feet from the Baia's stern. He was wearing board shorts and a cutoff tee shirt and had the keys to his Wrangler in his left hand. I stepped down past the transom, then over to the dock beside him.

"You alright?" he said. "Your face looks a little more purple than it was before you left."

I guess the scar from being slugged across the face by the Russian Devil was a little obvious.

"Fine," I said.

After a short moment of silence, he said, "So, you're still not gonna tell me what's going on?"

"We ran into trouble in Cay Sal."

Jack shook his head. "Wish I had a quarter for every time I heard that."

"No, not the usual trouble." I moved in closer and lowered my voice. Jack was one of my best and oldest friends; I owed him an explanation. "We ran into a small group of trained killers who had us as their marks."

"Do you know why they were after you?"

I nodded. "Look, I wanted to tell you before. It's just very complicated. But basically, they were after Kyle. Let's just say that years ago, he managed to piss off people on both sides of the law."

"Did you kill them? The guys that were after you."

"At least two escaped. They're just north of Knockemdown Key, and we're going after them in a few hours."

He paused a moment and glanced down at his keys. It looked like he had something he wanted to tell me but was debating whether or not to.

"You told Ange any of this?" he finally said.

I sighed. "I don't want her to worry. And I don't want you guys involved."

"Well, that's too damn bad," he fired back. "I'm your best friend, bro. Besides, it's not like this is the first time we've been in dangerous situations together."

I smiled, then relented and gave him a quick rundown of the plan.

"Alright," he said with a grin. "Keep me updated. I'll be close by on the *Calypso* and I'll have my Glock ready."

I patted him on the shoulder and thanked him, then he continued down the dock towards the parking lot.

TWENTY-ONE

At 1300, I parked my black Tacoma 4x4 at the northern tip of Summerland Key, where Niles Road dead-ends right at the water. There's a small boat launch there, and there was a guy standing beside an old red pickup with a trailer hauling a handful of kayaks hitched to it. The side of the truck had the words Mike's Coastal Adventures in white faded letters across the passenger-side door. The guy standing beside the trailer looked like he was in his late forties, with tanned skin, a decent-sized gut, and curly brown hair.

"You Logan?" he said when I stepped out of the Tacoma.

His accent made me assume that he was originally from up north, way up north.

He was Mike, the guy I'd spoken with on the phone, and he already had our kayaks unloaded and on the beach with their front ends touching the clear water. We read over a few papers and signed the waivers, then I paid a deposit for each boat that I wasn't confident I'd be getting back. At the line asking how long we'd be out, I checked four hours.

He glanced over at the extended bed of my Tacoma. "You want me to meet you guys back here when you're done?"

I shook my head. "We'll take them back."

He nodded. "Alright. The shop's open till seven. If you're later than that, we'll have to charge you for a full day."

"No problem," I said.

Once he started up his diesel engine and cruised south back toward the center of the island, we donned our disguises, then grabbed the rest of the gear from the Tacoma. We each had a long-sleeved shirt with a windbreaker over it. We each wore a hat, me sporting the Miami Marlins ballcap and Kyle the round-rimmed hiker hat. We both put our dark sunglasses on and dabbed a generous amount of sunscreen onto our faces. Along with the binos around my neck and a digital camera around Kyle's, we looked like a couple of tourists who dressed by the book and did everything possible to prevent the harsh tropical sun from doing damage to their skin. I even put a glob of sunscreen on my nose.

Once we were dressed the part, we each strapped on a lifejacket, then grabbed paddles and slid our kayaks forward a few more feet. Climbing inside, we adjusted our weapons so that they were readily accessible but out of sight. We each had a Sig with an extra mag, and I had my M4 to boot and Kyle had my MP5N. I'd also grabbed an M67 frag grenade that I'd swiped off a Black Venom cartel member on

Lignumvitae Key and kept stowed away in my safe ever since, just in case. I handed it over to Kyle, and he stashed it in his lap. Holding our paddles in front of us, we shifted our bodies forward and back, sliding the plastic hulls over the old gravel-covered slab of rock and into the water.

The sun was beating down on us, but a slight breeze over the water made our attire bearable. We moved quickly, cutting through the water, weaving our way around various islands then paddling between Little Knockemdown Key and Toptree Hammock Key. This part of the Lower Keys is a maze of scattered islands both big and small, interwoven with waterways, narrow channels, and man-made cuts. A pretty good place to hide out and wait for a good moment to strike. We were only about ten miles southwest of Blackett Key, the small island, owned by movie star Tom Steel, that had been taken over by the drug-running Campos brothers.

We hugged our way north along the eastern shore of Knockemdown Key, keeping to a smooth and strong rhythm. Had I been there for any other reason, I would have enjoyed the peaceful scene around me. The gulls flying and landing on nearby shores, the water gently lapping against the hulls, and the mangrove-riddled plots of land surrounding me. But we had business to attend to, and my mind was focused on playing over scenarios in my head, as I always did before a coming engagement.

Forty-five minutes after pushing off at the tip of Summerland, we slowly rounded the northern edge of Knockemdown and caught our first glimpse of the trawler. It was only about a quarter of a mile away and was anchored down in a small channel, surrounded by patches of mangroves. I grabbed my binos from around my neck and took a look. The bow was facing us, into a strong current, so I couldn't see much. But I could see the dark outline of bodies inside, and there was a guy with his back up against the windscreen, facing forward as he puffed on a cigarette.

We paddled across a narrow cut and used the cover of overgrown mangroves to move up close to the trawler without them spotting us. Grabbing my sat phone, I made quick calls to Jack and Wilson, letting them know we were about to move in. Jack told me that he was watching the trawler from the edge of Budd Key. He had a line of poles in their holders at the stern for an alibi and said he could reach the boat in just a few minutes once shit hit the fan. Wilson informed me that the Coast Guard was also nearby and ready to spring into action at the sound of gunshots.

Kyle and I glanced at each other.

"Alright," I said. "Time to take these assholes down."

We both loosened our lifejackets and unclipped all but one of the buckles so we could remove them easily. I moved my Sig into my lap, then grabbed my paddle and rounded the mangroves, bringing the trawler into view. It was only a few hundred feet away, and we paddled towards it as nonchalantly as possible. We weren't exactly professional actors, but we'd both worked undercover before and looked convincing enough. Perception is crucial if you want to take your enemy by surprise. To anyone aboard the trawler, we looked like nothing more than a pair of wandering tourists out for a day of bird-watching.

We paddled close enough to make out the features of the guy on the bow. He looked young, with tanned skin and a lean, athletic body. I didn't recognize him from our previous encounter with Drago. As soon as he noticed us, he pushed his back off from the windscreen and stepped towards the bow. I grabbed my binos from around my neck and looked innocently off towards a nearby flock of cormorants.

He stood at the bow a moment as if he were wondering what to do. I lowered my binos, glanced his way as if I'd just realized he was there, and was the first to speak.

"Hello there," I said in a friendly tone. "Would you happen to know if those are double-crested cormorants or greats? I checked my bird-watching manual, but I still can't tell."

The young man looked at me in bewilderment. He glanced over at the birds for only a second and shook his head.

"I don't know shit about birds," he said. "Now, piss off!"

His accent wasn't Russian. It sounded American, though he was clearly of Hispanic descent. Probably from Miami. I lifted my paddle slowly out of the water but continued to drift closer and closer to the trawler.

"I'm sorry," I said, in a passive and nonthreatening tone. "This is my first time in the Keys and I'm just very excited. I'm from—"

"I don't care where you're from," he said, getting irritated. "Now get the fuck out of here. Go look at birds somewhere else."

Kyle's kayak moved ahead of mine about a boat length. The front of his kayak was just about to make contact with the trawler. The young guy flicked his cigarette and hovered his hand over his waistband. I couldn't see what was there beneath his shirt, but I didn't have to.

"Hey, leave now!" he said, raising his voice. "I'm not gonna say it again."

I raised my hands in the air. "I'm sorry, I'm very sorry," I said frantically. "We're leaving. Come on, Curtis, let's leave these people be."

I could see a few guys moving about inside the trawler. They were looking and pointing towards us.

Here we go, I thought.

The exact moment the front of Kyle's kayak made contact with the metal hull, I reached my right hand under the plastic coaming and into my lap. Without taking my eyes off the guy, my fingers gripped the cool metal of my Sig like they had thousands of times before. With no wasted movement, my hand sprang into action, raising my Sig up out of the cockpit, and I quickly lined the sights up on the guy's chest. All he had time to do was drop his jaw in surprise as I pulled the trigger, sending a round into his abdomen and another into his upper chest. The sounds of the powder exploding and the subsequent sonic booms as the bullets broke the sound barrier echoed across the water. The guy let out a muffled grunt as his body fell backward against a spray of his own blood on the windscreen behind him. Then he fell forward, and gravity slammed his lifeless face into the metal deck.

In my peripheral vision, I could see Kyle climbing up out of his kayak and grabbing the port bow handrail. Keeping my gaze drawn towards the pilothouse, I raised my Sig towards the windscreen and fired off four rounds that shattered the glass and caused the guys inside to drop down for cover.

Just as we'd planned, Kyle pulled his upper body

up onto the handrail far enough for him to plant his left knee onto the deck. Rearing back his right arm, he hurled the frag grenade as hard as he could into the partly shattered windscreen. The heavy grenade broke through the remaining glass with ease, and I could hear it thump against the deck inside the pilothouse. Kyle leaned over the edge so that the hull could provide cover as the grenade exploded, sending a swarm of metal fragments shooting through the air in all directions at lethal speeds.

What remained of the windscreen shattered from the explosion, and I could hear the loud screeching of metal rattling against metal. A few men yelled out from inside as the mayhem went quiet. With the guy on the bow down and the guys inside either taking cover, dead, or sprawling on the deck in pain, it was time to move in. Kyle had already ripped the lifejacket from his body and snatched the Sig from under his windbreaker. He pulled himself up and over the railing, planted his feet, and took an athletic stance on the bow with his Sig raised.

It only took a few seconds for the current to push my kayak into the hull. I quickly switched my half-empty mag for a full one, pulled off my lifejacket, and rose to my feet. The railing at the bow was about seven feet above the surface of the water. I balanced myself, then grabbed hold of the handrail high over my head and pulled my body up, ignoring the pain in my shoulder as I maneuvered over the edge and landed softly on the deck beside Kyle.

Side by side and with our weapons raised, we moved in. The scene was still and perfectly quiet aside from the occasional groans of the unfortunate thug who hadn't managed to escape the blasting shards of metal. We stepped over the guy who lay flat in a pool of his own blood and peeked in through the shattered glass. The pilothouse was empty aside from two dead guys on the deck. Their bodies were mangled, but it was clear that neither of them was Drago. Looking around, I saw a streak of blood on the deck that went around the corner and down a set of stairs.

I motioned to Kyle, then moved down the port side, keeping my eyes drawn into the pilothouse all the way until I reached the stern of the trawler. We turned and stepped towards a wooden door, and I grabbed the brass handle as Kyle hovered behind to cover me. After a quiet count of three, I ripped it open and we both stormed inside like a SWAT team. The smell of warm, coppery blood filled my nostrils as we glanced around the pilothouse, which looked like a tornado had blown through it. The electronics near the helm had shattered screens and sparking wires. The cushioned seats were full of pieces of shrapnel and had cotton padding exposed. We listened and heard nothing.

For a moment, I thought about whether the whole thing was a trap, an intricate plan to lure us in, then blow us sky-high once we'd boarded the trawler. I felt a sudden urge to disembark, to hop back onto my kayak before it drifted too far away and wait for backup to arrive. By the look in Kyle's eyes, I could tell that he was thinking the same thing.

We turned back towards the door, but before we'd taken a single step, we heard shuffling feet and guys talking quietly to each other down below. A loud hissing sound suddenly ruptured the stillness, and my eyes grew wide as thick white gas burst forth from various corners of the room. The faint smell of the gas had just managed to reach my nose when my legs instinctively bolted the rest of my body for the door. But the small pilothouse quickly turned into a thick cloud. I held my breath, not wanting to let the teargas into my lungs as Kyle and I bolted out the door. My eyes quickly welled up and my nostrils burned. It was a painful, miserable, and all-too-familiar sensation. I'd first been teargassed years ago during Navy Basic Training and had been exposed to the stuff again a few times during SEAL training. It wasn't something I ever wanted to experience again, and I felt a surge of relief as we sprang out into the fresh sea air.

My eyes watery, I turned and saw two dark and blurry figures appear out of the white veil of gas. Both were tall guys, and they each wore black gas masks as they stepped out. The guy on the left held a blacked-out pump-action KS-23 Russian shotgun, the guy on the right a classic TEC-9 complete with extended mag.

Grabbing hold of the shotgun, I forced it up away from me by the barrel with my left hand, then aimed my Sig to fill his body with lead. But as I pulled the trigger, he jerked his body sideways, causing my rounds to soar past his body and pound against the metal door frame behind him. With the skill of a trained martial artist, he shifted his weight, then brought his left leg up and slammed the heel of his boot into my right hand, causing my Sig to break free of my grasp and rattle up against the transom.

Still gripping tightly to the barrel of his shotgun, I bent down and threw him over the top of me, slamming his back into the hard metal at our feet. We rolled a few times, each struggling for the upper hand, then crashed into the corner where the port gunwale met the transom. I felt like I was experiencing déjà vu. I'd just fought this guy in this exact same place the previous night. This time, I resolved, he wouldn't get away.

In the corner of my eye, I saw Kyle fighting the other guy. I knew Kyle had landed one round into his enemy's body, but it was clear that he was a highly trained killer, just like Drago. Men who knew what it was to feel extreme pain, push through it, and take life without batting an eye.

We struggled back and forth, fighting for control over the shotgun between us while each landing a few punches. The gas bled out from the pilothouse, and though much of it was carried away with the ocean breeze, I felt the burn within my lungs as I gagged a few times.

"You're a bloody fool for intervening!" Drago barked from behind his mask. "I always kill my target!" The gas seeped its way into my breaths, making it difficult for me to speak.

"Not… this… time… dirtbag!" I said.

Using all of my strength, I held the shotgun in place with my left hand, and reached with my right for my dive knife sheathed to the back of my waistband. Pulling the titanium blade free, I stabbed it towards Drago's masked face. He snapped sideways and the blade cut through the side of the mask, cutting a large hole that allowed the gas to crawl its way inside.

As I brought my knife back for another blow, he coughed, then slammed my hand into the deck. With my body pinned against the gunwale, he reached behind his leather jacket and pulled out his own knife. Its sharp, narrow blade glistened in the afternoon sun. With a loud grunt, he jabbed it towards my chest. I let go of the shotgun, let it fall lifelessly to the deck beside us, then jammed my hands around his wrists. The long blade stopped just a few inches from my heart. Drago shifted his body, put all of his weight into the hilt, and slowly the blade came closer.

My mind struggled to think of a way out as my lungs burned and my eyes watered so bad I could barely see. Drago's eyes were wild as he stared back at me. They seemed to pop out of his face like the veins in his forehead. Again I felt a surge of recognition burst forth from within me. My eyes grew wide as, at that moment, I remembered where I'd seen him before.

He shot me a sinister smile as he continued to force the blade towards me with all of his strength.

"Now that you are going to die, there's something I'd like you to know," he said. "You recognize me, don't you? We've seen each other before." He laughed sadistically and added, "You spotted me through your scope in Colombia years ago." Anger surged forth from deep within me. I could still see him through my scope, standing there over a village of massacred innocent people. "Now, you will die knowing that it was me and Carson's men who killed those people in the village. That she was the one who ordered the trap."

I breathed heavily. I fought with every ounce of my strength to keep him off me. Just as the blade was about to meet my flesh, a loud boom resonated across the air, and Drago's face exploded. Blood sprayed out the back of his head, along with a handful of brain and half of his skull. His body lurched back violently, then hit the deck hard and went motionless.

As a seemingly never-ending supply of blood flowed out and puddled on the deck beside me, I jumped to my feet just in time to see Kyle finish his man. They too were caught in a rolling scuffle, and Kyle ended the fight by reaching out, grabbing hold of the guy's TEC-9, and turning his torso into a cheese grater. Pushing the dead guy off him, he labored to his feet as well and we moved together towards the bow, into the wind and away from the cloudy nightmare of gas.

Once there, I rubbed my eyes and gagged until the gas was clear from my lungs.

"Fuck that," Kyle said, leaning over as he spat and cleared his sinuses.

It was as good of a reaction as any to being exposed to excessive amounts of teargas. The stuff is just plain nasty. As you try to breathe in air, your lungs instead get suffocated by burning, toxic fumes.

Once I could see relatively well, I looked around, searching for the source of the shot that had taken down Drago. He'd been hit by a high-caliber rifle, no doubt about that. And I knew it must have been someone that was very confident in their aim. After just a few seconds of peering over the bright horizon, I smiled as I saw the *Calypso* cruising quickly straight toward us from the northwest. Angelina Fox, my mercenary warrior woman girlfriend, was standing on the bow, holding her Lapua sniper rifle in her hands.

TWENTY-TWO

By the time the *Calypso* pulled up to the trawler, the teargas had stopped billowing out of the pilothouse. With the cloudy layer of white gone, I could easily see Drago's body twisted up in a pool of blood that was dripping through the holes in the transom and splashing into the water below.

The *Calypso* eased up along the port side. Jack was at the helm, looking over at Kyle and me. Ange had moved down into the cockpit and was staring at me with her hands on her hips.

Hell hath no fury, I thought.

Not keeping her in the loop the past few days was about to come back to bite me.

I smiled towards her. "Talk about cutting it close," I said as playfully as I could.

"I think what you mean to say is thank you," she said.

Her tone was stern, her voice raised. I was pretty sure that she was more angry at the fact that I'd lied to her than anything else.

"Thank you," I said. "And I'm sorry."

She was a sight for sore eyes. She was wearing a black tank top and a pair of athletic shorts that adequately showed off her lean figure, and her blond hair was pulled back in a ponytail. Her skin was even more tanned than usual from her backpacking trip to California.

She stepped against the edge of the stairs that led up to the *Calypso*'s pilothouse. Taking in a deep breath, she let it all out and her shoulders dropped a few inches.

"When are you going to learn that you need me, Dodge?" she said.

For a moment I'd forgotten where we were and what was happening, but that moment ended suddenly when I heard the sound of two Coast Guard patrol boats cruising towards us from the north. I asked Jack to retrieve the kayaks, and he motored a few hundred feet south of the trawler, picked them both up, and brought them back over to us. Without a word, Kyle slipped his sunglasses back on, climbed into his kayak, and grabbed the paddle. I reached into a small zipper pocket in my cargo shorts, grabbed my ring of just three keys, and handed them to Kyle. I didn't know how long clearing up the incident was going to take, but I knew that it wouldn't be timely. Nothing ever is when dealing with the government.

"I'll see you back at the marina," I said.

He nodded, then paddled as quickly as he could, heading south. In less than a minute, he'd disappeared from view around a few small islands covered in mangroves. The two forty-five-foot Coast Guard response boats thundered up and each performed a quick lap around the trawler before idling near the stern. The boats were both new and had deep-V double-chine hulls, giving them better balance and stability than previous models. Most of the boats' surfaces were silver, but they each had a thick orange lip that stretched all the way around and had white letters that said U.S. Coast Guard.

I spotted three guys on each boat. They were wearing full tactical attire, which included black Kevlar vests. Once they could see that the excitement was over, they quickly went about taking care of the scene. Sheriff Wilkes showed up on a police boat just a few minutes after the Coast Guard, and I was glad for it. Though I recognized a few of the Coast Guard guys, I knew that Charles had my back and would make it his priority to handle the situation as efficiently as possible.

The Coast Guardsmen were ordered by higher-ups in the chain of command to bring the trawler to a private dock on Big Torch Key. A handful of CIA agents met us there and quickly took over. Drago was a high-value target, and I was sure that they'd want confirmation of his death, as well as whoever else happened to be on that trawler. The remains of Drago and his buddies were put in body bags and hauled into the back of a light cargo military truck.

The agents handled everything smoothly, wanting to take the bodies and get rid of the trawler as quickly as possible. It felt good to have Scott, Wilson, and Charles all in my corner. Given the dead guys' track records, I was barely even questioned by the CIA agents. In fact, they seemed genuinely happy with the situation, which was strange considering my only other interactions with government agents had painted them to be serious people who showed little or no emotion.

"We've got it all taken care of from here," a bald agent who looked about forty said. "The Agency thanks you for your continued service to the nation."

"Don't mention it," I said.

I thought he was done, but as I turned to head back to the *Calypso*, he spoke again.

"You'll be contacted regarding payment once we've verified the body," he said.

I looked back at him, eyebrows raised.

"Payment?" I said. "What payment?"

The experienced agent gave a slight smile.

"Drago here was on our most wanted list. He had a generous bounty on his head. I'd say you can expect to be contacted and paid within a few weeks."

I smiled at that. I'd worked for the government for eight years. If they told me to expect money in a few weeks, I knew it would really be more like a few months. But seeing as how I hadn't expected anything in return, I was pleasantly surprised.

Killing bad guys and getting paid good money for it? I felt like I was working as a mercenary all over again.

I didn't bother asking how much the bounty was. I simply thanked him, then waved and walked down the private dock towards the end where the *Calypso* was tied off. Jack was sitting in the shade up in the cockpit. He glanced over at me through big dark sunglasses and waved at me. His curly hair was a mess as usual, and he looked as though he was just going about a normal beach bum day. Not like someone who'd just aided in the killing of a criminal on the most wanted list.

"Hey, bro," he said. "Everything good with the

feds?"

I nodded. "Yeah. They've got it from here."

"Good," he said, grinning down at me. "Cuz I've got a cooler full of Paradise Sunsets with our names all over it. Now that those disturbers of the peace are gone, I'd say it's time you kicked back a little."

I smiled back at him. He was right. It had been a long and demanding forty-eight hours, both mentally and physically. But I knew that we weren't exactly in the clear yet. Drago was dead, sure, but there was nothing stopping Carson from sending others. As long as Kyle was breathing and as long as I was by his side, the troubles would continue.

Ange stood up beside Jack and moved barefoot down the staircase, stopping at the first step so that we were the same height. I pushed back a few loose strands of hair from her face, then kissed her forehead. She smiled.

"I'm sorry, Ange," I said, wrapping an arm around her. "You're right, I should have told you about all this. What can I do to make it up to you?"

She thought for a moment.

"Well, for starters you can tell me everything that happened in Cay Sal," she said. Then she looked down at her perfectly toned legs and added, "Then you can give me a massage. Half Dome did a number on my calves."

I grinned, then pressed my lips against hers. After a few seconds in heaven, I said, "Deal."

Ange never ceased to amaze me. I'd had my share of girlfriends in the past, but none of them had made me feel the way that Ange did. There was no drama with her. She wore her heart on her sleeve, but rarely let negative things linger. She was smart and great at understanding me. She knew the only reason I hadn't told her was because I didn't want to put her in danger. Admittedly, she would have flown back to Key West much earlier had she known what I was up to. I cared deeply about her and I knew she felt the same.

But did she love me?

I thought about the ring stowed in the back of my nightstand drawer on the Baia.

Was she looking for marriage and all that a future with me would entail?

I hoped so. With all my heart I hoped so. But analyzing and overthinking scenarios was a facet ingrained in my character. It was a part of me that had kept me alive many times over the years. I couldn't help but think about every possible outcome in a given situation, even the worst-case scenarios.

We climbed up to the pilothouse and plopped down on the port side, across from Jack. The cooler was resting at our feet, and before we'd said a word to my old friend, he had the lid open and was cracking open two cold ones. His bottle was in the cup holder beside him, the outer glass covered in a layer of condensation. He and Ange had also cut up some fresh mango and pineapple, which they offered me in a bowl.

"And this is some of the last lobster of the season," Jack said, handing me a plate of grilled lobster along with a small dish of melted butter, garlic, and salt.

I had my fill as Jack brought us away from the private dock, then motored us into Niles Channel, heading south. Within a few minutes, we cruised under US-1 between Ramrod Key and Summerland Key, then entered the Atlantic. He had the forty-five-foot Sea Ray at her cruising speed of just over twenty knots as he banked us on a southwest heading towards Key West. With the nice breeze coming off the water, Jack decided to furl up the canvas, letting the warm sun bake our bodies as we finished off the food and downed my favorite brew.

This is just what I needed, I thought as I lay against the cushion. *Sun beating down on my face, fresh ocean air, delicious food, and great company.*

I wrapped an arm around Ange, then leaned back and closed my eyes, relishing the moment.

"So," Ange said, nudging my shoulder. "You were about to tell us what you've been up to these past few days, and who your friend is."

TWENTY-THREE

I gave Jack and Ange a brief synopsis of what had happened, starting from when Kyle had shown up out of nowhere, back from the dead, and ending when George had helped us in Cay Sal. They both asked question after question, trying to figure out as much of the backstory as they could. I decided to tell them everything, and for the first time since I'd been on a witness stand in a military courtroom ten years earlier, I talked about Kyle and what had happened in Colombia.

"Jeez, bro," Jack said. "I thought I recognized him from someplace. He was all over the news."

Ange turned to me with raised eyebrows as I grabbed my beer and took a few swigs.

"So, why did you trust him?" Ange asked. "I mean, since you didn't turn him in. He's a fugitive and deemed an enemy of the state, right?"

I took in a deep breath and let it out. It was a good question. One I'd wrestled with myself when he'd first shown up.

"I didn't really at first," I said. "But we'd been great friends in the SEALs, and I wanted to get to the bottom of it. But my opinion soon changed and now I know he's telling the truth."

"How?" Ange said. "How did your opinion change so quickly and so drastically?"

I told them about the Russian Devil and what he'd told me just before he'd tried to skewer me with his blade. I also told them how I'd seen him before, during the mission in Colombia years earlier. They listened intently as I spoke. I also explained to them both that if the accusations against Kyle had been true, they would have simply notified the government of his position rather than send hitmen to kill him and his family. It proved that their hands were dirty and that they were trying to cover something up by getting rid of Kyle for good. He was the one who'd managed to figure out what had really been going on in Colombia. It was still difficult for me to wrap my head around it; that so many high-ups in both the military and political arena would be tied into such a corrupt conspiracy. I vowed to help Kyle get to the bottom of it all, no matter how deep the rabbit hole went.

I finished the rest of my story, and they both went silent for a few minutes.

"What are you going to do now?" Ange asked.

It was one of those questions that she already knew the answer to but wanted to hear me say it out loud. She knew me well.

"This isn't the end of it," I said. "Drago, all of those hired guns. Carson won't stop going after him until he's dead. We need to take her down somehow. We need to prove what she was up to and what she's probably been up to elsewhere for years."

Ange sneered and killed the rest of her beer.

"Carson Richmond?" she said, though again she already knew the answer.

Ange knew Carson only a little better than me. She'd met her a few times, and Carson had offered to hire her for a major job the last time they had spoken a few years earlier. Ange detested the woman, both professionally and personally, and had turned her down by telling the rich Southern belle to shove her proposition where the sun didn't shine.

"Are you going to kill her?" Ange asked, her face stern and resolute.

I shook my head. "No. But we're gonna find a way to bring her down."

Kyle and I had discussed it briefly, and the truth was, neither of us wanted Carson dead. That would be letting her off too easy. She was a person who lived and breathed for her reputation. Public relations was her game, so that was what we'd attack. Ideally, we'd tarnish her name and put her behind bars for a very long time. Poetic justice. And if she still managed to come after us once her life as she knew it was ruined, then we'd look into other options.

"How do you plan to do that, bro?" Jack asked.

I shrugged. "Not sure yet. We've been preoccupied with Drago, but now that he's gone, we can go to work. She travels around a lot. We can try and track her down or hack into one of her computers. It's going to be difficult no matter how we go about it. She's rich, smart, and she's been doing this for a very long time."

At around 1700, Jack brought the *Calypso* into

slip forty-seven at the Conch Harbor Marina. I hopped onto the dock, tied her off and connected the shore power cable, then the three of us walked down the dock to where the Baia was moored. I spotted my Tacoma in the lot, and as we walked towards my boat, I saw Kyle sitting beside the dinette. Upon seeing us approach, he slid out onto the deck and turned to head down into the salon.

"It's okay, Kyle," I said. "You can trust them."

He turned slowly and shot me a skeptical look. Even though Jack and Ange had just saved us, he was still in survival mode and didn't seem to want to interact with anyone.

Ange held out her hand to Kyle.

"It's good to meet you," she said. He sauntered over, and they shook hands briefly. "I'm gonna help you boys take down Carson, whether you want me to or not."

I went and got Atticus from Gus at the marina office, then we loaded up my Tacoma with the kayaks and hauled them off to Mike's Coastal Adventures on Lower Sugarloaf Key. When we got back to the Baia, the four of us migrated down into the salon, and I brought out my laptop. It was time for us to take a crash course on Carson Richmond. We performed various searches, called a few contacts, and shot off a few emails. Gradually, we formulated the basic structure of a plan, though we hadn't decided on a location yet. It was clear that she spent most of her time split between Atlantic City and Miami. She owned casinos and fancy hotels in both cities, along with a fashion magazine and makeup line. It was difficult to think that the same woman who discussed her nails in flashy articles also owned a large stake in one of the largest private militaries in the world.

After a few hours of work, my phone vibrated to life in my pocket. Sliding it out, I saw that Scott was calling, pressed the answer button, and held the speaker up to my ear.

"Hey, thanks for calling back," I said. I could hear him breathing softly on the other end. "Is this an okay time? I have a few questions you might be able to help me with."

"Can you step outside for a moment?" he said, his voice calm but stern. "I'd rather have this conversation face-to-face."

I glanced towards the stairs, then slid off the cushion and rose to my feet.

"I'll be right back," I said, ending the call and dropping my phone back into my pocket. When I reached the cockpit, I saw Scott standing on the dock beside the Baia's stern. Scott was just an inch or so shorter than my six-foot-two. He had a strong jawline, short dark hair, and an athletic build despite the number of hours he'd spent behind a desk. Instead of his usual casual attire of jeans and a nice long-sleeved shirt, he was wearing his work clothes: a black suit with a red tie and an American flag pin on the left lapel.

I hopped onto the dock beside him and patted him on the back.

"Hey, Scotty," I said. "What brings you down here?"

Though he'd visited the Keys a few times since I'd moved there, he spent most of his time in D.C. and Orlando.

He motioned toward the parking lot.

"We need to talk, Logan," he said.

We walked side by side down the dock, up the perforated metal walkway, and into the parking lot.

There was a blacked-out SUV parked in one of the visitor spaces, and we hopped inside, me in the passenger seat and Scott in the driver's seat. After we both shut our doors, he took a quick look around. I'd fought alongside Scott for just over two years while in the Navy, and it was clear that something was bothering him.

"What is it, Scott?" I said.

"I should ask you the same thing," he replied, his light brown eyes meeting mine. "I just figured I'd come down here and try to dissuade you from making a very big mistake."

I shook my head. "What do you mean?"

He took in a deep breath and let it out slowly.

"Look, I'm impressed that you managed to take down Drago. It must have been difficult, even for you. But Carson is a different breed. She has connections you couldn't begin to understand." He paused a moment, then looked out the window, running something around in his mind. "What I don't understand is how you managed to encounter Drago in the first place. The guy's a ghost, and he only pops up on the grid when he's sent to kill somebody. I mean, I know you've made your share of enemies since moving down here, but Black Venom is all but finished, and Salazar's gang in Cuba has disbanded and most of those guys now hate his guts."

"He wasn't sent for me," I said, the words jumping out of my mouth before I'd even thought them over. Scott looked over, his eyes asking me for an explanation. "Alright, it's a good thing you're sitting down because this would knock you on your ass. I was trying to ensure you had plausible deniability, but it's time you knew. Kyle Quinn is still alive."

His reaction was just as I'd expected. At first, he didn't seem to believe it was possible. He stayed silent for what felt like ten minutes, his mind racing.

"That can't be true," he said. "He was killed in the plane crash. They found his body."

"No, they didn't," I said. "They found the other bodies, but not Kyle's. He's alive, Scott. He's on my boat right now."

He swallowed hard.

"So, what, now you're on some mission to help him? Do you have any idea what you're really up against here?"

"Yes," I said. "And with or without your help, we're gonna get to the bottom of this."

"What's your plan to do that? Do you have any idea the kind of security Carson has? She practically has a small army protecting her at all times."

"We're working on it," I said.

He nodded unconvincingly.

"Well, your plan better be a good one. As your friend, I'd ask you to reconsider, but since I know you too well for that, I'll say that if there's any way I can help, give me a call."

"How much longer will you be in the Keys?"

"Two days," he said. "I need to meet with a few of the local mayors anyway."

"Thanks, Scott," I said, then reached for the door. "I'll be in touch."

He placed a hand on my shoulder and I turned back to him.

"Look, I fought alongside him too," he said. "But before I risk my career for him again, I need to know, how sure are you that he's telling the truth?"

I looked deep into his eyes.

"I'm certain."

TWENTY-FOUR

I headed back to the Baia, and we worked for a few more hours before Jack rose to his feet and headed to his house, saying that his nephew, Isaac, would be getting home soon. Ange and I decided to head over to Salty Pete's for dinner. We were getting too deep into the situation, and sometimes the best thing to do is step away from a problem for a few hours and let your mind think about other things. Kyle was tired after practically pulling an all-nighter on the Baia during the crossing from Cay Sal, so he said he'd be hitting the sack soon. I told him I'd bring him back some food just in case.

Ange and I sat outside on the second-story balcony of Pete's. It was Friday night, so the place was pretty packed. In fact, most of the tables on the balcony were taken. Then I glanced over at the stage and saw that Pete had hired live music for the night, as he had been doing more and more lately.

We sat at a corner table, the farthest one from the stage, and listened as a local guy with dreadlocks strummed his acoustic guitar and played his own songs. He sang about island living, about beaches, palm trees, hammocks, and crashing waves. I really liked it. He reminded me a little of Jack Johnson. Kinda looked like him too, aside from the dreads.

Ange wore a nice-looking white shirt and jean shorts while I sported my navy cargo shorts and a plain gray tee shirt. She looked great in the glow of the hanging lighting overhead. We enjoyed the music and each other's company as we scarfed down the fresh seafood. She told me all about California while we dipped and ate our coconut shrimp, washing them down with a mojito and a tequila sunrise. For our entrees, we ordered up a few blackened grouper sandwiches and three fish tacos.

I saw Pete walk out through the sliding glass door. He smiled when he saw us, then strolled over to our table.

"There you guys are," Pete said. "You two hiding over here?"

"They were the only seats available," I said. "You run the hottest joint in town."

Pete smiled. "I have you to thank for it." After a few seconds' pause, he turned to me and added, "Jack told me you made a trip to Cay Sal. You run into any refugees?"

I shook my head. "Not one."

"You're lucky, then," he said. "Some of the best fishing in the Caribbean around there, if you don't mind the danger, of course."

Pete turned away from us and faced the stage as the guy went into the chorus of what I'd been told was one of his most popular songs.

"This guy's like Mozart," he said. "Yep, the Keys attract some of the most talented people around. That's for sure." He tilted his head back, then winked at Ange. "And the most beautiful."

I was about to joke and tell the old conch to put some ice on it when the folded-up newspaper sticking out of his back pocket caught my eye. There was only a small portion visible, but I noticed that it was the front-page article of the *Keynoter* he'd been going on about a few days earlier. All I could see was part of a picture of a beautiful beachfront location, along with part of a short bold caption. One word, in particular, caught my full attention and made my eyes grow wide.

"What?" Pete said, craning his neck and looking behind him. "Did I sit in cocktail sauce again? It always spills over on the chairs."

I shook my head slightly, then looked over at Ange.

"Are you okay?" she said with a smile.

I was silent for a few more seconds, my brain going to work, then looked back at Pete.

"Is that the article you were showing me a few days ago?" I said, motioning towards the rolled-up paper in his back pocket.

"That's right," he said, reaching back and snatching it. "Ridley was just doing her job writing it, but the front page of this issue serves only one useful purpose: swattin' skeeters."

"Can I see it?" I said.

He must have thought I was joking at first, but after seeing my expression, he handed it over.

"Yeah, sure," he said as I grabbed it. "But it's really a depressing read. These big-time developers are gonna ruin this paradise." I unrolled it and flattened it on the table, front page up. Pete continued as I read. "Mark my words. If the government doesn't do something, it'll be nothing but sterile buildings from Largo to here. Damn shame. A real damn shame."

Ange tried to block out Pete as she hunched over the table and peered at the article. After reading the caption, her eyes grew wide as well and she looked up at me.

I smiled. "You thinking what I'm thinking?"

It was an article about a brand-new high-end resort that was having its grand opening the following day. The article explained how the resort was located on an island off North Key Largo and that it was owned by Richmond Hotel and Resorts. The resort was also proud to announce that the company's owner, Carson Richmond, would be in attendance. It was like fate had orchestrated things in our favor to place an opportunity right in our laps.

Ange chugged the rest of her tequila sunrise, then wiped her lips.

"Crashing a spoiled rich criminal's party?" she said. "I can't think of a better way to spend a Saturday night."

TWENTY-FIVE

"Does one of you want to fill an old man in here?" Pete said, looking at both of us, confused.

I glanced over at Ange, who shrugged as if to say *don't look at me*. I thought for a second, then cleared my throat.

"This Richmond woman is an old friend of Ange's," I said with a grin. "They go way back."

Pete looked back and forth between us.

"Oh great," he said sarcastically. "Well, maybe you can tell your friend to take her spray-tanned butt back up north where she belongs."

"Alright, easy," I said, raising a hand. "I know it's your swatter, but you mind if I keep this?"

He raised his hands in the air. "Fine. Go right ahead. I'll be just fine if I never read another thing about it."

As we finished up our food, I ordered a few items

to go. When the bag of boxed food arrived, I handed the young waitress, who I hadn't seen before, a fifty and told her to keep the change. She smiled and turned on her heels, and before she was able to take two steps, Mia barged over and stripped the bill from her hands.

"Nice try, Logan," she said with a smile. "But Pete won't have it. And you better not leave cash on the table like the last time."

I smiled. It was like trying to pay for a meal when I used to go out with my dad. No matter how old I was or how much money I was making, it didn't matter. He never let me pay.

I shrugged playfully, not wanting to argue with her. She nodded triumphantly as Ange and I headed in through the big sliding glass door, past rows of glass cases containing various artifacts from around the Keys, and down the open staircase to the first floor. Dreadlocks hadn't finished, and we could hear his voice and guitar chords as we crunched our way towards my Tacoma in the seashell driveway. He was good. Any other night and I'd have stayed until the mike got cold, but it wasn't any other night. We had a lot of work to do the following day.

When we reached the marina, I parked and we headed down the dock to the Baia, food in hand. After stepping aboard, I unlocked the salon door, stepped down, and realized that Kyle was asleep. Atticus had been asleep too. He was lying beside the dinette, and his head and ears rose as I entered.

"There's some for you too, boy," I said, riffling around in the bag of food and pulling out a box for him. It had a few unseasoned hogfish filets inside, his favorite. I opened the lid and, after I gave him permission, he dug in. As I set the rest of the food in the galley, I heard Kyle shuffling in the guest cabin, then the door opened.

"It's really good," I said.

He was wearing black sweatpants and nothing else. I could see his heavily tattooed upper body by the dim light overhead. His eyes were slits.

He looked at the food and nodded. "You have a house, right?" he said.

"Yeah. About five minutes from here."

"You should go," he said. "Don't worry about me."

I smiled. He'd read my mind.

He walked over and opened one of the boxes of food, savoring the smell. I reached behind me and pulled out the folded-up *Keynoter* Pete had given me back at the restaurant. Flattening it on the table beside Kyle, I pointed at the article. After a few seconds of reading and eating, he stopped chewing and looked up at me, his eyes wide.

"We'll be here early tomorrow," I said.

He nodded, and I patted Atticus on the top of his head. He'd already finished his food and looked ready to go back to bed.

"Stay," I said.

I moved aft and up through the salon door. I locked it, then, after switching on the security system, Ange and I headed back down the dock to my Tacoma. Just a few minutes later, we pulled into my driveway off Palmetto Street. My house was two stories, the second being propped up on stilts like many homes near the water in southern Florida. I parked underneath beside my hanging heavy bag and a row of kettlebells. Before I'd even switched off the engine, Ange leaned over the center console and pressed her sweet, soft lips to mine.

We couldn't keep our hands off each other. Eventually, I managed to twist the key back and turn off the truck lights, and we both sauntered out and up the stairs while embracing. She'd stripped me half-naked before we'd even made it through the side door. We were usually very passionate when it came to our intimacy with each other, but this was another level. It was a powerful and overwhelming case of absence makes the heart grow fonder. We couldn't control ourselves, and we didn't want to.

I shut the door and locked it, then Ange pulled me and we stumbled across the living room towards the master bedroom. We didn't flick on a single light. We rolled onto the king-sized bed, kissed passionately, and smiled back at each other. Wrapping my arms around her and feeling her warm body pressed against mine was indescribable.

TWENTY-SIX

I'm not sure what time we eventually passed out. The evening had been a blur. An amazing and deeply satisfying blur. I awoke around 0800 with Ange lying on her side beside me. She looked incredible in the morning light that glowed in from my bedroom windows that looked out over my backyard and the channel beyond it. I spent a few minutes just watching her sleep. I wondered how such an amazing woman could even exist, and why she'd ever chosen me.

I kissed her on the forehead, then made my way quietly into the kitchen. I put on a pot of coffee and whipped up some pancakes and a smoothie comprised of frozen strawberries, banana, orange juice, and vanilla yogurt. Ange walked out from the bedroom wearing nothing but one of my old tee shirts. She smiled at me seductively as she leaned against the door frame, then peeked over the counter to see what I'd prepared.

It was a slightly overcast day, but it was already in the mid-sixties, so we ate out on the back patio. I brought out a tablet and we both did a quick search of the new Richmond resort. If what Scott had told me about her security was true, and I was sure that it was, getting into the party without an invitation wasn't going to be easy. I also gave Scott a call and told him I needed all the intel he could scrounge up on Carson Richmond and her new resort. He said he'd do what he could, then told me he'd be by the marina that afternoon to discuss what we were going to do.

After a few minutes, Ange leaned back in her white wicker chair, then looked up at me and smiled.

"What is it?" I said, smiling back at her.

"I was just thinking how this is a very formal event," she said. "That means I get to wear that new maroon dress I got last month. And I get to see you in a tux."

She eyed me up and down. If she was in any way nervous about what we were planning to do, she didn't show it in the slightest. She has nerves of steel, that woman, and more confidence than Pete Rose.

After breakfast, we showered, changed, and drove back over to the marina. When we entered the Baia, I saw that Kyle was sitting in the salon with my laptop open on the table in front of him. Atticus was lying beside him, but he jumped to his feet and ran over to greet us as we stepped down. You'd think I hadn't seen him in a week the way he spun, wagged his tail, and jumped up to lick my face. I glanced over at the counter and saw a half-empty pot of coffee. There was a map unfolded beneath the laptop along with a notepad with scribbles all over it. It looked like

Kyle had been up for a while.

I poured a mug of coffee, then we sat down beside him and went to work. We checked over every inch of the island resort, making written and mental notes of every path, structure, hill, patch of trees, and just about everything else. We wanted to know the place by heart so there would be no surprises. It was a relentless attention to detail that had been hardwired into our brains during our time in the SEALs. A facet of our characters that had become as natural as breathing.

Scott showed up around 1300. When he knocked on the door and stepped down, I welcomed him into the salon. He was no longer wearing his professional attire. Instead, he sported a faded pair of blue jeans and a thin flannel shirt with the sleeves rolled up to his elbows. In his right hand, he held a leather satchel. Kyle fell silent at the sight of Scott, and his face contorted with anger. Scott nodded towards each of us, then his gaze froze on Kyle's.

"It's good to see you're alive," Scott said. "I'm sorry about everything."

Kyle shook his head. "You're sorry. Well, that's great to hear." He paused a moment, then continued, "Logan, how could you bring him here?"

"That's enough," I said, raising my voice. "I trust Scott more than just about anyone alive. He's saved my ass countless times and he tried to save yours! Like I told you before, having your back lost him his career in the Navy. He would never be looked at by his superiors the same way again." Kyle began to rise, and I stepped towards him, placed my hand on his chest, and pushed him back down. "He's trying to help, Kyle! And we need him if we're going to pull this off, understand?"

Kyle was fuming. I knew that it wasn't really Scott that he was angry at; it was the government as a whole. The government that he'd fought for, bled for, and in the end, the government that had turned its back on him.

Kyle raised his hands in the air as if to say, "Alright, well, get on with it, then."

I glanced over at Scott. "What did you find out, Scott?"

He paused a moment, then said, "As you all know, Carson's good, really good. It's hard to find a chink in her armor. She's an anomaly when it comes to her privacy. The woman doesn't even have a cellphone, so far as I know. But I may have found a way to hack into her files." He reached into his leather satchel and pulled out a file. Inside the file, he showed a few pictures of Carson from different places around the world. "Wherever she goes," Scott continued, "her aides bring along a secured case that contains her private, personal computer. The bad news is she only takes it out of the case when she needs to make a private conference call. We also won't be able to tell where she's keeping it on the island. Lastly, if she was smart, and she is, she'd be unlikely to have any information on her computer that could tie her to illegal activity. Though if we were able to hack into her online database somehow, that would be a different story."

There was a short silence that followed as we each processed the information. The odds were most definitely stacked against us, but we hoped to at least have the element of surprise. After our encounter, Carson would likely suspect Kyle and I would split up and go into hiding. That was what her enemies usually did. But we weren't the hiding type. We were both more of the *face the mountain of a problem head-on* type.

"Well," I said, after letting out a deep breath. "One way to find out for sure whether her computer is there or not is to call and try and get ahold of her." I paused for a moment. All three of them were looking at me for an explanation. "I'd say the grand opening of a five-star resort deserves the recognition and congratulations of key figures within this state. That would include high political representatives."

Scott smiled. "That could work."

"And if the computer isn't there?" Kyle said.

I sighed. "Then we improvise. Maybe even get her to say something to instigate an investigation against her."

I'd planned to bring along my top-of-the-line pen recorder, just in case either Carson or someone in her circle slipped up.

"You're forgetting," Ange said, "that none of us are hackers. I'm sure each of us in this room has basic knowledge, but Carson won't have basic security. She'll have the best."

Kyle nodded and grinned slightly. "That's why we've got Murph."

The room went quiet. Scott had reacted slightly to hearing the name.

"He's a tech guru and hacker," I explained before the question popped up. "We knew him back in the Navy. He did private contract work and was brilliant at hacking into enemy systems. He's been working on his own for a while now, though."

"He left the service less than a month after the plane crashed," Scott said. "You've been in touch with him all these years?"

"Not me," I said, then looked over at Kyle.

Kyle nodded. “A little.”

He was still being short, not wanting to disclose too much. I was the only person in the room, one of the few in the world, that he trusted.

The room fell silent and I nudged Kyle’s shoulder softly. When he didn’t want to say any more, I took over as best as I could.

“Murph created a device that will help us hack her computer,” I said. “All we’ve got to do is get to it without anyone knowing we’re there.”

“When I told him I was going after Carson, he sent me a few tools to help hack into her system,” Kyle said, his stubbornness finally wearing away a little. “One is a small piece of equipment that he just recently finished. He calls it the Plague. It looks like an ordinary USB thumb drive, but once it’s connected, it attacks the computer and uses the computer’s own RAM against itself to search for keywords, even in heavily protected files. Essentially, it can turn a computer into a cannibal that attacks itself for specified intel.”

“Specified intel?” Ange said.

“Keywords, names, dates, et cetera,” Kyle replied.

“So it’s basically a hacker in your pocket?” Ange said.

Kyle nodded.

“That sounds incredible,” Scott said, genuinely amazed. “If that’s the case, then getting one of you near her computer is the mission. How long does this Plague take?”

“Depends,” Kyle said. “Murph told me it usually takes anywhere from five to fifteen minutes, depending on the amount of intel you’re trying to get and depending on the computer’s security. With

Carson’s computer, I’d wager it’ll be closer to the fifteen side of things.”

We continued like that for a few hours, going over every scenario until the makings of a plan were formed. It was crazy to think that we were about to go after one of the most powerful and dangerous women in America. If I’d been told a few days earlier everything that was about to happen, I would have responded that I had a better chance of winning the lottery.

TWENTY-SEVEN

At 1800, Scott took off, telling us he'd be standing by for his role. After a quick dinner, we stopped by a local men's formal shop called Jimmy Tuxedos. At first, we were planning to rent something for Kyle, but after seeing the selection, Ange insisted I buy a new suit as well. I picked out a black Italian regular fit, and Ange insisted that I get a bow tie as well. Kyle got the same one, and Ange said that we both looked pretty good for a couple of frogmen.

Once we had our appropriate attire on lock, we headed back to the marina, then prepped our weapons and equipment. Unlike most of the infiltrations and attacks I'd prepared for over the past few years, this one required everything to be compact. We'd each have one handgun, an extra mag, and an assortment of well-placed knives.

Just as the sun was beginning to fall into the Gulf

of Mexico, we cast the Baia's lines and cruised the 120 miles from Key West to North Key Largo, keeping to the Atlantic side of the Keys. The sky was dark, the moon nearly full, as we motored past Old Rhodes Key and into Card Sound. We were just south of Biscayne Bay and about thirty miles south of Miami. It was a calm evening, with less than five knots whispering over the water around us.

At just before 2200, Richmond Key came into view. It was pretty good-sized for a privately owned island, roughly thirty acres and round in shape. Much of the island was dark, featuring densely packed palm trees and thick underbrush. But the southern part of the island, where the heart of the resort was located, was brightly lit and full of activity. Elegant classical music was playing, boats were traveling back and forth to and from the mainland, and well-dressed people walked down both of the massive wooden docks extending from the main building of the resort out into the sound.

We cruised towards the key at about twenty knots, not wanting to draw any unwanted attention to ourselves. The sleek, dark hull of the Baia would blend in well with the other fancy boats, allowing us to reach the island without drawing suspicion. We counted three patrol boats, clearly part of Carson's private security detail, doing laps around the key. Timing our approach so as to avoid them as best as we could, I put us on an arched approach for the northern part of the island.

I'd already changed into my black tuxedo, and Ange had changed into her maroon dress. We had the topside lights switched off, but I could see her well enough in the moonlight to know that she looked amazing. We finished arming ourselves for the inevitable confrontations we were going to have with Carson's men. I had my Sig concealed under the right side of my waistband, fully loaded with fifteen 9mm rounds. I also had my dive knife secured around my left lower calf, strapped close to my body using a neoprene sheath. Ange had her Glock on her right hip, hidden by her dress, along with a few throwing knives.

Right before reaching the island, I grabbed a pair of drysuits from the guest cabin, one for each of us. Unlike the pristine white sandy beaches of the southern part of Richmond Key, the northern part was rockier, and I didn't want to get mud on our shoes and clothes as we made our way inland. We put our shoes in a plastic drybag, then pulled the drysuits up over our bodies.

Jack brought us as close as he could to the shore, then idled the engines. All four of us took a final look around, and when we didn't see any of the patrols, I gave a thumbs-up to Kyle and Jack.

"See you in there," Kyle said.

I stepped down into about two feet of water, gaining my balance on the rocky bottom. Turning around, I offered a hand to Ange.

"What a gentleman," she said with a smile.

As soon as she'd cleared the Baia's swim platform, Jack eased up on the throttles, and they were soon out of view as they wrapped around the key, heading for the other side. Ange and I held hands for stability as we sloshed through the water and soon reached the shoreline. We moved up off the sand and onto a layer of fallen leaves. We both went absolutely silent for about thirty seconds. Not a word or a sound was made by either of us as we stood frozen, listening to the world around us. It was quiet aside from the soft rustling of wind through the palm leaves above and the rummaging land crabs all around us. In the distance, we could hear the music playing from the resort along with a few occasional voices.

Just a hundred feet or so from the shore, we came to a paved pathway. From the satellite imagery, we'd been able to see that it traversed all the way around the island. My guess was that it was designed mostly as a bike and running path, and for groundskeepers to use as they golf carted their way around the island. As we'd suspected, there was no security on that part of the island, at least none that we could see.

Seeing that the coast was clear, Ange and I quickly shuffled out of our dry suits, grabbed our dress shoes from the dry bag, and put them on. The path looked new and well maintained, with only the occasional palm leaves scattered about. We moved side by side, heading south towards the main part of the resort. The dark water to our left made intermittent appearances through the trees, but for the first few minutes we were surrounded by nothing but dense, tropical jungle.

After five minutes we reached the outdoor recreation area which consisted of four tennis courts, a full-sized basketball court, and an indoor fitness center. As we passed the tall metal fence surrounding the tennis courts, we caught our first glimpse of security personnel. Two guys, both dressed in matching suits, stood about two hundred feet away from us right where the path forked. Part of the path continued south; the other turned west toward the heart of the island.

We noticed that each of the guys had an earpiece and that they were routinely checking in and giving the status of their watch station. They were too far away for us to tell what they were talking about, but I figured it was far from serious. I'd stood long hours on watch before and knew that boredom was usually the only enemy you had to worry about.

"Ange," I said quietly. We were both standing still beside the trunk of a palm tree. Her head swiveled and her eyes met mine. "I think this calls for the drunk lover."

I couldn't help but smile as I said the words. She paused a moment, then her lips formed a smile as well. Drunk lover was her favorite cover character.

"Wine or tequila?" she said with a wink.

"Well, it's a nice party," I said. "Open bar, no doubt. I'd go with champagne."

Her smile broadened. She took a short step away from me, then dramatically cleared her throat a few times. Bringing her right hand over her head, she proceeded to hover it down over her face like a TSA member using a metal detector wand. Her expression went from normal to plastered out of her mind in the blink of an eye.

"That was some great champagne," she said, wobbling side to side to complete the act. "Don't you agree, baby?"

I wrapped an arm around her to keep her from toppling over.

"Some of the best," I said. "Now let's get you back inside."

I kept helping her stay up as we moved slowly along the pathway, heading right past the two security guys. Normally, I'd have preferred a more aggressive approach. But the last thing we wanted was to put all of Carson's security detail on high alert before we'd even reached the resort. Plus it had been a while since I'd seen Ange as the drunk lover, and it was always entertaining.

"Where are we going?" Ange slurred, raising her voice loud enough for the two guys to hear. "I wanna play tennis. You're just embarrassed I'm gonna beat you at tennis."

"Hey," one of the guys said. "What are you two doing out here?"

They were each only about fifty feet from us by then. We kept walking south and didn't stop or divert our movements in the slightest.

"She's had a little too much to drink," I said. "Sometimes she goes wandering off."

"You've had too much to drink," Ange said, glaring at me playfully before dropping her head and waving it side to side.

The two guys froze and watched us for a few seconds before their stern gazes shifted to more annoyance than anything else.

"I'm just gonna get her back inside," I said. "Maybe find a place for her to lie down."

"I don't need to lie down," she fired back. "What I need is more glasses of bubbly."

She tripped and almost fell right on her face. I barely reacted fast enough to keep her from smashing her nose in. I was impressed and thought her performance deserved an Oscar nomination.

"I don't know how you managed to get by us, but this part of the island's off-limits tonight," one of the guys said. "That's why we have the path roped off."

"I'm sorry," I said. "She's not really herself right now."

As we moved past them, Ange tilted her head sideways and glanced at the two guys.

"Wow, hubba hubba," she said, looking the guys over from head to toe. "Look at those strapping men.

I like the bald one best."

Both men smiled and shook their heads. Neither one of them were bald. We continued down the path, me keeping her balanced as she swayed from side to side. About a hundred feet past the two guys, we reached a low-hanging rope that stretched across the path. We stepped over carefully, and Ange continued to talk nonsense until we turned a corner and were out of sight of the guys.

"Ange, there's no one like you," I said.

She came out of character in an instant and walked beside me normally.

"Thank you, thank you," she said, giving a slight bow.

We entered a large courtyard with magnificent fountains, cobblestone walkways, blooming flowers, and hanging white lights overhead. It was stunningly beautiful, a true feast for the eyes. It looked like it belonged to a royal family and I could only imagine how many professional gardeners and landscapers it took to create and maintain such a place.

There were a number of guests walking around admiring the gardens along with a few security guards standing by. We blended in nicely as we walked casually, admiring the grounds and smelling an occasional flower.

"I'm so glad you booked us a villa for the weekend," Ange said as we passed by a group of four very rich-looking people and a guard standing stoically behind them.

I glanced at my dive watch as we made our way across the courtyard to the main building of the resort. It had been fifteen minutes since we'd been dropped off on the island. I ran through the plan in my head and figured that Jack would be pulling the Baia up to the dock in about ten minutes and dropping Kyle off. Part of me really wanted to see the look on Carson's face when one of her security guards informed her that Kyle Quinn had just shown up to her party. She'd probably be less surprised if the president popped in.

We made our way off the cobblestones and onto a set of wide granite stairs that led up to a large veranda and a propped open set of impressive French doors. People spilled out from the doors, socializing and admiring the gardens from above. We moved inside, arm in arm, cool and confident. I hadn't spent a lot of time at fancy gatherings in my life. I preferred live music and rounds of beer at Salty Pete's. But if there's one thing I've learned when it comes to pretending like you know what you're doing, fake it till you make it usually rings true. In my experience, as long as you look and act the part, no one will notice.

The main hall of the building was filled with people intermixed among an army of servants carrying trays of drinks and food. There was expensive furniture, elegant paintings on the walls, and a large glass chandelier that I estimated cost more than my boat. On the eastern side of the room was the bar, a massive waxed mahogany number with a selection of alcohol that covered the entire wall behind it. On the western side of the room, a musical ensemble consisting of over thirty musicians played some of the most intricate and complex music I'd ever heard.

Ange and I made our way through the heart of the room towards the bar. I caught more than one person staring at Ange as we walked, and it didn't surprise me in the least. I couldn't help checking her out myself. Her maroon dress hugged her tanned skin in all the right places. Her hair looked like it was the product of three hours with a professional stylist. And her toned legs took my breath away in her high heels. She was hands down the most beautiful woman on the island, in the entire world for that matter.

When we reached the counter, two of the male bartenders moved towards Ange like they were being sucked in by tractor beams.

"What'll it be tonight, miss?" one of the guys said.

He had long black hair that was slicked back. The way he looked and spoke kinda reminded me of the Fonz, which caused me to smirk.

"A Manhattan, please," she said with a smile.

If Ange hadn't glanced at me, the guy probably would've never noticed that I existed. Ange had that effect sometimes.

"Make that two," I said.

The guy didn't even look my way. He shot Ange a wink, then turned and went to work making our drinks.

Ange and I leaned with our backs against the counter. I could tell she was looking at me, and I just smiled.

"What?" she said.

I turned and looked into her beautiful blue eyes.

"You look incredible," I said. "That's what."

After what had felt like ten seconds, the guy set our drinks on the counter. Another smile for Ange. Another wink too. We grabbed the small fancy glasses and spent a few minutes facing the wide open room, making note of every detail and observing the movements of the security guys while we made playful small talk.

Just as we each were getting to the bottom of our

drinks, the music quieted down and the large group focused their attention towards the main entrance. My eyes focused as if I were hunting and had just caught a first glimpse of my prey. Carson Richmond had just walked into view.

She was a tall, imposing woman, the kind who instantly commands the attention of everyone in a room. She walked elegantly but confidently as she greeted people at either side of her. She had fiery red hair, an athletic body, and strong facial features. She was wearing a dark blue dress and high heels, which made her look even taller than she was. She was a beautiful woman, there was no denying that. Even though she was in her early fifties, she looked twenty years younger, a feat she'd undoubtedly achieved through surgeries and the use of heavy makeup. She reminded me of the sirens in Homer's *Odyssey*; the beautiful creatures that lure you in close, then eat you alive.

As she neared the center of the room, her eyes scanned around her and stopped momentarily as they met mine. She smiled at me and I smiled back, then she continued greeting the rest of her guests.

Shit, I thought. *What are the chances that she recognizes me somehow?*

She was a big shot, I reminded myself. Someone who probably recognized important people only. I convinced myself that she wouldn't have wasted her time learning about me, that Drago might not even have revealed that I'd been with Kyle. Her look and her expression hadn't been one of recognition but of curiosity. Of genuine interest.

Was this woman into me? I shook my head and brushed off the idea.

Carson stopped in the center of the room and

gave a quick speech, welcoming everyone and thanking them for attending the grand opening of her new resort. She had a Southern accent and was good at speaking to a crowd. Her words were articulate, her voice smooth. She came across as the most inviting and nonthreatening person alive. When she finished, she raised a glass in the air and gave a toast.

After downing half the contents of her glass, she again looked over at me. I smiled back again, then turned to order another Manhattan.

"Holy shit," Ange said. She was still at the bar, though she'd been facing the other way and standing a body length away from me. Though she'd only met Carson briefly a few years ago, she didn't want to risk being recognized.

I glanced over at Ange and saw that her mouth had dropped open.

"Smile back at her, Dodge," she said. "I don't want her to recognize me, but smile back."

Before I could reply, she'd moved even farther away from me down the bar and turned to face the courtyard through a window, looking away from where Carson was walking. I felt my phone vibrate to life in my pocket, indicating that I'd received a message. It would have to wait.

I saw that Carson was looking and walking straight towards me. The guests around her parted like the Red Sea, letting her move towards me without breaking stride. Her light green eyes scanned away from mine only momentarily as she greeted someone who'd said hello. She stepped right up to me, her heels allowing our faces to be at the same level. The intoxicating scent of her perfume flowed into my nose. She grinned at me again, this time bigger.

"How'd I do?" she said in a playful tone.

I assumed that she was referring to her speech.

"The room's wrapped around your finger," I said, feeding her ego.

She beamed at that.

"Are you here just for the party, or are you planning to stay a few nights?" she said. "I do believe you will enjoy yourself if you stay."

She winked at me, and took another drink of her champagne.

"I have a villa for the weekend, Miss Richmond," I said. "Your resort is very beautiful, as are you."

Ange wasn't the only one who could lay on the charm if needed.

"Why, thank you," she said, her cheeks reddening a little. "I've decided to stay for a few nights myself. Maybe I'll run into you again, Mr.…?"

My mind raced. I couldn't tell her my name. No, that would jeopardize the entire plan. And she'd no doubt have one of her boys search whatever name I did give her, which meant that if I gave her a fake name, it'd blow the whole thing.

"Miss Richmond," one of her security guards said just a foot behind her. He was a big guy with unnaturally wide shoulders, muscles that pressed firmly against his suit, and a deep low voice.

Carson smiled at me, then turned her head to look at the guy. He moved in closer and whispered something into her ear. Carson nodded, then looked back at me.

"I'm sorry, but I have some business to attend to," she said.

"Duty calls," I said. "I understand." I grabbed her hand softly, brought it up to my lips. "I'll find you later and we can chat some more."

She smiled. "I'd like that."

She turned and moved across the room to where two more security guards were standing beside a hallway. They followed her as she passed, then they all disappeared from view. I turned to look at Ange, but she was no longer where she'd been standing just moments earlier. I quickly scanned the room and spotted her on the other side. She was moving casually beside a row of potted palm trees, her gaze directed down the hallway where Carson had disappeared from view.

I set my glass on the counter and moved towards her, weaving casually through the group. As I moved, I slid my phone from my pocket and quickly read the message. It was from Scott, and it was just a small silhouette of a thumbs-up. He was making the conference call with Carson, which was why she'd slipped away.

Just as I reached Ange, she drew her gaze away from the corridor and looked at me. She placed a hand on my chest, then smiled seductively and wrapped her other arm around me.

"Well, I'll say one thing about her," Ange said. "She's got good taste in men."

Without another word or a reply from me, she grabbed my hand in hers and moved toward the orchestra, pulling me with her.

"If you're not going to ask me to dance," she said, "then I guess I'll have to force you."

The music had started up again, and a handful of couples were dancing on the granite floor right in front of the musicians.

"By the way, Dodge," she whispered in my ear, "you were way too good at that."

"All part of the act," I said as we moved into the

center of the open floor, surrounded by other partners.

We embraced and joined the others in a waltz. I recognized the song and Ange told me that it was Waltz No. 2 by Dmitri Shostakovich. I smiled, enjoying the side of her that few people ever got to see. Based on her previous occupation, it was sometimes difficult to imagine that she'd once been a rich private school girl living in Sweden.

I enjoyed the dance immensely. I wasn't a great dancer by any means, but I could hold my own, especially with as great a partner as Ange.

"They went into the elevator," Ange said, reading my mind as I kept glancing towards the corridor where Carson had disappeared. "Two floors down."

We continued dancing through the next song, swaying our bodies slowly and enjoying each other's company. Ange loved to dance, and I realized then that I hadn't indulged her in it very much over the past year. When the orchestra stopped and the crowd clapped quietly, we made our way back to the bar. For a few minutes, I was so engrossed in the moment that I'd almost forgotten where we were and what we were doing. That while we were pretending to be guests at a party, we were there for other, more dangerous reasons.

My mood shifted in an instant as I glanced across toward the far side of the room and spotted Kyle. I focused my gaze on him and watched as he was escorted by a group of four security personnel through a door that led into the kitchen. My heart rate spiked and a timer started ticking down in my head, reminding me we'd have to move quickly. Ange and I both knew that they weren't taking him out of sight to question him. They were going to try and get rid of him, quickly and quietly.

I glanced over at Ange, then motioned toward the door as the guards led Kyle through. Before I could take a step in that direction, Ange grabbed me by the arm.

"No," she said. "I'll go help Kyle. You get to the computer."

"Ange, we—"

"We need to split up," she said. "It's almost kind of cute the way you try and protect me. As if you've forgotten what I've been doing for a living for most of my adult life."

"Just be careful, alright?"

She grinned. "I knew you were going to say that. You're getting too predictable, Dodge. You know I like a guy who can surprise me now and then."

As she started to walk away, I grabbed her hand softly and pulled her back towards me. Pulling her body close to mine, I looked deep into her beautiful blue eyes and smiled.

"Will you marry me?" I said, just loud enough so that her perfect ears were the only ones to hear me.

She paused for a moment, returning my smile. For a second, I could tell that she thought I was playing with her, but my eyes soon convinced her that I was serious. She gasped, then brought me in for a quick, passionate kiss.

"Well, that did it," she said into my ear.

TWENTY-EIGHT

Ange pressed her right hand against my chest, shot me one more sexy look, then walked past me. She made a beeline toward the door where the four guys had escorted Kyle moments earlier. I took off just a few strides behind her, then turned towards the corridor where Carson had gone earlier. At the end of the hall, I spotted a gold elevator, and as I moved closer, I saw that the red digital numbers were counting up from negative two.

I cut a sharp left, turning on my heels and entering what looked like a library. There were shelves of books from floor to ceiling, old-style couches, and a fireplace that would probably never be used. I took cover behind a potted cat palm and peeked through the thin leaves down the corridor towards the elevator. The shiny gold doors parted when the red number indicated zero, and Carson stepped out, flanked on either side by one of her security guards. I adjusted my position as they walked by, keeping myself covered behind the plant as I watched their every move.

My cellphone vibrated to life again, and I slipped it out of my pocket. Scott again. "We're go," was all it said. I watched as Carson moved back into the main room, her high heels clapping against the granite floors. I moved out of the library toward the elevator. After pressing the button, I waited just a fraction of a second before the doors opened, then stepped inside. Once in, I quickly pressed the button to shut the doors, followed by the negative two. The doors shut, and I could feel the elevator take me down. I debated grabbing my Sig but decided against it. I still had the element of surprise on my side, a valuable ally that I didn't want to compromise. Nevertheless, when I reached the bottom floor and the doors slid open, I had my right hand hovering over my Sig just in case. A habit, I suppose.

The doors opened to reveal a hallway that was far less glamorous than the one upstairs. The floor was polished concrete instead of granite. The walls were freshly painted and new but lacked any fancy artwork. It was also silent. There appeared to be nobody home.

I stepped out and took a quick look around. I had two options, left or right. Both ways appeared to turn ninety degrees after fifty feet, and both had the occasional closed door. I spotted two security cameras and knew that if anyone was watching those, they'd send a guy after me any second. Right about then, I wished that the plans we'd received of the resort had shown the lower floor. I hadn't even known there was a floor this far down. I looked at the ground and, seeing that there were more shoe smudges heading right, chose right.

I moved quickly and took the sharp left. Up ahead of me, I spotted a pair of large wooden double doors at the end.

Must be it, I thought.

I took one step forward, then one of the doors slammed open in front of me. A security guard stepped out, cutting me off. He was about my height, had pale skin, and probably had thirty pounds on me. In the dark room he'd stepped out of, I could hear radio chatter and saw rows of flat screens showing various locations in the resort. I couldn't tell how many more guys were in the room but could see the outline of at least two other guys.

"Hey," the guy said, his right hand hovering over his holstered Ruger handgun. "Where do you think you're going?"

He stood in front of me like a wall and I stopped just a foot away. I no longer had Ange by my side to help diffuse them. There was nothing I could say that would allow me to get by while they were still standing. Carson probably had a strict rule that only she was allowed inside her office. I glanced to my right and was able to see the inside of what had to be their main surveillance room. There were three guys inside, one standing and two sitting in front of a row of monitors. All four pairs of eyes were locked on me.

I needed to make a move, and I needed to do it quickly and efficiently. Strike fast and hard. No hesitation, no time for them to call in backup.

I took a casual step closer to the guy in front of me and he gripped his Ruger. Before he could pull it free, I grabbed the lapels of his jacket with a firm grip, muscled his upper body towards me, and slammed my forehead into his nose. His fragile nose was no match for my thick skull. It crunched as the guy's body fell backward, blood spewing out. The blow had caught him with such force that he collapsed unconscious as I stormed into the room, shifting my attention to the three other guys.

Faster than the standing guy could blink, I reached down and pulled my dive knife from its sheath under my left pant leg. He swung a big meaty fist straight at my face as I lifted the blade, and just as it was about to make painful contact with my right eye, I weaved to my left and stabbed my knife straight into his flying knuckles. The sharpened tip of the titanium blade cut deep into his fist, cutting bones and severing veins as the guy grunted in agony.

He froze for a fraction of a second, in awe of what had just happened. I grabbed his wrist, ripped my knife free, then manhandled his body around and sliced a gash in the back of his neck. His body jerked forward as one of the seated guys spun his chair towards me and tried to jump to his feet. Before he could extend his knees, I spun and side-kicked my right heel into his neck, causing his trachea to crunch audibly.

He struggled desperately for breath, and I saw that the fourth and final guy had already grabbed his Ruger and was raising it towards me. He was too far away for me to reach him without getting shot, so I hurled my dive knife through the air with everything I had. The blade soared in a blur and struck him in the chest. His eyes grew big and he fired off two shots as he fell back. The sound was deafening, and I hit the deck as one round slammed against the wall behind me while the other put a hole in the ceiling. As he jerked back, his roller chair flew out from under him, causing his back and head to slam against the hard floor.

With all four guys down, I took a few seconds to ensure that they wouldn't be getting up anytime soon. The guy whose neck I'd sliced and the guy with my knife sticking out of his heart were both goners, but the other two had a chance if they received medical attention within the next hour or so. I stepped across the room, pulled my knife free, and wiped the blood on the guy's suit. After putting it back in its sheath, I grabbed my Sig, stepped to the doorway, and fell silent for a few seconds.

They had to have heard the gunshots, I thought. *Someone had to have heard the gunshots*.

I held my Sig at the ready as I strode towards the wooden double doors at the end of the hall, assuming that at any moment, an army of footsteps would storm towards me. Halfway there, I noticed that the door required a badge to enter, so I turned back and pulled the badge off the guy whose nose I'd crunched and who lay passed out in a pool of his blood in the hall. Once I scanned the card, the light turned green and I pulled the right door open. Once inside, a few overhead lights turned on automatically, illuminating a decent-sized office with a large oak desk on the side across from me. There was a large desk chair and a leather couch along the wall to the right. Like the rest of the resort, everything looked and smelled brand-new.

I moved around the desk, where a seventeen-inch laptop sat folded shut on top of the desk. Knowing that it wouldn't take long for the rest of Carson's security to realize that four of their guys were down, I went to work as quickly as possible. I pried open the laptop, then watched as the main screen came up, prompting for a password. Grabbing the Plague from my pocket, I stuck it into the USB drive on the left side of the laptop. After a few seconds, the screen went blank, then displayed intricate lines of code. I remembered what Kyle had relayed from Murph, that it could take up to fifteen minutes. With my Sig firmly in hand, I kept my eyes on the door, knowing that I wouldn't have that long.

TWENTY-NINE

Angelina strode confidently through a swinging door, narrowly colliding into a waiter as he passed by balancing a round tray of appetizers. She'd entered a busy and seemingly chaotic kitchen. Chefs were hard at work cooking up massive amounts of tantalizing food, while waiters and waitresses shuffled in and out of the doors. Ange watched as the four guards escorted Kyle towards the back of the kitchen and down a set of metal stairs. She followed, keeping her distance and avoiding the occasional staff member who asked her if she needed anything.

When she reached the top of the stairs, she leaned against the railing and glanced down. The group was just walking out of view below, so she moved forward and headed down, her heels landing softly against the steps so they wouldn't hear her. She continued to follow the group past the doors of a large walk-in refrigerator and shelves of stored food. The farther they went, the quieter it got as the sounds of chatter and footsteps from the floor above became indistinct background noise.

Angelina watched as the group rounded a corner and entered what appeared to be a storage room. It was dark at first, but one of the guys flicked on a row of overhead lights. There were wooden crates on one wall filled with various kitchen essentials; garbage bags, cleaning supplies, mops, and so forth. On the far side of the room were what looked like massive hot water tanks with pipes that tangled up through the ceiling. The room had two concrete support columns that extended floor to ceiling for structural support of the building. They led Kyle over to the far one, uncuffed one of his wrists, and reconnected it so that he was bound to the column. Kyle noticed Angelina out of the corner of his eye and suppressed his urge to fight back.

One of the guards, a big Samoan guy whose face was covered in tattoos, grabbed a pair of pruning shears from his pocket. Holding it in front of him so that Kyle could see, he stepped towards his captive and growled at him.

"No fucking games, Quinn," the big guy said. "We're going to kill you. That's a fact. But you have a choice as to whether it's quick, or long and drawn out." He moved another step closer and stared deep into Kyle's eyes. "Where is the plane?"

Kyle tilted his head in surprise, then laughed.

"You're telling me that Drago didn't tell you guys?" Kyle said, not intimidated in the slightest by his captors. The Samoan guy's face burned with rage. Kyle shrugged. "What the hell does it matter? That asshole destroyed the important stuff."

Without a second's hesitation, the Samoan guy slammed his right fist into Kyle's abdomen. It knocked the air from his lungs and caused his body to lurch forward. The pain was immense, but nothing he couldn't handle. He brushed it off as best as he could, caught his breath, and looked back up at the guy.

"I don't give a rat's ass what he did," the Samoan guy barked. "You'll fucking tell me where it is or I'll cut you apart, piece by piece, starting with your fingers." He glanced over at one of the other guards, who carried a leather bag over one shoulder. "We brought plenty of zip ties and even a few tourniquets. We can do this all night, Quinn."

Angelina watched and listened intently as the scene unfolded. Knowing that a confrontation was imminent, she reached down quietly, slid out of her high heels, and stepped barefoot onto the cold floor.

Kyle paused a moment, then shot the big guy a cocky smile. "Then what the hell are you waiting for?"

The anger within the big guy boiled over. He grabbed Kyle's right wrist and pressed it forcefully against the column behind him. Holding it in place with his left hand, he brought the pruning shears up with his right, placing the sharp edges on either side of Kyle's thumb. Angelina knew she couldn't wait any longer. It was time for her to make her grand entrance and introduce herself to the guards.

She reached under her dress and grabbed one of the throwing knives strapped to her right thigh.

"Have it your way, Quinn," the Samoan guy snarled.

Just as he began to squeeze the shears, Angelina's knife caught him in the neck, its sharpened blade stabbing through the soft tissue and sticking out the other side. The big guy gagged, his eyes grew wide, and his head snapped back as blood flowed out from both sides of his neck. He dropped the shears and toppled over as Angelina ran into the room.

The guard closest to the door froze for a split second, then turned to look towards the door. He was barely able to focus his gaze on Angelina before she jumped and slammed her elbow into the side of his head. The powerful blow caused his body to twist uncontrollably. His eyes shot up and he collapsed, his lights knocked out before he'd even known what was happening.

As Angelina moved towards the remaining guards, the one closest to Kyle grabbed his Kimbro Micro 9 pistol and quickly raised it towards her. Kyle turned, leaned his upper body back, and jumped his legs into the air. Wrapping his feet around the guy's neck, he pressed hard and twisted his body with as much speed and strength as he could. The guy's neck cracked audibly as he whipped backward and hit the ground with a loud thud. He'd managed to get one shot off, firing a lone 9mm round into the ceiling above. Once on the ground, Kyle kicked him across his face, then knocked the Kimbro from his hands.

The fourth and final guard had pulled a six-inch knife from his leather bag before dropping it to the floor. He engaged Angelina, grunting violently as he stepped towards her. Instead of reaching for her Glock or another throwing knife, Angelina opted for a more convenient weapon. After swooping to the side to avoid the guy's blade as it sliced through the air, she wrapped her hands around the end of a mop handle. Spinning around, she slammed the narrow piece of hardwood into the guy's ear, a painful blow that caused him to wince in pain.

Angelina stepped towards him, planted her left leg and snapped her right into the air. The strong sidekick hit the guy square in the chest and caused him to drop his knife and take a few steps backward to regain his balance. He'd moved too far, however. Without realizing it, he'd moved within Kyle's striking distance. Kyle jumped his feet up again and slammed his heels into the guy's back. It looked like a game of pinball the way the guy bounced back and forth. But as he fell back towards Angelina, she brought the fight to an abrupt and gruesome end. Having snatched the guy's tactical knife from the floor, she sprang towards him and stabbed its blade straight through his heart. Blood dripped out of his mouth, his eyes went lifeless, and he collapsed to the floor at Angelina's feet.

Angelina dropped the knife, grabbed her Glock from under her dress, and took a quick look around the room, making sure all four guys were down. Once she could see that it was over, she searched the big Samoan guy's body for a key to the handcuffs. It was obvious that he'd been their leader, and after a few seconds of patting, she found the keys in his front pants pocket.

"That was a hell of a throw," Kyle said, genuinely impressed.

It was his first time ever seeing Angelina in action, and it was easy for him to understand why Logan had spoken so highly of her combat abilities.

Angelina inserted the key into the cuffs one at a time, clicked them loose, and let them drop to the floor. Kyle bent down, grabbed one of the guy's Kimber 9mms, and stuck it into the back of his waistband.

"Alright, let's go find Logan," Angelina said.

She moved over to the doorway and put her shoes back on. Then they both walked with purpose down the hall, up the metal stairs, through the kitchen, and back into the main room, where the party was still going on. A few of the staff had heard the gunshot and were frozen with fear when they moved past them in the kitchen. But the music had drowned it out in the main room, leaving all of the guests blissfully unaware of what was going on.

"This way," Angelina said, motioning towards the hallway that led to the elevator.

As they moved towards it, Carson stepped out from a large group of people, flanked on either side by two of her guards. Kyle and Angelina both spotted her at the same time. They diverted their course casually and turned to where a waiter was handing out tuna cucumber bites. They watched Carson intently as they each grabbed one. She was heading down the hall, straight for the elevator.

"Shit," Angelina said a little louder than she'd intended to.

The waiter looked at her quizzically and apologized that the dish wasn't to her liking.

"It's great," Kyle said. "She's just allergic to seafood."

The waiter handed her a napkin, and she spat it out unhappily. He apologized again as Kyle and Angelina watched the elevator doors open. Carson and two of her men stepped inside, the doors closed, and the red numbers transitioned from zero down to negative two.

Angelina's heart began to race. She knew that Logan would still be down there. They had to find another way down as quickly as possible if they were going to help him.

"Stairwell," Kyle said, motioning towards a set of doors beside the elevator.

He didn't have to tell her twice. In the blink of an eye, they both moved across the room towards the doors, hoping they could make it down in time. Hoping that they wouldn't be too late.

THIRTY

I stood beside the desk, watching the laptop screen as lines of code appeared, then vanished, replaced by more lines. Might as well have been Greek to me; I couldn't understand any of it. I could only hope that the Plague was doing its job and that it would be over soon. It had already been at it for a few minutes. I expected the doors to swing open and Carson's security to swarm inside any second.

With nothing to do but wait, I reached into my pocket and pulled out my cellphone. I quickly turned to Jack's contact page, then pressed the call button. No signal. Not even an attempted call, the service was so bad.

What the hell?

I'd received Scott's message just fine in the main hall.

Did Carson have some kind of signal blocker in

place in her private office?

I reached for a landline phone that was hooked up on the desk. I remembered what Scott had said, how Carson didn't even have a cellphone. She certainly was a unique character, unlike any evil and powerful person I'd ever encountered before.

I grabbed the handset and quickly dialed Scott's number. He answered after the first ring.

"Hey, Scott," I said. I switched on speakerphone and set the handset on the desk. "I'm in her office now. You with Jack?"

"Yeah," he said. "We're at the Anglers Club, about a mile south of Richmond Key. Are you ready for us to cruise over?"

"Not yet," I said, staring at the laptop screen and trying to will the device to work faster.

If I couldn't get the intel uploaded onto the USB before Carson and her guards showed up, the entire plan would crumble. The only other option we had was to get Carson to say something that could incriminate her. I shifted my gaze to my jacket, where my seemingly ordinary pen was clipped inside my left breast pocket. After making sure it was on and still recording, I looked back at the laptop. It started making sounds.

Was it almost finished?

I had no way of knowing. I'd never used it before, and the only crash course I'd received regarding its operation was to insert it into the computer and wait. Suddenly, the screen went black for a split second before going back to its default page; the same page I'd seen when I'd first pried it open. The one that asked for a password.

Must be done.

Whether it was or not, I was ready to get the hell

out of there. I worried about Ange. No matter how deadly and experienced she was, I still worried. Couldn't help it. I pulled the small thumb drive out of the computer and dropped it into my pants pocket.

"All set," I said. "Leaving now. I'll meet you at the dock."

I heard a faint, muffled reply as I grabbed a small notepad, placed it on the stand and set the handset down.

With my Sig in hand, I took a step around the desk, then froze. In a flash of movement, the double doors flew open and slammed into the wall. A group of security guards poured in like sand falling through an hourglass. For a moment, I thought about trying to take them out. I could have gotten a few shots off, then dropped beneath the desk for cover. But there were too many of them. At best, I'd take a few of them out before being surrounded and riddled with bullets.

"Drop the gun!" one of the guys yelled.

There were at least six of them, and they all had their weapons raised straight at me. My grip loosened on my Sig and it fell, rattling on the hardwood floor at my feet. Two of the guys moved around the desk as the other four provided cover. They grabbed me, slammed my upper body against the desk beside the laptop, and searched me. They came prepared. One of them had a metal detector wand and was hovering it over every inch of my body, stopping and searching every time it beeped to life.

After a full and thorough search, they'd grabbed my dive knife, cellphone, the Plague flash drive, and my pen. They also grabbed my Sig off the floor. Once they were done searching me over, they stepped back. All six of their weapons were aiming at me when I heard the familiar sound of high heels striking the concrete floor just outside the doors. A second later, Carson appeared.

She looked as strong and confident as she had upstairs, but her expression was different. As she moved into the office, I saw that her persona had shifted so drastically from what it had been up in the foyer that I could hardly believe it. Her eyes were no longer looking at me with lust, but with pure disgust and hatred. She stormed across the office and stopped across the desk from me.

"Well, well, well," she said, her eyes shooting daggers at me. "So you must be Logan Dodge." She shook her head slightly. "I can only assume that you are, since you're here with Quinn. I would've thought you'd both be halfway around the world by now, hiding out someplace. I guess you're not as smart as people say you are." There was a short pause, then she added, "What the hell are you doing here?"

Her voice was much different than before. Her tone harder, more sadistic. If I'd been blindfolded, I would've sworn that I was talking to a different person altogether.

I didn't answer, and one of the guys stepped towards her and set the contents of my pockets on the desk in front of her. She went through each item, one at a time. Grabbing the flash drive, she held it in the air, then dropped it to the floor and slammed her heel down. The small device cracked to pieces, then she grabbed the pen and examined it carefully.

"Now, that's very clever," she said before snapping it in two and handing it back to the guard. "I'm not mad, Mr. Dodge. I'm only disappointed. I was looking forward to enjoying your company this weekend." She sighed. "Alas, I'm not going to kill you. Quinn I will kill, but not you. You killed two of my men and nearly killed two others. You will rot in jail for what you've done today."

"You and your group are responsible for the deaths of countless innocent people, including children," I said sternly, speaking for the first time in what felt like ages. "Yeah. I know all about your corrupt deals. I know that you were the one who ordered the massacre of that entire village in Colombia and that you made it look as though FARC rebels were responsible." I paused a moment, letting the fact sink in that I'd been a SEAL fighting alongside Kyle years earlier. "I know that the only reason we were in Colombia was so that we would be ambushed, killed, and used as pawns to further your own corrupt agenda."

She paused a moment, then smiled devilishly and began clapping her hands.

"Bravo, Logan," she said mockingly. "Bravo. And it only took you ten years to figure it out. It's too bad for you that no one will ever believe you. It must hurt to know that you'll be the one jailed after all of this." She looked down at the broken USB. "Did you really think that you could take me down? Do you have any idea how powerful I am, how many people adore me?"

She laughed villainously.

"Look," I said, "you're a murderer, and a big-time criminal, nothing more. You make your living by ruining people's lives, by killing, and by deceiving. You're nothing more than a—"

My words were cut off by a strong punch to my jaw landed by the guard at my left. The room went blurry and my head snapped back. The pain was explosive. It caught me completely off guard and almost knocked me to the floor. If it wasn't for the guy holding me from behind, I probably would've fallen over.

I tried my best to shake the pain and dizziness away, then turned my gaze back to Carson. She'd moved right up to me, allowing me to smell her strong perfume as she stared at me like a lion about to take down its prey.

"Keep it up, Logan," she said. "You'll be watching more of my schemes unfold on a staticky old television while a group of fat inmates use you for pleasure."

She snarled, then slapped her hand across my face. It hurt more than I thought it would. Her nails cut deep, drawing blood that streaked down my cheek. It was the first time I'd seen her break away from her usual calm and collected demeanor.

"Take him out of my sight and off my island," she said. "Contact the police and let them know that there have been multiple homicides, but make sure that this is handled tomorrow, and on the mainland. I'd hate for my new resort to receive bad press on its opening weekend."

"We'll take care of it," one of her guards said. "What about Quinn?"

"Kill him," she said. "That is, if they haven't killed him already."

She shot me a final evil look, then turned her head. She took just two steps when a foreign voice cut the silence of the office.

"Miss Richmond," Scott's voice said through the speakerphone.

Carson froze in place. She whipped around, her eyes zeroing in on her phone resting beside the computer. I glanced down at it and smiled. I'd blocked the disconnect button with the small notepad, making it look as though the phone had been hung up while in reality, Scott and Jack had been listening the entire time. They'd also been recording the entire conversation. Carson was frozen still and kept quiet for a few seconds. She'd been quick-witted and seemingly on top of things all evening until Scott's voice came through the speaker.

The guards on either side of me leaned over the desk, then looked up at Carson in amazement that they hadn't noticed it was on. I didn't really blame them. The small LCD screen was counting up, but it was dark and difficult to notice unless you really looked at it. The phone looked like it was dead.

"Miss Richmond," Scott said again loudly. "Are you still there?"

She collected herself as best as she could.

"Who is this?" she said, trying her best to sound confident. But her persona was dwindling with every passing second.

"That's not important," Scott said. "What's important is that you know that we've been recording everything. You should expect a call from the CIA in the morning. I suggest you contact your lawyer."

Filled with anger, Carson stomped towards the desk, removed the notepad, and hung up the phone with a loud slam of the handset. She paused for a moment, then looked up at me. Before she could say a word, a scuffle broke out at the door. I looked up just in time to see two guards as they toppled over and slammed hard facefirst against the ground. Angelina and Kyle came into view, each raising their weapons towards Carson. For a moment, the guards on either side of me didn't know what to do. They raised their weapons towards Angelina and Kyle. A big mistake.

Without hesitating, I dropped down and swung my right leg forcefully towards the guard to my right. My shin crashed into the back of his legs, causing him to topple backward and his head to bang against the hard floor. As the guard to my left tried to engage me, I held his handgun, forcing it to aim away from me. With my left hand, I pressed firmly into the back of his skull, forcing him down, and slammed his forehead into the corner of the desk. I ripped the handgun from his hands, spun around, and had Carson in my sights before the guy had even hit the floor. Only Carson and two of her guards were still standing. The tables had turned in the blink of an eye.

My narrowed and focused eyes shifted from Carson to the two remaining guards.

"Drop 'em!" I said.

They paused a moment, not knowing what to do.

Carson raised a hand. "Just do what he said."

The two guards let go of their weapons, letting them fall and rattle at their feet. Angelina and Kyle moved into the office. I strode over to them, and the three of us stood in front of Carson. It was clear that she was pissed off beyond belief, but she was still trying her best to look as though she was in control of the situation—an act that was as much of a habit as breathing for her.

"This is Kyle Quinn," I said, placing my left hand on his shoulder while my right held up the snoozing guard's Ruger. "He was a first class petty officer in the United States Navy. Former Special Forces. He served nine years active duty, including four deployments. He's a patriot, an American hero, and an all-around badass. He's married to a loving and faithful wife and is the father of two girls." I paused a moment, then continued, "I just thought you should meet the man whose life you destroyed. Or tried to, at least. You're also responsible for the death of Petty Officer Manuel Estrada, as well as countless others."

I was breathing heavily and didn't even realize it. Carson was still staring back at both of us. If she'd been affected at all by anything I'd said, she hadn't shown it.

"So what, you're going to kill me now?" she said.

I shook my head. "Nope." I stepped over to the desk, hinged the laptop shut and picked it up. "We're just gonna walk right out of here." The three of us made for the door. I stared down Carson as we walked by her. "And if you do anything to try and stop us, well..." I paused for a second. "I think you know how that will end."

We kept walking, and just as we reached the door, Kyle stopped and turned back to look at her.

"You messed with the wrong fucking people," he said. "If you send just one more of your guys after me or my family, I'll hunt you down, look you in the eyes just as I am now, and put a bullet in your surgically altered face."

Carson remained motionless and silent as we moved out of the office and down the hall.

THIRTY-ONE

The three of us headed up to the main level via the elevator. When the gold doors opened, we stepped out and walked towards the main entrance of the resort. The party was still alive, the band still playing, the guests still enjoying themselves. We stepped through a massive archway, then out an automatic sliding glass door. The beach was just a short stone's throw away. We headed down a wide granite staircase toward a cobblestone path that led to the resort's private beach as well as its two docks. The Baia was just cruising up to the end of the nearest dock when we shuffled down a few more steps and headed toward it over the cedar planks.

We only saw a few of Carson's men, but none of them stopped us or even said so much as a word. The two staff members at the end of the dock greeted us and lent a hand to Angelina as we stepped over to the

Baia. Scott greeted each of us at the stern, telling us that we'd done one hell of a job. Jack was at the helm. He twisted his body around and revealed a massive smile covering most of his face.

"How was the party?" he said in his usual laid-back tone.

"Short and sweet," I said, "just how I like them." I handed Scott the laptop and added, "It's Carson's. Let's see what we can get out of it."

Scott smiled.

"Alright, Jack," Angelina said. "Let's get the hell out of here."

Jack grinned, backed away from the dock, and punched the throttles. In just a few seconds, he accelerated us up on plane, heading northeast around Richmond Key.

We all sat in the cockpit, with Jack in the helm seat and the rest of us around the dinette. Kyle had been silent since we'd left Carson's office, but after a few minutes, he looked at each of us and expressed his gratitude.

"Thank you guys," he said. "For everything. None of you had to do anything, but you did. You risked your lives and your careers for me." Turning to Scott, he held out his hand.

Scott shook it, then patted Kyle on the back.

"I only wish we could've fixed this mess sooner," Scott said. "I hate to rain on this parade, but it's not over yet. You're still a wanted criminal, Kyle. You will be taken into custody, nothing we can do about that. But, I'm confident that you won't be held for very long. I've already contacted Wilson as well as other government and military officials that I know and trust. We will do everything we can to get you free and to fix the damage this shit has caused your reputation."

Kyle nodded and looked out over the dark ocean around us. We cruised back around North Key Largo and into the Atlantic, then turned south and followed the Keys down towards Key West. I grabbed a blanket for Ange, then we nestled up alongside each other on the sunbed. I leaned back into the soft cushioned backrest and wrapped an arm around her, bringing her beautiful body in close. I thought back on what we'd just done and had a hard time believing we'd actually pulled it off. But then, that wasn't the first time I'd felt that way in my life. With Ange at my side, with guys like Jack, Scott, and Kyle fighting in my corner, I felt like there was nothing I couldn't do. It was a chilling feeling, an empowering feeling.

I kissed Ange on the forehead and thought about the question I'd asked her while in the resort.

She never answered me, I thought. Though she had smiled. A good sign.

I was close to asking her again but figured sitting at the stern of my boat beside my friends with a loud engine roaring beneath us wasn't exactly the best moment. I tabled it for another time and just enjoyed the moment and the great company.

We arrived back at the Conch Harbor Marina and pulled into my slip a few minutes before one in the morning. Scott headed straight for Key West International, where his private jet was parked. He took the laptop with him and said he'd get back to us soon. After I thanked Jack for everything, he flip-flopped down the dock and hopped into his blue Jeep Wrangler, heading to his house. I locked up the Baia and switched on the security system, then Ange, Kyle, and I hopped into my Tacoma and cruised over to my house. We had a quick bite to eat, then Kyle had a long and emotional phone call with his wife as Ange and I passed out on my king-sized bed.

The next morning, I woke up to a phone call from Sheriff Wilkes. He informed me as a friendly courtesy that he and a group of other law enforcement would be coming by my house to get Kyle and take him into custody.

"I understand," was all I said.

At 1100, I heard a squad of police cars as they pulled into my driveway.

A group of CIA agents and police officers filed into my backyard. They cuffed Kyle and hauled him off. Charles was there, and he looked uncomfortable. Once Kyle was out of sight, a few of the agents approached Ange and me and said that they'd need us to make statements. I sighed. I wasn't looking forward to having to deal with so many government employees. I'd worked for the government for eight years and there'd been a reason I'd been so anxious to get out. The protocols, the paperwork, the never-ending red tape. But I was ready to do everything I could to help Kyle and to fuel the karma that was cracking down on Carson.

Within two weeks, the evidence of Kyle's innocence became overwhelming. There was the recording of Carson admitting to being responsible, the intel recovered from her private laptop, and the cockpit recorder from the crashed flight that was found and salvaged by MDSU 2. The charges against Kyle were dropped and, following his continued involvement in the investigation, he'd be free to go. He was even working with the Department of Veteran's Affairs to have his discharge upgraded to honorable, the one he rightfully deserved after years of honorable service.

The story had garnered so much attention that the president himself had mentioned the situation during a briefing, stating: "The tarnishing of Petty Officer First Class Quinn's reputation and the impact this has had on him and his family is a stain on our nation's history. We will do everything we can to rectify this situation and restore this American hero to his rightful position within our nation."

The president was then asked by a reporter what he had to say about Carson Richmond, her involvement in illegal activity, and the supposed corruption within certain political and military chains of command. He refused to comment on specifics, saying only that there was an extensive investigation taking place.

The day Kyle was released from his temporary holding cell at the Jacksonville Naval Complex, Ange and I surprised him by picking him up in her Cessna and flying him back down to Key West. We'd also worked with Scott to fly his wife and two daughters via private jet from Southeast Asia, where they'd been living in hiding for much of the past ten years. They were standing on the tarmac in Key West when we landed. His wife was smiling and crying tears of joy; his daughters were waving. Kyle was one of the toughest and most masculine guys I'd ever met, and as soon as he saw them, he broke down.

Ange slowed the Cessna, bringing it to within just a few hundred feet of them. Before we'd come to a stop, Kyle opened the door and hopped out. Ange brought us to a stop, and we both watched through the windshield as Kyle wrapped his arms around his family. Uncontrollable tears streaked down the sides of my face. I couldn't take my blurry eyes off them.

Ange wiped a tear from my cheek, then leaned

over and kissed me.

"You did a good thing, Logan Dodge," she said.

I smiled as I turned to look back at her. Her eyes had welled up as well. Watching Kyle and his family was one of the best things I'd ever seen in my life.

"We did a good thing," I said, then brought her in for another kiss.

A longer and more passionate kiss.

EPILOGUE

A week after Kyle's release, I surprised Ange with breakfast in bed and told her I'd booked her for a full spa package at Paradise Spa. It included an aroma tub soak, a facial, a foot scrub, and an hour-and-a-half-long Swedish massage. It was her birthday, and I wanted everything to be perfect.

While she was at the spa, I packed up both our bags for a little getaway I had in mind. The past week had been a blur. We'd spent the days celebrating Kyle's freedom with barbeques, evenings at Salty Pete's, and boat rides around the Keys. We fished, we dove, we snorkeled, and we island-hopped our way around our beautiful paradise. It had been a hell of a time spent with the best friends a guy could ask for.

The previous day, Kyle and his family had left for their hometown of Newark to reconnect with family they hadn't seen in ages. I realized that I hadn't spent very much alone time with Ange since she'd gotten back from California and figured that her birthday would be the perfect occasion to spend just the two of us.

By the time Ange had finished at the spa and met me over at the marina, it was midafternoon and I had us ready to go. In the salon, I had our two bags along with my four-person tent, a big sleeping bag, a hammock, tiki torches, and my portable propane grill. My Yeti was resting on the deck in the cockpit, filled with food, drinks, and ice. And lashed against the port gunwale was my two-person sit-a-top kayak and two paddles that I usually kept stored over in Gus's shed. I'd also gotten Jack to watch Atticus for a day or two, depending on how much we were enjoying ourselves.

Ange looked incredible as she walked down the dock. I met her at the swim platform and held out my hand to help her aboard. She was wearing a white sundress and leather sandals and had a pair of aviator sunglasses covering her eyes. She was relaxed and refreshed and had a big cherry-red-lipped smile on her face.

"A girl could get used to this," she said as she stepped towards me.

She pressed her chest against mine, wrapped a hand behind my head, and pulled me in. I wasn't sure how long we stood there, and I didn't care. All I knew was that I was enjoying the company of the most beautiful and amazing woman in the world. She stepped down into the salon and I prepared the Baia to make way. She came back up just as I started up the twin six-hundreds.

"What have you got planned, Dodge?" she said in her sexy, smooth Swedish accent.

She motioned her head towards the kayak, then

looked back at me.

"It's a surprise," I said. "Just sit back and relax. I've got everything taken care of."

I opened my Yeti, grabbed a coconut water, and handed it to her. Grabbing the helm, I eased the throttles forward and cruised us out of the harbor. Once we were clear of the no-wake zone, I quickly brought us up on plane, heading west into Key West National Wildlife Refuge. It was a beautiful day in paradise, clear blue skies from horizon to horizon, barely any wind, and temperatures in the mid-seventies. The following day's forecast called for perfect weather as well, making it an ideal time to enjoy a night out in the great outdoors.

After two hours of cruising west through the Gulf, we reached Dry Tortugas National Park, a remote one-hundred-square-mile park consisting of beautiful blue waters, an abundance of bird and marine life, and picturesque islands. The area is also rich in history. Off the port bow, we could see the impressive Fort Jefferson. Brilliant red brick walls rise up forty-five feet from the water and sand below, creating a massive hexagon that encloses over sixteen acres. In recent years, you'll spot mainly tourists brought in by the ferry that runs back and forth from just down the street from Conch Harbor Marina. But in its heyday during the Civil War, nearly two thousand Confederate soldiers lived in the fort.

Up ahead, I could see the largest of the seven islands in Dry Tortugas: Loggerhead Key, its black-and-white-striped lighthouse rising high into the air. After passing the northern tip of Loggerhead, Ange looked over and shot me a confused look. I smiled, enjoying her reaction. She'd assumed that we would be camping out on Fort Jefferson or Loggerhead, but I had a better, more private location in mind.

After fifteen more miles of blue open water, my desired destination came into view. By outward appearances alone, the island was nothing more than tall cliffs jutting up into the air, reaching sixty feet at their tallest point. According to any map or chart I'd ever seen, the island we were heading for didn't even exist. I cruised us around to the northern side of the island, then killed the Baia's engines. After dropping anchor, I climbed down into the salon and took a few trips bringing our gear up on deck.

"So what's the name of this pile of rocks?" Ange asked.

She was sprawled out on the sunbed, wearing a turquoise bikini, and had her hair down. Her right hand shielded the side of her face from the sun as she looked towards the island.

"Well, officially I don't think it has a name. But my dad and I always called it Monte Cristo."

Ange laughed. "An excellent book. I love Dumas. But what exactly made you name it that?"

"I've always loved the book as well. And we called it that because this pile of rocks shares a few similarities with the fictitious island."

"Like?"

I leaned over her body, unlashed the kayak, and slid it over to the swim platform.

"Well, from all appearances, this island looks barren and uninhabitable, just like the island from the book. It also holds a secret, like the one in the book did."

Her curious reaction was just as I'd hoped.

"Alright, you've got my interest. What secret does this sorry excuse for an island have?"

I grinned. "You'll see."

We loaded down the kayak with all of our gear, including my cooler and grill, then I headed down into the main cabin to grab a few final things. Pulling open my nightstand drawer, I reached all the way back and grabbed a small wooden box. I stashed it away in my Camelbak, then returned topside and locked up the Baia. I kept the kayak steady as Ange sat down, then handed her a paddle and sat down in the seat behind her. Reaching behind me, I pushed against the Baia's hull to give us momentum, then we paddled towards the island.

"Those are some sharp cliffs," Ange said. "You got any rock climbing gear in those bags?"

I smiled. It had been the same thing Scott had said when I'd first taken him to the island last summer. She was right, though. The cliffs were sheer and would be a challenge even for an experienced climber.

"We won't need it," I assured her.

She chuckled, and shook her head, no doubt thinking that I was out of my mind. But as we came closer and closer to the rocks, a narrow opening revealed itself. It was difficult to spot even up close and practically impossible from far away. A small cut in the rock no more than ten feet wide that turned twice and blended in well with the rocks surrounding it.

Ange picked up her pace. We paddled through the opening, following its turns, then entered an untouched tropical oasis. Ange froze, unable to believe what she was seeing.

Not so crazy anymore, am I? I thought as I continued to paddle us slowly into the beautiful lagoon.

The water was crystal clear beneath us, allowing

us to see the various colorful marine life below. I paddled us up onto a brilliant white sandy beach roughly thirty feet wide. I sloshed up onto the sand, then helped Ange to her feet and kissed her. She was stunned speechless and kept looking around us at the beautiful secret island oasis.

After dragging the kayak all the way up onto the beach, we unloaded the gear and hauled it up a steady slope towards the top of the island. Most of the ground was covered in palm trees and various other tropical plants, but there was a narrow path that my dad and I had created, which led up to our favorite place to camp.

We soon reached a small patch of grass with views looking out over the empty blue ocean to the west. We set up the tent, strung the hammock across two palms, and set up a perimeter of tiki torches. We spent a few hours swimming in the lagoon, enjoying each other's company as we splashed down from the cliffs and snorkeled our way back and forth.

As the sun began to fall, we toweled off, then made our way back up to our campsite and cooked a delicious dinner of steak, baked potatoes, and corn on the cob, all cooked on my portable propane grill. To watch the sunset, we climbed up onto the rock face, allowing us to have a 360-degree view as the red sun sank into the ocean.

I grabbed Ange's hand in mine softly, then kissed her on the cheek and looked into her blue eyes.

"You know," I said, "you never gave me an answer back at the resort."

She gave me a big smile and turned to look out over the brilliant artwork nature was creating.

"Well, you never showed me a ring," she said playfully.

She glanced back at me and took my breath away. I couldn't speak, so instead I bent down to one knee in front of her. I loved her and I knew that she loved me, so why was I so nervous? I'd spent much of my life going toe to toe with some of the baddest and deadliest guys around, but this was a whole other animal. This was commitment, lifelong commitment, and a promise to love her and only her forever. My heart pounded in my chest harder than it ever had before. Her eyes, her smile, her perfume, the way her hair danced in the ocean breeze. She leveled me.

"You know I'm not the most sentimental guy," I said, getting off to a rough start. "But you make me feel ways that I can't explain. I want to love you and hold you in my arms forever if you'll have me. My dad always said that there're a lot of people you can live with, but there's only one person you can't live without. That person is you, Ange." I reached into my pocket and pulled out a small handcrafted wooden box. Holding it in front of me, I hinged the top open, revealing the diamond and letting it sparkle in the distant, dark red sun. "Angelina Fox, will you marry me?"

We spent much of the night right there on the edge of the cliff, then moved down and nestled up in our tent with the rain fly off so we could look up at the sky full of stars. Ange had her body draped over my chest and pressed against mine as she slept. Her left hand rested gently on my right pec. Glancing down at her fingers, I smiled as her new piece of jewelry sparkled in the moonlight. Taking a deep and satisfied breath of the fresh evening air, I kissed her on the forehead, then closed my eyes, wondering how I'd managed to be so lucky.

THE END

Logan Dodge Adventures

Gold in the Keys
(Florida Keys Adventure Series Book 1)

Hunted in the Keys
(Florida Keys Adventure Series Book 2)

Revenge in the Keys
(Florida Keys Adventure Series Book 3)

Betrayed in the Keys
(Florida Keys Adventure Series Book 4)

Redemption in the Keys
(Florida Keys Adventure Series Book 5)

If you're interested in receiving my newsletter for updates on my upcoming books, you can sign up on my website:

matthewrief.com

About the Author

Matthew has a deep-rooted love for adventure and the ocean. He loves traveling, diving, rock climbing and writing adventure novels. Though he grew up in the Pacific Northwest, he currently lives in Virginia Beach with his wife, Jenny.

Made in the USA
Las Vegas, NV
06 August 2024